DEUS SANGUINIUS

Following his triumphs against the forces of Chaos on the planet Cybele, Brother Arkio of the Blood Angels is being worshipped as the reincarnation of Sanguinius, the Chapter's primarch. Only Rafen, Arkio's brother, has his doubts, but dare not voice them lest he himself be denounced as a traitor.

When Chief Librarian Mephiston arrives to investigate Arkio's claims, the forces of Chaos spring their cunning trap... Forced to the edge of no return, can the Blood Angels control their bloodthirsty nature or will this noble Chapter destroy itself in a vicious civil war?

A WARHAMMER 40,000 NOVEL

BLOOD ANGELS

DEUS SANGUINIUS

James Swallow

For The Tech Crew

A BLACK LIBRARY PUBLICATION

First published in Great Britain in 2005 by
BL Publishing,
Games Workshop Ltd.,
Willow Road, Nottingham,
NG7 2WS, UK.

10 9 8 7 6 5 4 3 2 1

Cover illustration by Phillip Sibbering.

A CIP record for this book is available from the British Library.

ISBN 10: 1 84416 155 2
ISBN 13: 978 1 84416 155 3

Distributed in the US by Simon & Schuster
1230 Avenue of the Americas, New York, NY 10020, US.

Printed and bound in Great Britain by
Bookmarque, Surrey, UK.

See the Black Library on the Internet at
www.blacklibrary.com

Find out more about Games Workshop
and the world of Warhammer 40,000 at
www.games-workshop.com

IT IS THE 41st millennium. For more than a hundred centuries the Emperor has sat immobile on the Golden Throne of Earth. He is the master of mankind by the will of the gods, and master of a million worlds by the might of his inexhaustible armies. He is a rotting carcass writhing invisibly with power from the Dark Age of Technology. He is the Carrion Lord of the Imperium for whom a thousand souls are sacrificed every day, so that he may never truly die.

YET EVEN IN his deathless state, the Emperor continues his eternal vigilance. Mighty battlefleets cross the daemon-infested miasma of the warp, the only route between distant stars, their way lit by the Astronomican, the psychic manifestation of the Emperor's will. Vast armies give battle in His name on uncounted worlds. Greatest amongst his soldiers are the Adeptus Astartes, the Space Marines, bio-engineered super-warriors. Their comrades in arms are legion: the Imperial Guard and countless planetary defence forces, the ever-vigilant Inquisition and the tech-priests of the Adeptus Mechanicus to name only a few. But for all their multitudes, they are barely enough to hold off the ever-present threat from aliens, heretics, mutants – and worse.

TO BE A man in such times is to be one amongst untold billions. It is to live in the cruellest and most bloody regime imaginable. These are the tales of those times. Forget the power of technology and science, for so much has been forgotten, never to be re-learned. Forget the promise of progress and understanding, for in the grim dark future there is only war. There is no peace amongst the stars, only an eternity of carnage and slaughter, and the laughter of thirsting gods.

CHAPTER ONE

IN THE MIDST of all the madness, the warrior found himself a small corner of darkness where he could shut himself off, a tiny sanctuary of silence. It was his shelter, after a fashion, a bolthole in which he could shutter away the churn of doubts and fears and concentrate instead on finding answers to the questions that plagued him. The room had once been a basement store for volatiles and dangerous chemicals, and it still carried the tang of free hydrocarbons in the thick air, the very stink of them embedded into the dull iron walls.

He peered out of the doorway to ensure that he was not being followed, and then shouldered shut the heavy hatch. It met the frame with a low booming, and he closed the latches. The biolume in the ceiling was cracked and dull, a thin trickle of greenish glow-fluid staining the cage around it. The chamber's only real light source was the grille near the top of the wall, which peered out at ground level to the streets beyond. Now and then, the faint snap-crack of a las-gun discharge passed through the vent, and the wave-like rush of a distant cheering crowd.

He removed the heavy hessian sack from the cord across his shoulder and dropped the bag to the floor. The delicacy he displayed seemed at odds with the huge, muscled figure he presented. Even out of the characteristic power armour of the Adeptus Astartes, the warrior manifested an impressive sight in his tunic and robes; he would tower over normal men even when barefoot, and the Space Marine filled the room with his presence. Gently and with reverence, he drew the sackcloth from the object he had so painstakingly recovered from the rubble of the street chapel. It had been buried there, forgotten by the people who had once paid fealty to it in favour of a new subject of devotion. That thought brought the beginnings of a glower to his hard, blunt features, and he forced it away.

The hessian bag fell away and in his cupped hands the Space Marine held an icon of the One True Master. It was a representation of the God-Emperor of Mankind, there in his infinite sagacity at rest atop the Golden Throne of Terra. He ran his fingers over the old, careworn idol; it had been made from brass off-cuts, from a factory that forged shells for the Leman Russ tanks of the Imperial Guard. He placed it on an upturned wooden box so that it rested in the shaft of light falling from the vent grille, the rays of the tepid orange sun casting it with a faint halo. He folded his arms over his chest, hands like flat blades, wrists crossed; the fingers and thumb taking on the shape of the double-headed Imperial aquila, one eye looking to the past, the other staring into the future, unblinking.

The Blood Angel bowed his head and sank to his knees before the Emperor, then spread his arms wide to show his wrists to the air. A mesh of faint scars caught the light on his forearms, the silent trophies of a hundred battles. Across one limb there was the red ink of a tattoo, showing a single drop of blood framed by two wings.

'In the name of Holy Terra,' he said, his voice low, 'in the name of Sanguinius, Lord of the Blood and the Red Angel, hear me, Master of Man. Grant me a fraction of your most perfect insight and guide me.' He closed his eyes. 'Hear these words, the contrition of your errant son Rafen, of Baal Secundus. I beseech you, Lord Emperor, hear me and my confession.'

THE INQUISITOR RAMIUS Stele rose to his feet, his meditation at an end, and gathered himself together. He rubbed a hand over his brow, touching the aquila electoo on his bald pate, and frowned. The closer he came toward the fruition of his plans, the more it seemed to fatigue him. He sniffed and his fingers wandered to his nostrils; they came away with a trickle of blood on them, and the inquisitor grimaced at the dark, purple-black fluid. Cautiously, he dabbed away the liquid with a kerchief and watched the stain spread across the cloth, moving like a cancer over the cotton threads.

Stele balled the kerchief and stuffed it into an inner pocket of his robes, dragging the heavy coat of his office about his shoulders. The symbol of the High Inquisition, the stylised capital 'I' in brass adorned with a white gold skull, hung from a chain about his neck, and Stele fingered it absently. There were times when it felt as if the medallion was a noose upon him, weighing him down, tying him to the petty world of men. He glanced at the emblem, rubbing away a faint bloodstain from its surface. Soon enough, he would be rid of it, rid off all the trappings that bound him to the corpse-god.

Stele took a moment to look about him, at the walls where dull brown handprints and splashes of old gore still marred the walls. In the battle for Shenlong, this place had been the site of one of the Word Bearers Chaos Marines' most brutal atrocities, where civilians had been gutted alive as a penitent sacrifice to the Ruinous Powers. While many of the chambers in the Ikari fortress had been cleaned and reconsecrated, Stele had quietly ensured that the death room had remained as it was. Here, where the screaming souls of the brutalised dead had etched their pain into the stone and mortar, the inquisitor found the membrane between the world and the warp to be thinner.

Resting here, letting his psyche drift free of its organic shell, Stele could taste the faint, seductive texture of the empyrean just tantalisingly beyond his reach. It was for him a far more divine experience than kneeling in false piety to the Emperor of Man.

Stele left the dank room behind and exited, to find his honour guards waiting outside. Towering above him in their crimson sheaths of ceramite armour, bolters at arms, they seemed less like men and more like animated statues cut from red rock. Only the brilliant polished gold of their helmets set them aside from the rank and file of the Blood Angels Space Marines. Stele paid them no heed. He had no idea of who these men were, their names, hopes and dreams, anything; in truth, he cared less for them than he did his automaton servo-skulls, which rose from the floor on gravity impellers as he strode away. The silver orbs hummed after him, watchful as hawks, with the Marines two steps behind.

At the junction of the corridor, Stele's lexmechanic stood waiting, lurch-a-backed. Its head bobbed by way of a greeting. 'Your meditation is concluded?' The servitor became nervous in the confines of the room and it had elected to remain outside for the duration. 'Matters present themselves for your attention.'

'Indeed,' he replied. The last traces of the dark miasma clouding Stele's mind faded away, the seductive vestiges of the warp's caress retreating. He missed it.

'Your servant Ulan has descended from the *Bellus* with news,' the lexmechanic continued. 'A concern which she was unwilling to confide to me.'

Was there wounded pride in the servitor's voice? Stele doubted it; his helot's mentality had been so thoroughly expunged in its service that there was little vestige in it that could be considered to be a personality. 'She waits in the chapel for your indulgence, inquisitor,' it added.

'Good, I will attend to her before I–'

An anxious, wordless shout broke through the air and Stele whirled in surprise. His hand drifted toward the butt of the elegant lasgun in his belt, but his action was slow and leisurely compared the whip-fast movements of the honour guards. The Blood Angels had their bolters to bear in an instant, training their weapons on a trio of figures framed in a side corridor.

At the head of the group was a man, florid-faced with watery eyes. His clothes, and those of the two women with him, were worn and slightly unkempt but in a rich, opulent style. Stele decided that they were most likely from Shenlong's mercantile class, dispossessed land-owners still clinging to the courtly ways of life from before the Word Bearers invasion. 'My-my lord inquisitor!' said the man, lips trembling. 'Forgive me, but–'

He took half a step closer to Stele and suddenly one of the Marines was there, blocking his path like a crimson wall. 'Stay back,' grated the Blood Angel.

The lexmechanic turned on the other Marine. 'How did these civilians get in here? These levels of the Ikari fortress are prohibited to all but the servants of Arkio the Blessed and the God-Emperor.'

A pair of gasps fled from the lips of the two women at the mention of Arkio's name. The man made the sign of the aquila and bowed his head. 'Please, forgive me, lords, but it was in devotion to his name that we dared to venture past the wards below…'

Stele raised a quizzical eyebrow and stepped forward, gently pushing the Marine's bolter away. 'Really? And what devotion do you have to share?'

The man licked his lips. 'I… We… Hoped to lay eyes upon the Blessed himself. To ask for his benediction.' He wiped a tear from his eye. 'All that we have was taken in the invasion. We have nothing now.'

Inwardly, Stele sneered. This pompous oaf was weeping over the loss of his money and chattels while others on Shenlong could barely feed themselves. The man's words did nothing but reinforce the inquisitor's hatred for the corruption of the Imperium, the maggot-ridden carcass of a society that served only to glorify the empowered and the rich. Stele betrayed none of these thoughts outwardly. 'Those of us who show our devotion to the Blessed will be rewarded,' said the inquisitor. 'Will you do so?'

A flurry of nods came from the merchant. 'Oh yes, yes! For the one who liberated us, I would gladly give all that I can, and ask only for his beneficence in return.'

'You would give all that you can,' Stele repeated, allowing the hint of a smile to cross his lips as he studied the women. The resemblance between them was clear. The younger of the two, perhaps no more than sixteen summers, watched him with wide eyes. She was attractive, in a virginal, parochial sort of way. The other, closer to his age, had the docile look of enforced pliancy about her. Stele considered them both; perhaps he could grant himself a distraction. 'This is your wife and daughter?' he asked, the question trailing away into the air.

'Uh…' The man fumbled at a response and found none.

Stele nodded. 'Take them to my chambers,' he told the honour guard, and the Marine obeyed, ushering the women away under the eye of a bolter. 'I'll call upon them at my leisure,' The inquisitor threw the man a nod. 'Your devotion is great. The Blessed has a worthy servant in you.'

As he continued on his way to the chapel, Stele heard the man mumble out ragged, broken words of thanks.

RAFEN HAD NOT dared to enter any of the tabernacles inside the Ikari fortress, all too aware of what he would see inside. Troops of Shenlongi had taken hammers and chisels to the intricate mosaics and the friezes that the Chaos invasion force hadn't already destroyed, and pulled them up. The enemy was gone now, routed and killed, but the people they had briefly subjugated completed the deconsecrations the Word Bearers had begun. Only the object of their veneration differed. In place of sanctioned Imperial idolatry they had daubed crude renditions of the Blood Angels sigil and the newly-created icon of their Blessed Arkio, the golden halo crossed by a shining spear. The sight of it burned in Rafen's heart like a torch, but he could not dare to speak openly of the doubts that thundered about him, much less even consider giving a confession in such a place. There was no doubt in his mind that any words he spoke would be spirited away to the ears of High Priest Sachiel, and to have him listening to Rafen's heartfelt thoughts would be a grave mistake.

Neither could Rafen visit one of the churches that the commoners and citizens used, down in the city-sprawls crammed into the gaps between Shenlong's kilometres-high factory cathedrals. The sight of a Space Marine, even one without his hallowed armour, would never pass unnoticed among the populace – and just as the people had taken Arkio to their hearts in the fortress, so the man they called the New Blood Lord had also supplanted the Emperor in chapels all across the forge-world.

So here, in a dim and ill-lit chamber, in a street ruined by shell fire and abandoned by life, Rafen had created his own place of worship, some small and safe conduit to his messiah where no prying ears would spy upon his prayers.

'I must confess,' he told the brass idol of the God-Emperor, 'I was forced to forsake my oath to the liege lord of my Chapter, to turn from Sanguinius to my sibling… the man they call Arkio the Blessed.' Rafen bit back the tremors in his voice. 'I know not what my brother has become, but only that my heart cannot accept what Sachiel and Stele claim to be self-evident. I cannot accede that Arkio is Sanguinius Reborn, and yet knowing this I took an oath of fealty to him.' He shook his head in answer to an unspoken question. 'This is not cowardice on my part, I swear. The Sanguinary High Priest Sachiel would surely have executed me had I not knelt before Arkio, but with my death there would be no voice to speak out against this insanity. Forgive me, lord, for this duplicity.'

Rafen drew a shuddering breath. 'Grant me insight,' he said, entreaty in his voice, 'show me a path. I ask of you, what do you wish of me? On Cybele, against the assaults of the foul Word Bearers I was ready to give my life and come to your right hand at the Throne, but in your wisdom the warship *Bellus* came to our aid and with it my young brother. I thought I was blessed to see my sibling after so long apart… Our ties of blood are as strong as the fellowship of my battle-brothers.'

The Blood Angel recalled the instant on the war grave world when Arkio rose in their moment of blackest despair, with a plan to turn the fight against the Traitor Marines; Arkio's uncanny flash of brilliance led them to bring down a Word Bearers warship and beat back the Corrupted from Cybele. At first, it seemed no more than a chance insight from Rafen's sibling, but then the young Marine had single-handedly saved Sachiel's life from a daemon creature, rallied the men and become the figurehead which turned the tide against the Chaos forces. By the time they had left Cybele aboard the *Bellus*, there were men wondering aloud if Arkio was not touched by Sanguinius himself, and then came the moment when the Spear of Telesto seemed to prove the truth behind the whispered rumours.

STELE LEFT HIS guard at the tall copper doors to the chapel and strode inside, the lexmechanic's clawed iron feet clattering after him. The astropath Ulan stood in the centre of the chamber, arms folded. Her sightless eyes glanced up from the hood of her dark robes and she gave a half-bow. 'My lord inquisitor,' she began, her quiet tones a whisper of wind through gravestones.

He approached her, for one brief moment letting his gaze stray to the titanium canister that lay atop the altar. The thought of the coiled power inside the long container made him thirst in a way that nothing else could slake. With a near physical effort, Stele turned his whole attention to the thin psyker girl. 'Speak to me.'

Ulan glanced at the lexmechanic, and Stele nodded, turning. 'Servitor, wait outside.'

The machine-slave turned on its heel and left them to their privacy. As the chapel door thudded shut, Ulan began to talk. 'Matters aboard the *Bellus* proceed, Lord Stele,' she said carefully. 'Questions as to the fate of the astropath Horin and his chorus have been suppressed. There is no other conduit to the galaxy at large now, save me.'

Stele made a dismissive gesture. 'You came to tell me that which I already know?' Without his notice, the inquisitor's trigger finger twitched, unconsciously repeating the action it had performed when Stele executed the *Bellus*'s cadre of telepaths. 'I installed you aboard the battle barge to be my eyes and ears.'

'And so I am,' she replied. 'I have news. The warning that was sent from Shenlong to Baal, the message to the Blood Angels Commander Dante... It has been heeded.'

'Dante has replied?'

She shook her head. 'The master of the monastery on Baal favours a more direct approach, Lord. A ship is on its way. I have intercepted the shadows of signals from the depths of the immaterium. It will arrive soon.'

Stele accepted this with a nod. 'Do you know what kind of vessel? Something more powerful than the *Bellus*?'

'Unlikely,' she noted. 'There is but one Blood Angels ship matching the tonnage of the *Bellus* within operational range of Shenlong, and that is the *Europae*, the Lord Mephiston's personal command.'

'Dante would not send his lieutenant Mephiston without good cause,' Stele spoke his thoughts aloud. 'Not yet, at any rate. No, it will be a smaller craft.'

'The advent of any Adeptus Astartes reinforcements will jeopardise the strategy,' Ulan said flatly. 'They will be outside our sphere of influence, an incalculable variable. The matter must be addressed.'

'Yes, and so it will be,' said the inquisitor, considering the situation. 'Return to orbit and maintain your post. You are to contact me the instant Dante's envoy reaches contact range.' Stele toyed with the silver purity seal stud in his ear. 'I must prepare.'

'New arrivals will not be turned so easily to loyalty to the Blessed,' the psyker warned. 'Termination presents the better option.'

'You are too narrow-minded, Ulan. Commander Dante is about to deliver me a valuable object lesson.' Stele dismissed her with a wave of his hand. 'Go now.'

When he was alone, the inquisitor let his control slip away and he crossed to the altar and the metal box upon it. The grey cylinder bore sigils and purity seals showing the oaths of the Ordo Hereticus and the Blood Angels, some engraved in the titanium itself, others on strips of sanctified parchment, fixed by fat discs of sealing wax embossed with devotional symbology. He laid his hands on the surface of the container and felt the warmth radiating out from the object inside. The Spear of Telesto, one of a handful of battle weapons and hallowed objects forged – so the myths would have it – by the very hand of the God-Emperor himself. The inquisitor felt himself drawn magnetically to the umbra of the device, even now as it lay in quietus.

Stele smothered a surge of jealousy; the reaction was the same each time he considered the Marine Arkio and his affinity with the artefact. On the mission of the *Bellus* into ork space to recover the archeotech weapon, it had been Stele who wrested it from the grip of a greenskin warlord, Stele who held it high in victory, but only in Arkio's hands had the Holy Lance awakened. On some basic, animalistic level, he could not excise the constant core of resentment he felt for the young Astartes.

He shook the thoughts away. The higher part of Stele's mind, the ice-cold engine that calculated the intricate clockwork of his schemes, knew better. Arkio was the ideal candidate to wield the spear, the perfect subject for veneration by his battle-brothers – and in the end, Stele's guidance of his path would lead the inquisitor to such power that would make the spear seem like a child's toy in comparison.

'My brother laid his hands on the Spear of Telesto,' Rafen's words echoed off the iron walls of his makeshift meditation cell. 'The Holy Lance that Sanguinius himself once commanded, and then...' His voice trailed off, the memory as fresh now weeks later as it had been the moment it happened. For a brief instant, Rafen felt the divine radiance of the spear on his face again, the golden light shining off the teardrop blade as Arkio held the haft high in the Great Chapel of the *Bellus*. Try as he might, Rafen could not explain what he had seen that day. The sudden vision of his sibling's face melting and merging into a brief incarnation of the long-perished primarch of the Blood Angels, the winged Lord Sanguinius.

'It was his example that lit the way to this blighted world.' The Blood Angel's head bobbed as he considered the desolation of Shenlong. 'Fired by the oratory of Inquisitor Stele, my brethren clamoured for a chance to visit retribution on the Word Bearers who had desecrated Cybele. It was only Brother-Sergeant Koris and his fellow veterans who spoke of caution, and they were censured for it.' The words were suddenly flowing from Rafen's lips in a torrent; it was as if speaking them aloud lifted a great weight from his shoulders. The icon of the God-Emperor watched him with calm and unmoving eyes, silently listening to the Marine as he unfolded the tale.

He opened his mouth to speak again and a knife of emotion cut into him. Rafen saw Koris's face there before him, the craggy old warhound, eyes hard but never without honour. It had been one of the greatest privileges of Rafen's service to count the veteran as a mentor and a friend, but all the strength the Marine could muster did not stop his former teacher from falling into the dark grip of the Blood Angels gene-curse, the warped berzerker battle lust known as the black rage. Inducted into the Death Company, as all men who succumbed to the red thirst were, Rafen had watched Koris as the old warrior relived the great battle of Sanguinius against the arch-traitor Horus, played out in the depths of the Ikari fortress. 'He died there,' Rafen told his god, 'and you took him to the peace he deserved... But he did not release his grip on life easily. His words... He left me with a warning.'

The moment replayed in the Marine's mind.

'Rafen. Lad, I see you.'

'I am here, old friend.'

'The Pure One calls me, but first I must… Warn…'

'Warn me? Of what?'

'Stele! Do not trust the ordos whoreson! He brought me to this, all of it! Arkio… Be wary of your sibling, lad. He has been cursed with the power to destroy the Blood Angels! I see it! I see–'

'Gone now,' Rafen admitted, 'and without him I felt cut adrift and alone, while my brothers took up Arkio's cause as their own. I saw no other path to take… I broke the disciplines we swore to and damned protocol…' He shook his head, calculating the enormity of his transgressions. 'Under cover of lies I sent word to the monastery on Baal and the Lord Commander Dante, in hopes that he might come to end this madness… But in your wisdom, you have yet to guide him here.'

Rafen opened his eyes and looked into the unmoving face of the God-Emperor. 'I beg of you, lord, I must know. Am I the heretic, the dissenter, the apostate deserving only of death? If Arkio truly is the Great Sanguinius reborn, then why do I doubt it so? Which of us is the one fallen from the path, he or I?'

'LORD INQUISITOR?'

Stele turned to see Sachiel approach, a questioning look on his face. The Sanguinary High Priest's battle armour caught the light through the chapel windows, glinting off the white detailing that marked his wargear. Stele stepped down from the altar and fixed him with a sullen eye. 'Sachiel. Where is Arkio?'

'The Blessed observes the trials in the plaza below, Lord Stele. He bade me to find you.' Sachiel paused, frowning. 'He has questions…'

Stele crossed to a set of stained-glass doors and waved his hand over a discreet wall sensor. On ancient mechanics, the glass gates parted to reveal a broad stone balcony jutting from the equator of the fortress. The instant the doors opened, a wall of sound thundered into the chapel; all at once, there were chants and cheers of victory, the screaming of the dying, the discharges of multiple weapons. The inquisitor walked out into the noise, to the lip of the balcony, and Sachiel followed.

Below them, the vast open plaza fronting the Ikari fortress was a ring of shanty-built grandstands and huts ringing a makeshift arena. The floor of the stadium was littered with the dead and a few pieces of broken cover. Gunfire flashed and snapped back and forth as figures swarmed over one another, some armed only with blunt clubs and crude knives, others clinging to lasrifles or ballistic stubber guns. In the stands, the faithful roared in approval as kills were made and the numbers of the fighters gradually diminished.

Stele glanced at Sachiel. The Blood Angel observed the unfolding battle with an arch look, clearly unimpressed by the crudity of the fighting. 'How many so far?' he demanded of the priest.

'Three hundred and nine chosen at last count,' he replied. 'The Blessed himself is making the selections.'

Stele saw the sunlight glinting as it touched a huge figure in golden armour, drifting over the battle on angelic wings. As he watched, the messianic shape singled out a wiry man wielding two swords and nodded to him. He dropped his weapons and wept with joy, the crowd chanting its accord once again. 'One more,' said Stele. 'We'll have the thousand soon enough.'

'As the Blessed chooses,' said the priest. 'He will have his army.'

The inquisitor looked away. 'You don't approve?'

Sachiel's face flushed red. 'How can you ask such a thing? It is as Arkio commands, and he is the Reborn. I would not question his wisdom.'

Stele smiled. 'The Warriors of the Reborn,' he said, gesturing to the men penned into a holding area at the edge of the arena. 'A thousand of the most zealous and devoted to the name of Arkio... And yet, there are Blood Angels who hesitate at his decision to raise this helot army.'

Sachiel blinked. 'We do not doubt,' he snapped, 'It is only... new to us. Understand, inquisitor, we have lived our lives to the tenets of the *Book of the Lords* and the *Codex Astartes*, and the recruiting of these commoners goes against those convictions.'

'We are past the time for ancient dogma,' Stele replied, 'Arkio the Blessed ushers in a new age for the Blood Angels, and the Warriors of the Reborn are merely an aspect of that.' He pointed into the crowd of tired, bloody fighters. 'Look at them, Sachiel. They have fought all day and still they would cut out their own hearts if Arkio demanded it of them. When he embarks on his glorious homecoming to Baal, the chosen thousand will accompany him. They will be the vanguard of a new breed of initiates to the Blood Angels, a new generation of the Adeptus Astartes.'

When the priest did not answer him, Stele turned to press him for a reply; but instead he saw the look of surprise on Sachiel's face.

'The Blessed...' began the priest.

From nowhere a sudden rumble of wind beat at Stele and he staggered back a step, forcing down the urge to shield himself with his hands. A shape, swift and brilliant, rushed up before the edge of the balcony and hung before him, blotting out the glow of the Shenlong sun. Sachiel fell into a deep bow and tapped his fist to the symbol of a winged blood droplet on his chest plate. The inquisitor looked up into a face of striking nobility, a countenance that combined a most patrician aspect with the promise of a darker heart beneath. A face that mirrored that of Sanguinius himself.

'Stele,' said Arkio, hovering there on wings spread like wide white sails. 'I would speak with you.'

'I SAW HIM turn death upon innocents,' Rafen's voice was heavy with anguish. 'By my blood, I watched my own brother cull men and women all too willing to accept murder, as if it were some horrific benediction. This is not the promise to which I granted my life as an aspirant. This is not the Emperor's will, I hope and pray that it is not. Arkio rules this world now by force of temper, with Sachiel as his instrument and the Inquisitor Stele as advisor forever at his side. It is not *right*. By the Red Grail, the marrow in my bones sings it is not so!' Anger boiled up inside Rafen and he came to his feet, fists balling, his words bouncing off the chamber walls. 'I pray that Lord Dante will have the grace and wisdom to end this matter before our Chapter is split asunder beneath its weight, but until that moment comes I must answer the call of my blood.' He took a breath, his burst of fury subsiding. 'Until a sign comes to me, bright and undeniable, my heart will set the compass of my deeds from this moment forth.'

Rafen laid a hand on the icon of the Emperor and bowed his head once again. 'Hear me, hear the pledge of Rafen, son of Axan, child of the Broken Mesa clan, Blood Angel and Adeptus Astartes. I recant the false oath I have taken to Arkio the Blessed and in its stead I restore my allegiance to Sanguinius and the God-Emperor of Mankind. This I swear, my blood, my body, my soul as the price.' The declaration seemed to take all the energy from him, and Rafen staggered back a step. 'This I swear,' he repeated.

After a long moment, he gathered himself together and opened the hatch, pausing to throw the holy icon a last glance. Here, in this forgotten place, the symbol would lie safe from the hands of those who sought to revise their beliefs in the face of Arkio's new Blood Crusade. 'There is one thing of which I have absolutely no doubt,' he told the statue. 'A single act for which I know I and I alone will be responsible. By what means and when are unclear to me, but my brother Arkio will perish and I shall be the one to end him. I know it in my blood, and it damns me.'

Rafen left the room behind, the leaden burden of his dilemma pressing down upon him as he stepped back into the Shenlong sunlight. He picked his way through the ruined streets and did not look back.

Before him, the vast cone of the Ikari fortress rose to fill the horizon like a monstrous volcanic mountain.

CHAPTER TWO

ARKIO DROPPED TO his feet on the balcony with a whisper of air through the wings at his back, and cocked his head. Sachiel fell to one knee and averted his gaze, while Stele gave a shallow bow. The gestures seemed to satisfy the Blood Angel. 'Lord inquisitor, I have questions.' His voice was cool, assured and direct, with none of the hesitation that had plagued him in the past as a youth.

Stele resisted the urge to smile. 'Blessed, I will answer them if I can.'

'Your counsel has meant much to me in these past few weeks,' Arkio began, 'and your guidance has helped me to understand the path Sanguinius has laid before me.'

'I am merely the lamp to light the way, Great One,' Stele allowed. 'I took on the governorship of this blighted world only because I saw it wanting. No honest servant of the Imperium would have done any less. That I could help you into the bargain…'

Arkio accepted this with a cursory nod. 'And we have done well here, have we not? The taint of Chaos has been burnt from the streets of Shenlong.'

Sachiel cleared his throat self-consciously. 'All the Word Bearers that intruded on this planet lie dead, lord, that is true… But our search still continues to find and purge any sympathisers.'

Stele watched Arkio assimilate the priest's words; only a short time ago, it had been Arkio who had suggested they annihilate this world completely rather than chance the survival of any cohorts of the Chaos Gods. But that was before his transformation, before Arkio's brutal duel with the Dark Apostle Iskavan the Hated in the manufactorium below the city. With his physical changes, Arkio had also altered within. He had become, to all intents and purposes, the living reincarnation of the Blood Angels primogenitor, and the former Space Marine revelled in his newly found divinity. He wore the sacred golden artificer armour of his Chapter with the arrogance and hauteur of one whom had been born to it. Yes, Stele told himself, I chose him well.

'The men speak in whispers and keep their fears from me,' Arkio turned his back on them and wandered to the edge of the balcony, watching the continual pit-fight. 'But yet I hear them.'

Sachiel's face twisted. 'What dissent is this? Lord Arkio, if there are weaklings and craven among our forces, I would know it. The honour guard will see them repudiated for such failings!'

Stele arched an eyebrow. With little prompting, Sachiel had stepped into the role the inquisitor had laid for him with gusto. So focussed was the priest on adhering to the word of his new master that he hardly noticed he was sanctioning the censure of his own battle-brothers.

Arkio shook his head slowly. 'No, Brother Sachiel, no. These men are not to be chastised for their fears. What leader would I be if turned away every Marine who dared to wonder? A fool myself.' The warrior's wings had folded back on themselves now, and they lay flat against Arkio's sun-bright armour.

'If it pleases the Blessed,' said Stele, 'what have you heard?'

'My brothers are conflicted, inquisitor,' said Arkio. 'They look upon me and see the truth of my change, of the Great Angel's hand on my soul, and they believe. But word spreads now among the ranks of the Blood Angels here on the planet and above on the *Bellus*.' He gestured toward the sky. 'I have heard men speaking of Dante and Mephiston, and questions of our Chapter brethren on Baal.'

'They fear you will not be accepted by the Lord Commander,' Stele said gently, providing the words to the rumour that he himself had quietly seeded. It had been a simple matter to fan the flames of righteousness in the Marines who had laid their fealty at Arkio's feet; it was the nature of the devout to seek enemies in all those who did not share their beliefs.

Sachiel made a negative noise. 'Lord, this matter trivialises your Ascension. I grant that yes, perhaps our battle-brothers at the Baal monastery may have their doubts about you, but when they lay eyes on you, they will know as I do – that you are the Deus Encarmine, the Reborn Angel.'

Arkio hung his head for a moment. 'Can you be sure, my friend? I still look to my own face and wonder at the changes wrought on me by fate. Mortal men could do no less.'

Stele took a calculated pause before answering. 'Blessed, as you speak of this now I must admit that I too have heard these misgivings among my comrade brethren. I chose to keep it from you as I believed it to be beneath your concern.' He shook his head, adopting a look of contrition. 'I am sorry.'

'Then tell me now, Stele. What is said?'

'As you say, Great Arkio. The men see themselves set apart from their brothers elsewhere, blessed by your arrival in their midst – but they fear Dante's reaction to your Emergence.'

The Blood Angel fixed him with a questioning look. 'But why, Stele? Why should they be afraid of that? Dante is a good and honourable commander. He has led our Chapter through adversity and strife for more than one thousand years, his character is impeccable.' Arkio gave a quick, bright smile. 'I welcome the moment when I will be able to face him with this miracle.'

And there it was, the opening Stele had been waiting for. With care, he marshalled his lies and pressed them home. 'But will Dante welcome you, Blessed? When you enter the grand annexe of the fortress-monastery, will Dante kneel and give you his fealty as we have? Will his Librarian Mephiston bow to you? What of Brothers Lemartes, Corbulo or Argastes? Will they see the truth of it?'

'Why would they do otherwise?' Arkio said darkly. 'Why would they doubt me?'

'Dante did not witness your miracle,' broke in Sachiel, 'He would ask for proof…'

'Proof?' Arkio snapped, and his wings unfurled in a flash of white, his eyes shining with sudden intensity. 'Proof denies faith, and faith is all that we are!'

'You yourself said that Lord Dante has commanded the Blood Angels for over a millennium,' Stele took a step closer to Arkio, 'and some might argue, too long. Such a man would not step aside easily, Blessed, even in the face of such divinity as yours. And Mephiston…' He shook his head. 'The psyker they call the Lord of Death has always held himself to be the heir apparent to the mastery of the Chapter. These men… I would not vouch for their magnanimity in this matter.'

Arkio shook his head again. 'No. I will not hear this. What has happened to me is a blessing from the Emperor for every Blood Angel, for our entire Chapter, not just the Marines here on Shenlong and the crew of *Bellus*. I have been chosen, Stele. Chosen by fate to be the vessel for a power far greater than myself! Sanguinius makes himself known through me, returns to us after so long departed. I will not conceive that this marvel…' He paused, his fangs bearing in a snarl as he fought down his anger. 'That *I* will be the cause of a schism among my brothers. No! It shall not be so.' In one single bound, Arkio stepped up on to the lip of the stone balcony and swept off it, a crash of air filling his wings. The golden figure dropped back into the arena, into the thunderous adulation of his warriors and his subjects.

Stele watched him go, aware of Sachiel as the priest came closer. 'Would that his wishes become reality,' said the inquisitor gravely, 'but it may not go as the Blessed would hope.'

Sachiel had a faraway look in his eyes, as if the Apothecary's mind was focussed on some distant vanishing point, on events yet to come. 'You… could be right, lord inquisitor. If Dante denies the Ascension of Arkio, it will split the Blood Angels asunder.' The sombre thoughts were hard for the priest to articulate. 'There could be a… a civil war. A severing greater than anything our Chapter has ever known before.'

'Indeed,' Stele intoned, 'and such a break would not be as congruous as those that created the Successor Chapters, the Blood Drinkers and the Flesh Tearers, the Angels Vermilion, Encarmine and Sanguine…'

'We will find adherents in those bands,' Sachiel said quickly, 'once word spreads of the Blessed. If what you suspect comes to pass, Dante will be unable to deny the Rebirth when all our battle-brothers give credence to it.'

The inquisitor gave a sigh. 'Perhaps, Sachiel, perhaps. I hope that these dark possibilities we consider now remain just that – but if not, we must be prepared.'

The priest watched Arkio as he swooped and dove over the great arena. 'To do what, lord? To go to war with our kinsmen? I hardly dare to speak such a thing.'

'If the Blood Angels on Baal are unwilling to accept Arkio for what he is, as the avatar of the Sanguine Messiah, they may need to be *encouraged* to believe.' Stele met Sachiel's gaze and held it with his cold, glittering eyes. 'If they do not, then those who resist the divine design must be purged.'

The High Priest replied with a slow, serious nod, and Stele drew away a smile.

* * *

RAFEN KEPT OFF the more heavily trafficked streets as much as he could, but eventually he was forced to walk out in the open, amid the endless confusion of markets, portable shrines and thronging Shenlongi citizens. He was on the far side of the Ikari fortress to the combat arena, but still the sounds of the chanting crowds were filling the air, humming up and down the octaves like distant surf breaking on a shore. The Marine spied several knots of excited natives clustered around jury-rigged speakers in shop doorways and windows, the sound boxes hastily tapped into the webs of lines from the factory-city's vox-net. Tinny commentaries issued out of the speakers, encouraging hoots of excitement from some and groans from others. The fruits of wagers, dog-eared handfuls of Imperial scrip, changed hands as candidates for the Warriors of the Reborn died off or were chosen for the thousand.

Rafen did his best to keep to the edges of the highway, head bowed and hood up; but there was little he could do to avoid towering over the civilians, the tallest of whom could barely reach the Marine's shoulder. With awed whispers they parted in front of him like water flowing around a rock. Some of them, the more daring, would reach out and run a finger over the hem of his garment. He considered giving them a flash of his teeth and a snarl to keep them at bay; but what good would it do to instil an even greater fear of his kind in these people?

Something crunched beneath the sole of his sandal and Rafen paused. With the tip of his foot he nudged a broken tin object out of the dirt. It had been cut from an old recaf can and bent into shape as… what? The Marine became aware of a skinny child watching him with an open, gap-toothed mouth. The street urchin was smeared with rusty dirt and bore a scarred cheek. In front of the child was a box filled with more tin shapes. Rafen looked closer. Some of the crafted things were crude copies of the Blood Angels crest, others a model of the Spear of Telesto, even a miniature figure of a winged Space Marine. He indicated the object at his feet. 'You made this?'

The child nodded once, with no change in expression. Rafen picked up the ruined effigy and deposited it back in the box. Closer, he could see that the juvenile was a girl. On the blemished side of her face she was missing a patch of hair. He nodded to himself; the child had been caught in the nimbus of a plasma shot. 'You are lucky to be alive,' he told her.

She nodded again, and closed her mouth. On her dirty tunic, Rafen saw a rendition of the spear-and-halo badge that Arkio's supporters were popularising and frowned. He surveyed the contents of her box, then looked up and met her gaze. 'There are no icons of the Emperor here,' he said quietly. 'You will make no more of these others from now on, understand? Only symbols of the God-Emperor.'

'Yes, lord.' At last she spoke, and it was with a piping, tremulous voice.

Rafen turned and walked away, resuming his path toward the fortress. Behind him, the people on the street scrambled to press money into the girl's hands, suddenly desperate to buy an icon that a Blood Angel had touched.

Chaplain Delos was waiting for him at the foot of the fortress tower. 'Rafen,' the black-armoured priest beckoned him closer. 'I did not see you at prayers–'

'Forgive me, but I took my devotion alone today, Chaplain,' he replied. 'I required… solitude.'

'Just so,' said Delos. 'The arming ritual demands your most serious mind. It is good that you have prepared.' The priest walked him into the massive inner atrium of the fortress, past the metre-high piles of devotional objects and invocation plaques left by the citizens. 'I know these times have been difficult for you.'

Rafen said nothing and walked on.

The Chaplain took his silence for assent. 'The deaths of your Captain Simeon on Cybele, the fall of Koris to the red thirst…' He shook his head. 'And your sibling… None of us have been through the maelstrom of things as you have. But it pleases me that you have come to understand the glory of Arkio's blessing.'

'Yes,' Rafen kept his voice neutral. Delos did not seem to notice.

'That you took his oath, that gladdens me, Brother Rafen. I was afraid you might also succumb to the red thirst as Koris did.'

'Were there any men who refused?' Rafen said suddenly. 'Did any battle-brother refuse to bend his knee to Arkio?'

Delos looked at Rafen with a confused smirk. 'Of course not. Not a single Blood Angel could deny his Ascension.'

'No,' said Rafen, 'of course not.'

The Chaplain stepped forward and opened the doors to the consecration chamber and beckoned him inside. It was gloomy in the room, the light of hovering biolumes casting a viridian haze over everything. A spider of metallic arms moved in the shadows and a Techmarine emerged.

'Brother Lucion,' said Rafen.

Lucion gave him a nod of acknowledgement and gestured to a low iron bench. Across the surface were the parts of a suit of Adeptus Astartes power armour, and around the table a trio of hunched servitors twitched, awaiting the Techmarine's command.

'We shall commence,' intoned Delos.

Without ceremony, Rafen disrobed, discarding his common cloth and sandals, revealing the glistening ebony sheath of his black carapace. A living compound of plastics and alloys, the dark material had been implanted under the skin of his upper torso in his seventeenth year, as the final part of his initiation and transformation from Baalite tribesman into Blood Angels Space Marine. The neural sensors and transfusion shunts that bloomed from the surface of the carapace opened like the yawning mouths of tiny birds, ready to accept the interface jacks of his new armour.

As Delos began the Litany of Armament, he set a grail-shaped censer swinging from his hands. Lucion gave a burst-command in chattering machine code, and as one the servitors went to work, fitting the components of the Mark VII codex power armour to Rafen's body. The Space Marine joined in the chant where his answers were needed to complete the rite. Thermonic garments slid across him; flexible myomer muscle encircled the meat of his limbs, arranging itself to enhance and augment his physical strength; over this came the outer layer of bonded ceramite and plasteel weave, tough enough to turn a glancing bolt shell at twenty paces. Rafen slid his bare feet into the hollows of his greaves, the gyroscopic stabilisers in the broad boots humming into life.

As the armour wrapped itself around him, the Blood Angel felt a measure of comfort from the familiar touch and scent of the wargear. The power armour he had worn since his initiation had been destroyed in combat with the Chaos champion Iskavan, the centuries-old hardware ruined by the claws and blades of the Word Bearer. Perhaps some elements of his old gear might remain among the components he now donned, but for the most part he was clothing himself in the armour of dead men. On the inner surfaces of the boots, the wrist sheaths, the chest plates, there were lines and lines of tiny scripture, etched there by blade-point over hundreds of years. Each piece of the codex armour carried the history of its wearers, a roll of honour naming the men that had borne it into countless battles. The gear that Rafen would now call his own had been in service to the Chapter for half a millennium or more.

One of the servitors handed him a gauntlet, and Rafen paused. Etched in the ceramite about the wrist guard was a name that he knew. 'Bennek,' he said softly.

'Brother?' Lucion gave him a questioning look. 'Is something amiss?'

Rafen shook his head, remembering Bennek's death on Cybele. His comrade had been struck by enemy plasma fire and crushed beneath a horde of Word Bearers. Rafen thrust his hand into the gauntlet and made a fist with it, silently vowing to avenge his battle-brother's death.

Lucion leaned in and attached Rafen's left shoulder guard, running his claw-hand over the winged tear of blood embossed on the surface. The Techmarine gripped the opposing piece and moved to place it over the right arm, but Rafen's eyes narrowed and he blocked Lucion with the flat of his hand. He pointed at the other shoulder guard. 'What is this?' Along with the traditional white teardrop design that symbolised the Third Company of the Blood Angels, the armour bore a new sigil – a golden spear surrounded by a halo.

The Chaplain and Techmarine exchanged glances. 'In honour of Arkio, brother,' said Delos. 'To signify our presence here as witnesses to his Emergence.'

Rafen hesitated, thinking of his oath, then looked away with a nod. Lucion attached the pad without comment. Finally, the litany concluded with the Chaplain's benediction over Rafen's helmet. The Marine allowed the servitors to place it over his head, and he heard the hiss and click of the neck ring sealing him into the wargear. Inside the accustomed confines of the armour he felt alive again, the second skin of metal and plastic as natural to him as breathing. Rafen dropped to one knee and made the sign of the aquila.

'I am armoured by the Emperor himself,' he said, recalling the words of Dante from the eve of the Alchonis Campaign. 'Righteousness is my shield. Faith is my armour and hatred my weapon. I fear not and I am proud, for I am a Son of Sanguinius, a protector of mankind. Aye, I am indeed an Angel of Death.'

'Blood for Sanguinius,' Lucion and Delos spoke together. 'Blood for the Emperor. Blood for Arkio, the Angel Reborn.'

Beneath the blank mask of his helmet's breather grille, Rafen's face soured at the last words, and he came to his feet. Lucion presented him with an object wrapped in red velvet. The Marine unfurled the cloth from his bolter and ran his fingers over the gun's surface. This was the only piece of his equipment that had survived the clash with Iskavan intact, and Rafen felt a curious sadness as he read the engravings he had placed on it during his years of service. The bolter was a remnant of the old Rafen, he realised, the Blood Angel who had been content in his service to

Chapter and God-Emperor, never daring to question his place in the scheme of things; not so now. He worked the slide on the weapon and loaded it, the last action in the ritual completed. Rafen brought the bolter to a battle-ready stance with a snap of boots on stone.

A voice came from the doorway. 'Ah, my brother is whole once more.' Delos and Lucion bowed as Arkio strode into the chamber. Even in the poor light of the room, the Blood Angel's golden armour seemed to glow with an inner luminescence.

'Blessed,' began the Chaplain, but Arkio waved him into silence.

'Delos, if you would permit me, I would speak with my sibling alone.'

'Of course.' The priest gestured to Lucion and the two Marines took their leave, the tech-servitors waddling out after them.

Arkio placed a hand on Rafen's shoulder and smiled. 'I promised you that you would live, did I not?'

Rafen recalled his brother's words in the wake of the duel with Iskavan. 'Yes. I thank you for my life.'

The smile broadened, and once again Rafen was struck by the uncanny similarities between Arkio's new aspect and the renditions of Sanguinius that hung in the chapels. 'Formality is not needed between us, Rafen. You are my blood kin as well as my battle-brother.' He tapped the sculpted breastplate of his armour. 'I want you close by my side. We have great works ahead of us, kinsman, high deeds that will be spoken of throughout the galaxy.'

The display inside Rafen's helmet told him the comparative positions of the nearest Blood Angels. There were four honour guards outside the chamber, along with Delos and Lucion; even the swiftest of them was a full ten seconds away. Arkio stood within arm's length of Rafen, his mood relaxed and his guard apparently lowered. His brother was without headgear, the bare skin of his throat visible. Rafen was aware of the weight of his bolter in his mailed fist, a full magazine of shells there in the clip. It would not take much; just a jerk of the wrist to bring the muzzle of the gun to press against Arkio's chest, one squeeze of the trigger to discharge a point-blank burst of fire. Even the hallowed gold artificer armour would not be able to withstand such a strike. In that moment, Rafen imagined the look of shock and pain on Arkio's face as the bolt shells tore into his torso, punching his organs through his back in a riot of fluid and matter. He could almost smell the hot blood, the taste of it on his tongue flaring as the red thirst caressed the edges of his mind. The opportunity was here, now. All Rafen need do was raise his weapon and murder his brother, and he would put an end to all question of this Emergence. The thought of it repelled and agitated him in equal measure.

'What... what deeds?' The words came out of his mouth of their own accord.

'A Blood Crusade,' Arkio said firmly. 'Once I have united the Chapter under our banner, we will draw together all the successors, all the Sons of Sanguinius. By the grail, we shall cut the cancerous heart of Chaos from our space.' He gave his sibling a clear-eyed look, the pure power of his disposition overwhelming at such close quarters. It was little wonder that lesser men would die for one such as he.

Rafen's bolter felt like it was as dense as neutronium, too heavy to move. 'How?'

'We'll begin with the Maelstrom, brother. Fitting that our first target will be the nest of the Word Bearers, yes? I will personally see to it that their foul cadre is purged to a man.' Like the monstrous Eye of Terror, the horrific realm of warped space known as the Maelstrom was a gateway into the chaotic realm of the Ruinous Powers, and it was in this twisted zone that the Sons of Lorgar had made their throneworld. Arkio nodded to himself. 'Commander Dante has allowed them the privilege of life too long, I think. As Sachiel said, it is not enough that we drove them from Cybele and Shenlong. We must drive them from existence.'

'The priest,' Rafen said in a chill voice. 'You value his words more than those of our Chapter's lord?'

Arkio's eyes narrowed. 'Dante is not here, Rafen. Dante did not see, as we did, the merciless intent of Iskavan's hordes. Had we not intervened, a world would have been put to death.' He looked away. 'I have always honoured Commander Dante in word and deed, but now I find my perspective changing, brother. During my time on the mission of the *Bellus*, away from Baal, perhaps it was then that I first began to wonder if his stewardship of our Legion was all it could be…'

Rafen stifled a gasp. 'Some would call that dissidence.'

'Who?' snapped Arkio, 'Who would dare say that to me? Was it not our old mentor Koris who said that men must question all that they believe, or else they are fools?'

'And what did it bring him?' Rafen said bitterly. 'Lord Dante is a fine commander.'

'Yes, perhaps. Perhaps he was, five hundred years ago at the peak of his powers, but what of now? It was the inquisitor who drew me to this fact, Rafen – among all their victories, have the Blood Angels truly assumed their place as the first among equals before the Emperor? Look back to the death of our Brother Tycho at Hive Tempestora. One of our greatest falls and nothing is done? We should have led a reprisal force to wipe out a dozen ork tribeworlds as payment in kind. And Dante did not!' He turned away, presenting his folded wings to his brother. 'In eleven hundred years at the head of the greatest Chapter of the Legion Astartes, what progress has he made toward the mastery of our gene-curse? None!'

Rafen could not believe what he was hearing, the open scorn in Arkio's voice. 'Brother, what has driven you to this?'

Arkio fixed him with a level gaze. 'I have had my eyes opened, Rafen.'

'By Stele? By *Sachiel*?' He tried and failed to keep a mocking tone from his voice.

The Blood Angel gave a snort of derision. 'Rafen, you are transparent to me. Now I see why you falter at these ideals – it is not your will that prevents you, it is your pride. Your... rivalry with the priest runs deep, yes? Neither of us will forget that it was he that almost cost you your chance to become a Chapter initiate.'

'You are right,' Rafen admitted. 'But it is not just my dislike of Sachiel that colours my words. I implore you, brother, do not follow the counsel of the priest and the inquisitor blindly–'

'Blind?' Arkio repeated, his mood turning stormy. 'Oh no, Rafen, it is you who refuses to see.' He paused, moderating his annoyance. 'But still we have time. I keep you close, brother, because you remind me that no path is the easy one. I question and you question me. You are the devil's advocate.' Arkio gave him another brilliant smile and patted him on the shoulder. 'Thank you.'

Rafen watched him leave, the hand around his bolter's pistol grip as rigid and immobile as cast iron.

IN THE SILENCE of the Sanctum Astropathica aboard the *Bellus*, Ulan drifted in zero gravity, a weave of mechadendrites and brassy cables snaking from slots on her skull to banks of murmuring cognitive engines. The psyker's mind was spread as thinly as she dared, the energy of it dispersed into a wide net. Her concentration was paramount; if she were to let her thoughts drift further for even an eye-blink, what little there was to call her personality would be picked apart on the winds of the empyrean. She was a spider now, settled at the nexus of a web she wove from her own psy-stuff. Ulan lurked there, sensitive to any perturbation in the rolling non-matter of the warp, looking and watching for patterns.

There were things out there. She was careful not to let her attention turn directly upon them, cautiously watching them only by the wakes they left in passing, the shimmers as the anti-space stretched under their weight. Ulan kept her terror for these things under the tightest control of all;

they liked the taste of fear. Even the tiniest speck of it could call them across the void like sea predators scenting drops of blood in the water.

Then they were gone as quickly as they had arrived. Ulan was listening again, watching, waiting.

And there was her target. Very distant but approaching quickly now, cutting through the immaterium like a sword blade. A man-made object, swift and deadly in aspect.

Ulan smiled and gathered herself back together. When she had recovered enough of her potency, she focused on her master and sent him a single word.

Soon.

IT WAS LATE for Firing Rites, and so the range was deserted. Rafen was inwardly pleased; he did not feel like company for the moment, and the questions and comments of his brethren would have not been welcomed. He loaded a fresh sickle magazine into the bolter and took aim with the naked eye, releasing a series of three-round bursts into the rotating target stands.

He frowned at the results. His weapon had been knocked off true when it fell from his hands in the manufactory. With care, Rafen adjusted the pitch of the foresight. The simple, disciplined action gave him focus away from the churning concerns in the back of his mind. Intent on the work, he realised too late that someone else had entered the chamber.

Rafen looked up and scowled.

'Here you are,' said Sachiel, with false lightness. 'Your new armour fits you well, brother.'

He returned to his bolter, unwilling to waste breath on pretended pleasantries with the Sanguinary High Priest. 'I will strive to be worthy of it.'

'I am pleased to hear you say that. The Blessed was quite concerned that you be returned to duty status. Arkio... It appears he has a greater degree of lenity for a blood relative, than for other men.'

Rafen reloaded the bolter and slammed the magazine home with force. 'Do not play word games with me, Sachiel,' he said sharply. All at once, his tolerance for the conceited priest vanished. 'You have come here to say something to me? Speak and be on your way.'

Sachiel's face reddened but he kept the annoyance from his voice. 'Your bluntness could be construed by some as insubordination, Rafen. I would pay it mind if I were you.' He leaned in to speak in a low, loaded whisper. 'The Blessed may have reason to endure your dispute of his divinity for now, but I would not test him further, brother. A wise man would do well to heed a warning and keep his silence.'

'Your words could be construed by some as a threat, Apothecary,' said Rafen, mimicking his tone.

'They might at that,' Sachiel agreed. 'If you continue to challenge Arkio, there will come a time when his favour will wane. And when that moment comes, it will be my pleasure to see you branded a heretic.'

Rafen angrily rose to his feet in a rush from his firing stance, the bolter still hot in his hands. Sachiel was caught by surprise and backed away a step. 'Your counsel is appreciated,' Rafen said coldly, shouldering his weapon. 'But if you forgive me, I have duties to attend to aboard the *Bellus*.'

'What duties?' demanded the priest.

'The memory of the dead, Sachiel. I must pay my respects to the fallen in the ship's great chapel.' He pushed past the Apothecary and walked away.

'Take care, Rafen,' Sachiel called out after him, 'lest you wish to join them too soon.'

CHAPTER THREE

RAFEN FELT THE pull of Shenlong's gravity lessen as the Thunderhawk rose out of the forge-world's atmospheric envelope. He glanced through the viewport – the dun-coloured sky beyond had faded to a dirty purple and now it was the black of space. Craning his neck, he could see the curvature of the planet, a blanket of rusty pollution over the industrial landscape.

The transport rocked as it changed course. Rafen knew the interiors of these craft as well as he did the words of the Chapter hymnals, many was the occasion that he had been crammed into the heavily armoured cargo deck of such a vessel, shoulder to shoulder with other Blood Angels. The vibration of the floor beneath his feet never failed to kindle a faint anticipatory thrill in his chest. It was so often the precursor to battle, but not today. The Thunderhawk carried only munitions on this journey. Rafen had half-expected not to find a flight back to *Bellus*'s anchor at high orbit, but by luck one of the barge's auxiliaries had been preparing for lift-off. The transport was taking advantage of the forge-world's full stocks of shells to rearm the warship, ferrying case after case of missiles where it might normally have loaded Rhinos and Marines for ground assault. The warheads filled the hull spaces, leaving scant room for anything else.

Rafen was not the only passenger. Personally supervising the cargo was the battle barge's second-in-command, Brother Solus. Rafen could not recall ever having seen the man outside the bridge of the *Bellus* before. Solus seemed more like an extension of the will of the ship's commander, Captain Ideon, than a person in his own right.

Solus threw him a cursory nod as he passed through the cabin. 'We'll dock soon,' he noted. The Space Marine paused and gave Rafen a questioning look. 'I was not aware you had been ordered to return to the ship.'

Much of the *Bellus's* crew had been granted planetfall leave in a gesture of magnanimity by Inquisitor Stele, following his assumption of the brevet governorship of Shenlong. In the wake of the Word Bearers invasion, the forge-world had declared a celebratory holiday and Chapter serfs and commoner crewmen had been only too happy to join the festivities. The carnival mood Rafen had glimpsed in the Ikari district was everywhere, all of it alive with the worship of Arkio. The pressure of that and the knowledge that Sachiel was surely watching Rafen's every move had driven him to look for solace somewhere – anywhere – away from Arkio. A spell aboard the quiet corridors of *Bellus* would give Rafen time to think, he hoped. None of this, however, he confided in Solus.

'My mentor, Brother-Sergeant Koris,' said Rafen. 'He lies in the grand chamber aboard the barge. I wish to pay my respects to him, and enter his name in the *Book of the Fallen*.'

Solus nodded. The ritual was typically performed by a Sanguinary Priest, but often men who had served closely with those who died would carry out the rite as a personal farewell, writing the dead man's name in their own blood as a lasting salute. 'I did not know him. From what I saw of him, he seemed an… outspoken warrior.'

'Indeed,' Rafen agreed, 'he was that.'

'A pity he did not live to see the Emergence,' Solus continued. 'A great many of our brothers fell for that piece of dirt.' He indicated Shenlong with the jerk of his chin. Even though he was Astartes to the core, Solus still had a spacer's dislike for planets.

A hatch hissed open to admit a bondman in flight crew gear. He bowed quickly to Solus. 'Lord, we are receiving an alert from *Bellus*.'

'To what end?' the Marine demanded.

'A starship is approaching the planet. Our cogitators believe it to be the strike cruiser *Amareo*.'

Rafen straightened. 'One of ours.' He felt his pulse quicken. The arrival of another Blood Angels vessel could mean only one thing: the clandestine message he had sent using Sergeant Koris's vox-net transmitter had got through to Baal. 'Is it known who is in command of the cruiser?'

The serf nodded. 'Yes, lord. The pennant of Brother-Captain Gallio flies from the *Amareo*'s bridge.'

'Gallio…' repeated Rafen.

'You know him?' said Solus.

'Only by reputation. He was a contemporary of my late commander, Captain Simeon.'

Solus considered this for a moment, then turned to the crewman. 'Contact *Bellus*. Inform Captain Ideon that we are diverting to intercept *Amareo*. Protocol requires that a ranking officer welcome Gallio to the system.'

The serf saluted and returned to the bridge. Rafen watched him go. 'Lord, should not the *Amareo* be received by a quorum of senior Marines?'

Solus nodded. 'Correct, Rafen, but with much of the crew planetside for the celebrations of the Ascension, I doubt Ideon could find others to be spared.' He beckoned him to his feet. 'You and I will have to suffice.'

The Thunderhawk's engines throbbed and the light through the window shifted as the ship changed course. Rafen looked out and saw a splinter of silver and red hanging in the dark like a thrown knife; his search for respite would have to be postponed.

ULAN'S WARNING BROUGHT a thin smile to Stele's bloodless lips. Seated cross-legged in the centre of the bloodstained death room, the inquisitor's dark grox-hide coat pooled out around him like spilled ink. In the dim half-light, he appeared to be some sort of strange extrusion growing out of the patches of dried crimson. Stele gave a quick look at the door; if he were disturbed, if his concentration was broken, then all of this would be for nothing. There was a shock-ward attached to the inside of the hatch, primed and ready to deliver a massive electric charge into anyone foolish enough to try to open it from the outside.

He reached into one of dozens of secret pockets in the coat and retrieved two vials of bright, fresh blood. Stele had drawn the fluid himself, from the necks of the merchant's wife and daughter as they had lain spent at his feet, compelling them into death so that the liquid might teem with the vital essence of their brutal, potent murder. Uncapping the vials, he licked his lips as the smell of the liquid reached him. Gently now, it was important not to waste even the smallest drop.

Stele closed his eyes and jerked his wrists; the contents of the vials flickered into the air in a wet arc, tracing precise lines that bisected one another. In that moment, the gloomy, meat-wet room quivered with the psychic fingerprints of agony, and Stele slipped his mind into the non-space at the edge of the warp. To the layman and the untrained, Ramius Stele appeared to possess formidable pskyer talents, but in truth he was a man of only middling mental power in comparison to many of the Imperium's telepathic agents. Stele's talents lay not in the brute force application of his psychic ability, like those of his servant Ulan, but in his subtle use of them. Stele's mind was less a sword, more a scalpel, but still utterly lethal when used correctly.

The inquisitor ignored the thrilling warmth of the energies around him, resisting the urge to dip into them like a welcoming ocean. His resolve firm, Stele let his abhuman senses map the space around Shenlong in shades of psionic force. Up above, where *Bellus* lay, was the faint ember glow of the latent minds aboard her. Flickering and wavering among them was Ulan's bright and dangerous psychic imprint. She was a firefly in a bottle, her power bouncing off the walls of the inhibitor coronet he forced her to wear. Had Stele chosen to channel his mind through hers, what he did now would have been far easier, but her erratic character was too unpredictable for something that required so delicate a touch.

He passed further out, ignoring the dots of light on a small craft suspended mid-way between *Bellus* and the new arrival, letting his spirit-self approach the *Amareo*. A dart of indistinct fear rose and fell in him as he sensed the clear, steady glow of a psyker mind on board the starship; on some level, he had been concerned that the arch-telepath Mephiston would be the first to come and confront Arkio. For all his arrogance, Stele was not so foolish as to think he could match wits with the Lord of Death – at least, not at the moment. But as he predicted, the Chief Librarian of the Blood Angels had sent a proxy in his place, and it was this trained psyche that glittered before him. It had none of the random, freakish coloration of Ulan's mentality. This was a keen, acute mind born of the psykana librarius.

All the more reason to tread carefully, Stele reminded himself. The inquisitor raised his hands so that his ghost-fingers barely touched the corona of the psyker's aura and let the surface details of the Librarian's mind reveal themselves. The Blood Angel was without his psychic hood for the moment, a piece of good fortune that would make his task easier. The inquisitor's subtlety was his greatest skill, his target would never suspect that Stele's dark touch was spreading over his mind like some dark sheen of oil.

'Your name…' Stele said aloud to the dank air, 'You are Brother Vode, Epistolary to Mephiston. He has sent you… Sent you to taste Arkio's mind…' And there it was, drifting inside Vode's thoughts, perhaps even too faint for the Space Marine to know himself, the cold splinter of doubt and suspicion. Stele made a low chuckle in the depths of his throat. Mephiston had dispatched the best of his Librarians on this mission, but in doing so opened Vode to the thought that he would be venturing into the souls of heretics. Stele laid his hands upon Vode's nascent misgivings and began to massage them, working them deeper. Even at such a distance, the taint of the Blood Angels psyker's loathing for apostates leaked into the mind-space like black ichor.

With ghostly pressure, Stele nurtured Vode's doubts, sweat beading his bald brow with effort and concentration.

BROTHER-CAPTAIN GALLIO entered the cruiser's training gallery and found Vode immediately. The Librarian was in the midst of a series of regimented *kata*, a complex dance of advances, parries, and blocks. In his hand, the psyker held a formidable-looking force axe, a full half of Gallio's height and forged from bright steel made in the foundries of Luna. The axe head quivered in the light, the crystalline blade flickering with the witch-fire of psionic energy.

The captain's eyes seemed to slide off the metallic curve, as if his vision could not hold the shape of the weapon in his gaze. Gallio, like most Adeptus Astartes, held a powerful distrust of anything that bore the mark of the psyker. To him, those who had this aberrant curse were to be considered a danger, or at the very best, to be pitied. It was through the lens of such minds that the first gateways to the warp had been opened, and with them the lurking powers of Chaos that made the immaterium their home. This was the fear that lay at the heart of the psychic 'gift'; those who were weak in spirit would find themselves seduced by the raw energy of the warp space. Such souls could become conduits for daemonic intelligences, flesh vessels for creatures that were hate incarnate.

Gallio approached Vode carefully, watching the precise ballet of the psyker's fighting style. There was no wasted movement there: each simulated blow of the axe was economical and clear-cut. Every iota of Gallio's battle instinct was keyed to the war against Chaos, and on some level he believed that such witch-minds deserved only death. And yet, here was a psyker who bore the mark of the Blood Angels. Before him stood a man that embodied both the magnificence of a Space Marine and the dark potential of a monstrous psychic. The duality of the matter perturbed him.

Vode came about and halted, the humming force axe hovering between the two men. Vode had eyes that were so pale as to be almost grey. Gallio resisted the automatic surge of revulsion in his gut as the faint glow from the weapon drew all the moisture from the air.

'Honoured captain,' said Vode quietly, showing no concern at Gallio's expression. 'I am prepared. What is your bidding?'

The Librarian was nothing like his master, the notorious Mephiston, Gallio noted. The Lord of Death was a gaunt, imposing figure in red-gold ceramite, where Vode was a rugged fireplug of a man with skin the colour of dark wood. 'A transport approaches from the *Bellus*. We must be prepared to receive them.' Unlike the rank and file of the Blood Angels, Librarians wore armour that was blue in coloration, with only a single crimson shoulder pad. It was another factor that set them apart from the rest of their brethren, thought Gallio.

Vode nodded. 'As you order.' With care, the psyker drew his axe back to a sling across his armour, the tiny licks of cerulean lightning fading from its surface. Vode's face twitched slightly and something moved inside the neck ring of his battle armour. From thick bulges about his head, panels made of fine circuitry and crystal matrices extended in a tripartite cowl. Gallio watched with slight distaste as the pieces of Vode's psychic hood connected themselves to brass sockets in the Marine's skull.

'Do you... sense anything?' said the captain.

Vode gave a slight smile. 'All the myriad ways of the traitor are subtle and complex, brother. I will root them out, if they conceal themselves here. But for now, there is no–' The expression on the psyker's face changed in a flash; his eyes narrowed and his lips thinned to a line.

Instinctively, Gallio's hand dropped to the bolt pistol in his belt holster. 'Brother Vode?'

Then the moment was gone, and the Librarian shook his head. 'A passing shadow,' he said. 'The taint of the Word Bearers lingers still in this star system, brother-captain. Faint, like fading smoke...'

The answer did little to satisfy Gallio. 'This way,' he indicated.

Vode strode after the officer, a frown threatening to form on his face. For an instant, just the smallest of moments, the psyker had felt the touch of something corrupt. He ran his fingers over the trio of purity seals on the breast of his armour, turning the sensation over in his mind, the weight of a new doubt preying on him.

THE DROP RAMP of the Thunderhawk opened like a yawning mouth and Rafen followed Solus down it. Glancing around the hangar bay of the *Amareo*, he saw a dozen more ships of the same class in launch cradles, armed and set for attack. A troop of Space Marines stood waiting for them in two tight lines, ostensibly an honour guard but just as easily a combat unit. There were other Blood Angels nearby in twos and threes, observing with cold, keen eyes. Rafen's impression was one of preparation; the men aboard *Amareo* were unsure what to expect on Shenlong, and they had taken to book and bolter in readiness. He felt a curious foreboding; these battle-brothers were here only because of a secret message that *he* had sent, and Rafen felt some measure of responsibility for them.

He caught sight of the dark hue of a Librarian's wargear as they set foot on the strike cruiser's deck. The psyker hovered at the shoulder of a senior Blood Angel who studied them with a hawkish manner.

Solus tapped his fist to the blood-drop symbol on his chest. 'Brother Solus and Brother Rafen, requesting permission to come aboard.'

The Space Marine returned the salute. 'Granted. I am Captain Gallio.' He nodded at the Librarian. 'Epistolary Vode, my adjutant.'

'Your arrival is unexpected,' said Solus.

Gallio gave Solus a penetrating stare. 'I think you know why we are here, brother. I have come on the express orders of Lord Commander Dante himself, to see with my own eyes what has transpired on Shenlong.'

'You come to venerate the Blessed Arkio, yes?' Solus replied. 'I suspected as much.'

'We shall see who will and will not be venerated,' Vode broke in, his voice thickening. He studied Solus and Rafen with open scrutiny, and both men felt the pressure of his mind upon them.

'Why did you depart Cybele when orders were sent that *Bellus* should remain there?' Gallio demanded. The captain wasted no time in cutting to the core of the matter.

Solus shook his head. 'I know of no such orders, Captain Gallio. My commander, Brother-Captain Ideon, followed the directives of Inquisitor Stele to weigh anchor and make best speed to this system. Our orders after the rout at Cybele were to contain and destroy the Word Bearers warband here.'

Gallio frowned. 'Those commands were not sanctioned by Baal.'

'If that is so,' Solus retorted, 'then how did you know to locate *Bellus* here?'

'A message was sent to the fortress-monastery,' said Vode. 'The contents of that message raised some questions of integrity.'

'There are only loyal Sons of Sanguinius here.' Solus said hotly. 'Who sent this signal? Tell me his name!'

'Brother-Sergeant Koris.'

'Koris is dead,' said Rafen, unable to keep an edge of pain from his words. 'He was killed in the attack on the Ikari fortress. I witnessed him pass from this life.'

Gallio and Vode exchanged glances. 'It is the content of the message that is of gravest concern to Lord Dante. Koris, if it were he, spoke of a "transformation". By Dante's order, I am to evaluate this occurrence in the commander's stead.'

Rafen felt his throat tighten. The Librarian's eyes had not strayed from him, and Vode's powerful gaze made the Marine feel like a tiny speck swarming under the lens of a microscope. *He knows.* The Blood Angel could sense Vode's inner sight picking at his mind.

Solus gestured at the Thunderhawk, his face taut with concern. 'Perhaps you should accompany me back to the *Bellus*, captain. We could provide you with a complete tactical report on the Cybele battle and—'

'If this "blessing" of which you speak is true, I will not tarry to debate the matters surrounding it,' Gallio interrupted sharply. 'Answer me, Solus. Where will I find Inquisitor Ramius Stele and Brother Arkio?'

The Marine's face darkened with anger. Gallio's bluntness rankled. 'Lord Stele has taken stewardship of Shenlong from the Ikari fortress in the capital district. Arkio the Blessed resides in the chapel there.'

Vode broke eye contact and nodded to the *Amareo*'s commander. 'Then that is where we will go.'

Solus took a step forward. 'He is the Angel Reborn. You cannot simply bid him to your beck and call.'

'Until we make our determination, he is nothing of the kind,' Vode replied with icy certainty.

Rafen saw an opportunity and spoke again. 'Brother Solus, this matter will be resolved with alacrity if we proceed as Captain Gallio demands. With your permission, I will accompany the captain back to the surface to assist him.'

Solus gave Gallio a hard look, then glanced at Rafen. 'Perhaps you are correct, brother.' He turned back to the

Thunderhawk. 'Once these men see the Blessed, any disagreeable hesitancy will become redundant.' He threw them a last look as he reached the hatchway. 'I will return to *Bellus* and inform the inquisitor of your impending arrival.'

Rafen turned away as the ramp slammed shut to find Vode watching him once again. 'I am at your command,' he said.

Gallio indicated a shuttlecraft parked nearby. 'This way. You will use the journey to tell me all you can about this Arkio.'

'Yes, Rafen,' added Vode. 'We would know more of your younger sibling.'

THE STATUE HAD been moved from the grand chamber of the *Bellus* and brought down to the chapel, there to stand in pride of place before the altar. With appropriate ceremony, the icon of the Emperor of Man had been shifted behind the statue, towering over it like a watchful father at the shoulder of a dutiful son. Arkio ran his bare fingers over the ancient stone. The pinkish marble came from a mountain range on Baal Primus.

He touched the face of the statue. The likeness was baring its throat in supplication, eyes closed and mouth slightly open, neck muscles taut. A crown of sculpted jags about the tousled hair of the head signified the solar glow of a halo. Arkio followed the line of the nose, the jaw, down the neck and to the sternum. Of its own accord, his hand came to his own face and traced the same course. The shapes of both were so close as to be almost identical.

He backed away a step, taking in the whole statue of the Blood Angel Sanguinius. His seraph wings arched over his shoulders, the Pure One wore the robes of an initiate priest – a sign of his humility – and his arms were outstretched. In the right, he grasped the skull-shape of the Red Grail, from which fell the four drops of blood that Sanguinius had shed for his Chapter; his left arm was upturned, and from the wrist fell a torrent of his blessed vitae.

With perfect grace, Arkio balanced on the uppermost step of the altar and raised the wings that folded from his own shoulders. The mighty pinions were no longer new and strange to him, now Arkio took his angelic limbs to be as much a part of him as any other. He extended his arms and mimicked the pose of the statue, tipping back his head and showing his throat.

'Magnificent.' Sachiel's voice was thick with barely contained emotion. Arkio opened his eyes and relaxed as the Sanguinary High Priest approached him. Sachiel dropped into a bow. 'Blessed, it is confirmed. A warship from Baal has taken up station alongside *Bellus* and a party from the vessel is on the way as we speak.'

Arkio bid Sachiel to his feet and listened intently as the priest relayed the message from Solus. 'Captain Gallio is joined by Librarian Vode and your brother,' he concluded, a slight annoyance colouring his tone at the mention of Rafen.

The Blood Angel paid it no concern. 'So soon,' he murmured. 'Dante has moved quicker than I had expected... But this shall not be an issue. Give the order to provide Gallio's shuttle a priority flight corridor.' Arkio indicated the ceiling above them. 'Have his ship vectored to the landing pad on the roof of the fortress.'

Sachiel swallowed hard. 'My lord, is that wise? Perhaps it might be more prudent to land him at the starport and bring the captain's party here in a convoy. We could... control them more easily if the circumstances required it.'

Arkio shook his head. 'What will come to pass, will come. I will look Gallio in the eye and offer him nothing but the truth. Where he goes from there will be his choice alone.'

The priest hesitated. 'Blessed, as ever you exhibit the wisdom of the Great Angel, but I must confess I fear the reaction of these new arrivals.'

The chapel doors opened as Sachiel spoke to admit Inquisitor Stele and the drifting shapes of his servo-skulls. 'I will add my voice to my comrade's,' said Stele as he approached. 'He speaks with concern for you and our enterprises, Arkio.'

'Thank you for attending me,' said Arkio. 'I would not wish to proceed without your counsel, Stele.'

The inquisitor gave a gracious nod. 'Forgive my delay, but I was meditating…' He patted his brow with a kerchief; there was a thin sheen of perspiration coating his bullet-like head from his mental exertions in the death room.

Arkio studied both men. 'Your considerations are noted, but I stand by my order. Gallio and Vode will come here to me, and I will answer all questions.' He straightened, glancing back at the statue of Sanguinius. 'It is my duty to the Chapter.'

'Of course,' Stele demurred, 'and to that end, might I suggest we proceed as ceremony demands? I have assembled the honour guard to attend you.'

Arkio gave him a cursory nod and stepped away, walking to the balcony where the battle trials still raged below.

Sachiel leant close to Stele's ear. 'The moment is upon us, lord inquisitor,' he said quietly. 'We will know where the loyalties of Dante's men lie.'

'Indeed,' Stele purred. 'Arkio hopes for the best, but we… we must prepare for the worst.'

'Of that, there is no question,' replied the priest, his eyes bright with righteous fervour.

'I SENT THE message.' Rafen watched the play of emotions over Gallio's face as the captain considered his words. 'As Koris lay in death, I used his vox to transmit a signal to the *Bellus* and beyond.'

'Subterfuge,' said Vode grimly. 'What you have done violates protocols of discipline and rituals of the fallen.'

Rafen gave a rueful nod as the shuttle rumbled through the atmosphere. 'I am only too aware of that.'

'The strictures are clear, only a Techmarine may handle the wargear of the deceased in anything other than the most desperate of circumstances,' Gallio replied.

'The future of our Chapter is in the balance,' Rafen snapped, a little more fiercely than he would have liked. 'What could be more desperate?'

Gallio considered the Marine's words. 'The issue of your actions is secondary to the issue at hand, Rafen. Any decision that you may or may not have behaved improperly is deferred, for the moment.' He looked away. 'What you have told us of this change in Arkio... it is remarkable.'

Vode nodded. 'Aye. And terrifying as well. I sense forces at work here that reach beyond my ability to define. Great powers, moving into conjunction.' The Librarian's hands had strayed to his force axe, unconsciously kneading the grip.

Gallio noted the psyker's small sign of agitation but let it pass unremarked. 'Rafen, you would know Arkio better than any man. These physical changes of which you speak are shocking enough, but his soul... I ask you, when you look into your brother's eyes, what do you see?'

An involuntary shudder passed through the Space Marine's massive frame. 'When we were youths, it was I that was the reckless one, captain. Arkio was open and guileless, he was pure of spirit... It was his influence that helped me to turn my ways, the younger helping the elder.' For a moment, Rafen lost himself in reverie. 'Now... now that youth is gone. It is still Arkio's soul that lives behind those eyes, brother, if that it what you truly wish to know... But for all the changes wrought upon him in these passing weeks, it is his manner that is most altered.'

'Explain,' demanded Vode, tension in his voice.

'Arkio is arrogant now, where before he was humble. Whatever the hand that guides his new path may be, Arkio himself *believes* in it. Within the halls of his heart, he has no doubt that he is the Deus Encarmine.'

'And if we must disabuse him of that belief,' Gallio said, 'what then?'

Rafen found he could not look the captain in the eye any longer. 'I dread to think,' he said. 'I dread to think.'

In the long silence that followed, the shuttle's deck canted as the craft dropped through thick cloudbanks and down over the factory sprawls.

'We are close,' Vode said abruptly.

Gallio gave Rafen a last, measuring look, and then signalled the other men in his personal guard. 'Prepare for landing.'

A BLACK-ARMOURED figure stood waiting for them as they strode off the shuttle pad, Gallio's four men in a line behind the captain, Vode and Rafen. The Chaplain saluted the officer and the Librarian, throwing Rafen a wary nod.

'I am Brother Delos. Welcome to Shenlong, Captain Gallio. It is an honour to receive a warrior of such noted standing within the Chapter.'

Gallio ignored the greeting, and held out a metallic scroll case. 'I carry the letter of Lord Commander Dante. In this place, I speak for him. Chaplain, I would see the warrior Arkio.'

Delos faltered for a moment, eyes flicking to the scroll case, then to Rafen and finally back to Gallio. 'As you wish, captain. The Blessed will receive you in the fortress chapel.' He turned. 'Follow me.'

Rafen remained silent as they ventured down through the Ikari fortress, boarding the recently repaired elevator platform to descend to the core levels. For the second time that day, he felt the pressure of scrutiny from eyes all around him. As they passed groups of Marines, helots and scattered packs of pilgrims, conversations fell silent and barely concealed suspicion greeted them at every turn.

'They know we have come to judge him,' Vode hissed. 'They resent us for even considering the fact.'

The copper doors of the chapel opened to admit them, and Gallio strode boldly past Delos to enter first. Arkio came to his feet from the dais where he sat and the shock of the sight of him almost staggered the captain to a halt.

'Emperor's blood!' Gallio breathed. It was a living, breathing rendering of Sanguinius that stood there, wings bright as sun-fire, the golden armour aglow with honeyed radiance. Arkio inclined his head in greeting and Gallio found himself physically resisting the urge to kneel. A palpable energy of personality crackled in the air, drawing all things to Arkio.

'By the Throne, it is the Pure One.' It was one of Gallio's men that had spoken, his voice hushed and reverent.

Vode smothered his words with a venomous rejoinder. 'That remains to be seen.' The Librarian still gripped his force axe; it was not quite in a battle-ready stance, but close enough to make any seasoned warrior wary of him.

Rafen felt a hand on his shoulder. Delos drew him back to halt at the doorway of the chapel. 'Stand down, lad. This is for the Blessed to decide.' He hesitated as Arkio approached the men from the *Amareo*. Beyond his brother, Sachiel looked on with obvious impatience, while Stele stood in the shadows. The inquisitor seemed muted, eyes distant and unfocussed.

'I am Arkio,' he began. 'I greet you as a brother, and honour you as Lord Dante's proxy.' The figure in gold gave a shallow bow, the tips of his wings touching the mosaic floor. 'What would you ask of me?'

'The truth,' Gallio replied. 'To know what force has brought you to…' He hesitated, searching for the right words, 'to this transformation.'

Sachiel bolted forward from the altar, an intense expression colouring his face. 'What *force*?' he repeated. 'Even the blind know the answer to that question. Do you not see him before you? He is the Blessed Angel Reborn.' Sachiel's eyes shone. 'Sanguinius has returned.'

'All of us carry the vitae of the Great Angel within us,' Vode snapped angrily at Arkio, 'but we do not claim to usurp his place. Our primarch lies millennia dead, yet you presume to take his name!'

Arkio gave a gentle shake of the head. 'I presume nothing. As you asked, so I offer only truth.'

'*Your* truth,' said Gallio. 'If you are what you say you are, then you will accompany us back to Baal, where the

veracity of your claim will be put to the question. You will
release this world and Inquisitor Stele will return governorship of Shenlong to the Imperium.' He paused.
'Commander Dante gives this order, and you are to heed
it.'

Rafen's gaze happened on Stele; the Hereticus agent
rubbed his brow, his gaze fixed on the Librarian Vode. The
Blood Angel looked to the psyker and saw him tense with
fury.

Then Arkio said the words that Rafen feared the most. 'I
am beyond Dante's authority now.'

'*Heretic!*' The curse exploded from Vode's lips, his dark
skin shading with rage. 'The hand of Chaos hides here. You
are *impure!*' The Librarian's words sent a shock through the
chapel, and white lightning crashed across the floor. It happened so fast that Rafen saw only a blur of blue and yellow.
Vode sprang at Arkio, his force axe flaring with psy-flame.
The curved blade met the gauntlet of the gold artificer
armour and deafening thunder assailed his ears.

CHAPTER FOUR

VODE'S MIND WAS drowning in thick streams of glutinous hatred and black, oily darkness. At first, in that moment aboard the strike cruiser, he had thought nothing of the brief contact that had wafted over his psychic senses, passing like a diaphanous veil. There one breath, vanished the next. The mind-space about Shenlong was still dirty with the passage of the Word Bearers, their disgusting mental footprints like profane scars only visible to a psyker such as he. The bright purity of his force axe was a comfort to him. It was a talisman, a badge of the Space Marine's charmed life in the Emperor's service.

Vode listened to Rafen's words as they approached the Ikari fortress, outwardly fixed on the Blood Angel's face, but inside, his preternatural intuition buzzed like a warning siren, louder and louder in his ears as they came ever closer to the chapel. The Librarian tried to hold on to the sensations, to cup them in his hands and make some sort of sense to them – but it was like trying to pick out the perfume of a single black orchid through a sea of charnel house stench. And then in the chapel, he laid eyes on the golden armour and knew instinctively that he had found his way to the epicentre of this great skein of corruption. The Blood Angels psyker had faced this breed of witch-kind before: outwardly flawless, perfect and beautiful. Within they were rotted corpse-flesh, maggoty hearts pumping spoiled blood through bone voids.

He struggled to banish the image, blinking it away. For a second, everything seemed to shift and waver, and part of him cried out, *No!* Deceit laced the air. He glimpsed the man from the Ordo Hereticus across the stone floor, half-clad by shadows. For an instant, it seemed as if he, not the winged one, was the source of all the darkness here. Confusion creased Vode's brow; he had to be sure.

Then, as quickly as it was there, the impression fled and the hissing pressure behind his eyes returned in tenfold force. Vode looked at Arkio as the armoured figure spoke in silky tones to Captain Gallio. The psyker saw two visions of him, one over the other, each warring for prominence in his mind's eye. There was the Reborn Angel, a new Sanguinius glorious and unblemished in his holy perfection, radiant as the Throne of Terra itself, and there was the other.

It turned his stomach to see it. The gold armour was scarred and dull, black with shed blood. There were no eyes in the face of cracked, white porcelain, only pits of empty space; and the wings, foul things flensed of skin and barbed with hooks and broken razors. It spoke and the noise made Vode's bile rise to his throat. 'I am beyond Dante's authority now,' it jeered.

If the others in the chapel saw Arkio as he did, then they were either struck dumb by his awfulness or else bewitched by the apostate's illusory beauty. From the corner of his eye he saw Stele twitch, but the surge in hate that flowed through him at the same moment made the inquisitor seem immaterial. If no man here could or would act, then it was only Vode that could end this parody of the primarch's majesty. The thunderous heat of the black rage came upon him and the Librarian sent it crackling into the haft of his force axe. He shouted his malediction at the top of his lungs. '*Heretic*. The hand of Chaos hides here. You are *impure!*'

Vode's weapon moved as if it were guided by the hand of the God-Emperor himself, cutting a flashing arc toward the skull of the pretender. Every ounce of mind-power from his Quickening channelled into the force axe. 'Hell spawn!' he spat. The crystal blade struck Arkio's wrist-guard with a roar of rended air. Like water pouring off a glass dome, the blue-white psy-fire fell away from the axe head, streaking around Arkio in harmless rivulets. An invulnerable sphere of crimson and gold danced around him at the edge of perception, the halo blunting Vode's attack into nothing.

SACHIEL'S REDUCTOR WAS in his hand as the Librarian struck, dancing, searching for a target. All about him, Arkio's golden-helmed honour guard brought up their weapons on reflex, and he glimpsed Gallio's retinue doing the same. The *Amareo*'s captain was crying out, reaching with one hand, his other skimming toward the butt of his holstered bolt pistol. A voice was shouting from the chapel doors, an indistinct red man-shape turning in the grip of a black figure; all this in a heart-beat.

Arkio's other hand came up and punched Vode away. The epistolary flew backwards, boots scraping across the stone as he struggled to keep his balance. With an eyebrow arched, Arkio reached for the force axe where it rested, lodged between plates of gold. The Blessed removed the weapon and, with a tightening of his fist, broke the axe handle in two.

Vode screamed and threw a curtain of lightning at him, racing back to leap at Arkio's bare throat, fangs flashing. Again, the Quickening parted around his golden form and he shot out a hand. Arkio's dart-sharp fingers impaled the ceramite chest plate of Vode's power armour and buried themselves to the knuckle. The Librarian's bolter was in his grip, and, even as blood bubbled from his mouth, Vode let shell fire crash out and flare across the room.

Unaimed, heedless bolts skipped close to Sachiel and the shock brought him to action. He lunged at Gallio with the reductor, clipping the Blood Angels captain's scalp. No word of command was uttered, but with the priest's gesture a tiny hell was unleashed in the chapel. The Blood Angels of Arkio's honour guard and Gallio's detachment alike opened fire on one another, burning rounds lancing back and forth across the room in a screaming web of death.

'*No!*' The cry was Rafen's, but it sank unheard under a tidal wave of gunfire, and with strength that belied his age, the Chaplain Delos shoved him back from the fray.

Arkio flicked Vode's corpse from his hand like a discarded piece of meat, aloof as bullets keened and hummed off his golden ceramite chest. Gallio's troop, outnumbered two to one by the honour guards, danced and spun as multiple bolter shells tore through their battlegear and cut them apart. Gallio was the last to fall, thick arterial blood running in rivers from every joint in his armour. His pistol dropped from nerveless fingers and the captain sank to his knees, eyes glazing.

Arkio came to him and cupped Gallio's chin in his hand. 'You have brought my worst fear to life,' he told the dying man. 'You will not be the last to perish.'

The captain gasped out a final breath, and with that it was ended; the entire exchange had lasted hardly a tick of the clock.

Rage filled Rafen and he punched Delos, turning the black-armoured Chaplain with the blow. He forced his way through the ranks of gold-helmed men and down to the blood-slick mosaic floor. Suddenly among the dead, he felt like weeping.

'What…' He could barely speak. '*What have you done?*'

Arkio looked him squarely in the eye and Rafen's veins filled with ice. 'These men,' said his sibling, casting an offhand wave at the steaming corpses, 'they were here to destroy us, kindred. I knew it from the moment they entered the room.' He glanced up, addressing every Blood Angel in the chapel. 'Hear me, brothers. We have been forsaken. These men came to condemn, not to know me.'

'There was to be no question of truth.' said Sachiel, taking up the call. 'Gallio's psyker was an assassin. Dante fears the Blessed Angel, he fears the threat that Arkio represents.'

'You have killed our battle-brothers,' Rafen said in a dead voice.

Arkio shook his head, a flicker of hurt in his eyes. 'No, Rafen. None of these men were brothers to me, or to any of us. In their blood I see the real truth of it. Dante denies me.'

From the altar came a strangled choke, and Stele stumbled forward, his face drawn and wet with perspiration. His eyes bulging with effort, the inquisitor gasped for air. Rafen felt the same actinic tang of psyker-taint in the air, just as he had when Stele tortured the Word Bearers prisoner they had captured on Cybele.

'Lord.' Sachiel said. 'What is wrong?'

'The ship...' Stele choked. 'May be more of Vode's kind... More aboard the ship... don't let them...'

Sachiel met Arkio's gaze and the figure in gold gave him a sharp nod. 'I will not put any more of my brethren at risk.' Arkio cocked his head and spoke into a hidden vox pick-up at his neck. '*Bellus*, heed me.'

The shock of his brother's intent startled Rafen. 'Arkio, you cannot–' Sachiel interposed himself between the two siblings, blocking Rafen's outstretched hand.

Arkio glanced at him. The weight of ages glittered in his eyes. '*Bellus*,' he said, his voice instantly carried to Captain Ideon aboard the battle barge, 'Captain Gallio and his men have revealed themselves as traitors to the way of Sanguinius. We shall not suffer the *Amareo* to live.'

Rafen's breath caught in his throat, and for one moment of hope he believed that Ideon would refuse such a command; the brother-captain was a veteran warrior, not a zealot so easily swayed as Sachiel.

Then that hope guttered out and died. 'Your will, Blessed,' said Ideon, his voice distant and mechanical through the vox.

HIGH ABOVE THEM, the battle barge's starboard side rippled with activity as cannon hatches irised open and guns ran out on firing cradles. Missile batteries, lances and lascannon twisted in cupolas and turrets, finding the blade-like profile of the rapid strike cruiser *Amareo* in their sights. In allied space, with no threat to be determined, the cruiser's commanding officer had placed no power to the ship's void shields and so *Amareo* was naked to the unleashed fire of a ship that dwarfed her by fifty magnitudes of tonnage. Ideon did not flinch from the order; the concept of such a thought never once entered his mind. He had seen Arkio with what remained of his own eyes, tasted the coruscating power of his aura through the sensor web of the *Bellus*. The brother-captain had no doubts, and he fired.

It was a small mercy, perhaps, that the men aboard the other ship never saw the attack coming. They died without knowing where the blow had come from, lives snuffed out in an instant. *Amareo* exploded beneath a hellstorm of energy, and once again the battle barge was alone in the skies over Shenlong.

RAFEN SAT AT the edge of the chapel chamber, on the shallow steps leading down to the mosaic floor, and he found he could not move. A distant flash of memory returned to him as he sat there, eyes unfocussed and shoulders hunched. As a boy, when his journey to Angel's Fall was still a dozen cycles away, Rafen had become separated from the tribe during a migration. As a sandstorm had descended on him, the child had become disoriented and lost, wandering through the stinging dust clouds until at last he beached himself on a rocky outcropping and waited for the end to come. Hours passed as he stared out into the roiling storm, and the lad had known then what it was like to be dwarfed by the force of things larger than he was.

Against the storm, his flesh and bone were ineffectual; the realisation of his own powerlessness had sobered him. Rescue had come, eventually. His father Axan emerged from the clouds and carried him to safety – but Rafen had never forgotten the hollow knowing that the storm had forced upon him.

Here and now, with the stink of spent cordite and spilled blood still lingering in the air, he felt that sensation all over again. For all his prowess, all the strength and fortitude granted to him as a Space Marine, Rafen felt powerless and weak as events rumbled on over him, crushing him beneath their passage. He looked but did not see the bodies of Gallio, Vode and the others. The Blood Angel felt empty inside, like the tin icons he had seen in the street urchin's box. It was his audacity that had summoned the *Amareo* to Shenlong, his daring to send the secret message to Commander Dante, and now his own warrior-kin were dead. *If I had kept my silence, these men would still be alive*, his inner voice tormented, *their blood is on my hands.*

Sachiel summoned a gaggle of servitors. 'Take these traitors and put them to the torch,' he ordered. 'They shall not soil the presence of the Blessed one moment longer.'

Arkio knelt on one knee close to Gallio's remains, studying the shattered face of the dead man. 'Wait,' he said quietly. His words were almost a whisper, but they carried like a thunderclap. 'Priest, you will harvest the progenoid glands of these men and see them preserved with our fallen aboard the *Bellus*.'

'My lord?' Sachiel blinked. 'But these recreants have proven themselves unworthy of your beneficence – they opposed you.'

Arkio's face was downturned. 'In life, yes. But perhaps in death they can be born anew to the will of Sanguinius.'

Stele mopped his brow with a delicate kerchief. 'You truly are the Angel's Son, Arkio. Even in the face of a turncoat, you show forgiveness…'

The figure in gold armour raised his head; tears glittered on his face. 'I weep for the destiny lost, Lord Stele,' he told him. 'These men might have stood beside us if they had been granted the choice. Instead, Dante has indoctrinated them with his fear. Fear of *me*.'

The inquisitor spied the silent Rafen from the corner of his eye, but he continued on to Arkio. 'Blessed, it is as I had expected it to be. While the will of the God-Emperor would make our species masters of the galaxy, there are those who turn his words to their own selfish ends...' He hesitated, breathing hard. The effort Stele had expended influencing Vode's mind had left him weakened. 'The noble purpose of the Imperium is smothered under the prejudice of men with limited vision... and you, you are the embodiment of a threat to that.' He gestured to the dead. 'Here is proof of it.'

'What does this mean?' Delos voiced the question on the minds of all the Space Marines in the room. Each of them having seen the miracle of Arkio's Emergence themselves, they had no doubts about rallying to his side, but the bloody line they had crossed this day gave each and every one pause. Like the Chaplain, they looked to Arkio for guidance.

Sachiel spoke for him. 'It means there is a schism in our Chapter, brothers. Commander Dante sought not to learn from the Blessed, but to judge him as wanting and put him to the sword. Dante denies the Ascension, and he must be forced to see the error of his ways.'

'I have met the commander,' said Delos, 'and in his eyes I saw a man not easily swayed. If he will not recant and join the banner of Great Arkio, what then?'

Sachiel scanned the room, meeting the eyes of every man there – all except Rafen. 'All those who oppose the dominion of the Reborn Angel are faithless, and they do not deserve to bear the hallowed legacy of Sanguinius. The only reward for those men is to share in the fate of Gallio and his assassins.'

Another Marine spoke up. 'What you suggest...' he was hesitant and afraid, 'it is tantamount to civil war. We would be forced to turn against those of our own Chapter.'

'Look around you, comrade brothers,' Stele broke in. 'Your hand has been forced. You have already done that!' The inquisitor stabbed a finger at the broken remains of Vode's force axe. 'They came to kill. They came to murder Arkio in order to preserve Dante's command of the Blood Angels.'

'But Vode was a decorated warrior,' said Delos. 'He would not simply–'

'Brother,' said Arkio, and the Chaplain instantly fell silent. 'The psyker looked upon me and saw nothing but murder.'

Delos gave a slow nod. 'Forgive me, Blessed. As you say, so it is.'

With an abrupt flash of movement, Rafen came to his feet. 'So what now, my brothers? Do we declare a holy war against our own kind? Shall we take up arms and lead an invasion to Baal, or perhaps even to Terra itself?'

'Be careful, Rafen–' Sachiel began, but Arkio silenced him with a look.

'No, no, priest. Rafen's questions deserve answers.'

'We must not follow this path, Arkio.' Rafen's voice was desperate. 'Turn back and reject it. We cannot have war among the Blood Angels – if we fight amongst ourselves, we will be destroyed as surely as if our enemies wiped us from existence.'

Stele took a shuddering breath, watching the two men carefully. The future came to a balance point here in this moment; the inquisitor's delicate plans were caught like a fly in amber. Arkio's response to his blood brother would either release them or shatter Stele's careful machinations utterly.

'As ever, my elder kinsman cuts to the heart of the matter, and for that I am grateful.' He shook his head. 'No, Rafen, I do not wish to sow insurrection among our Chapter. This matter must be resolved before more blood is shed. You are right, we must strive against war.' Arkio turned to Sachiel. 'Dante's proxy wished to bring me in chains to Baal where I could be prodded and toyed with like some addled mutant. I will not submit to that.'

'What do you suggest, Blessed?' the priest replied.

'Select a location in neutral territory,' he ordered. 'Find a world where we can meet face-to-face, on equal terms. Send Dante a message that I wish to resolve this division between us.' He glanced at Rafen, eyes afire. 'I would not have embraced the glory of the Deus Encarmine only to see it spent turning Blood Angel against Blood Angel.'

'Your will be done,' Sachiel bowed. 'And what of our followers among the commoners?'

Arkio came up to his full height and strode toward the ornate glassteel doors that led to the chapel's balcony. 'I will address the people and my Warriors of the Reborn. They deserve to understand what has transpired here today, and to where it may take them.' Honour guards opened the doors as he approached. 'I shall take my thousand with me,' he declared, 'and then on to Baal.' Arkio stepped out into the wan sunlight of Shenlong's day and the adulation of the crowds blotted out all other sound.

Rafen watched his sibling bask in the glow of their reverence. 'Do you seek death?' said a voice close to his ear, and he turned to face Sachiel. The Sanguinary High Priest was standing at his shoulder, his face red with restrained anger. 'It would be my pleasure to provide it to you, if that is what you wish.'

He ignored Sachiel's loaded reductor, there in his grip. All other eyes were on Arkio as he began his speech to the factory city. 'What are you afraid of, priest?' he said in a low voice. 'Is your faith in Arkio so fragile that the breath of my voice could send it tumbling?'

Sachiel's face clouded. 'It is you who is without conviction!' he hissed. 'Even in the face of fact, you refuse to give yourself fully to Arkio's fealty.'

'I took his oath–'

'Did you?' The priest prodded him in the chest. 'Did you take it *in here*?' Rafen hesitated for a split-second, and Sachiel gave a twisted smile. 'I thought not.'

Movement caught the Marine's eye; unseen by Arkio and the others, the inquisitor was silently making his way through the shady cloisters of the chapel, toward the copper doors. 'I am a loyal Blood Angel and a Son of Sanguinius,' Rafen said to the priest, in tones filled with absolute conviction. 'That has never been in doubt.'

Now it was Sachiel's turn to hesitate. 'I... I have been the Pure One's most pious servant for as many years as you, Rafen.'

'Yes,' Rafen agreed, 'but piety alone may blind you.' He pushed Sachiel's pistol away and stepped past him, following Stele out of the chamber. 'Remember that, the next time you are drawn to shed another brother's blood.'

Rafen left the priest standing alone. Sachiel's brow furrowed and he cradled the reductor, losing himself in the fine tooling and curves of the sanctified device. In the depths of the Sanguinary High Priest's mind, the smallest splinters of doubt lay waiting.

THE EFFORT OF each step was weighing heavily on Stele as he moved through the shadowed corridors of the fortress, a casual observer would have seen nothing amiss, perhaps a slight hurry in his walk, a deepness in his breathing. He was a credit to his Ordo Hereticus training. The inquisitor was fatigued, far more so than he dared to show to Arkio and the Blood Angels. Their kind were animal predators. They could smell weakness like the scent of an open wound. His performance had reached a critical phase and he could not afford to be seen as wanting.

Stele paused for a moment and patted at his brow once more with his kerchief, rubbing at the aquila electoo. The knots of tension in his muscles were waning, but he still ached from the sheer physical effort of expending his psychic reserves on Vode. He took a deep breath. There had been a flash there in the chapel when Stele's keen psychic focus had slipped, just for a second. The epistolary instantly knew it, and turned his inner eye on the inquisitor, for one brief moment seeing him for what he was – the manipulator behind the unfolding events. Stele's whole plan had almost unravelled right there; if Vode had realised that it was he, not Arkio, that was the source of the dark energies in the room, the inquisitor would have died on the end of Vode's axe. *Thank the warp, it was not so*, he told himself. Stele managed to recover, pressing Vode to turn his ire on Arkio once more, and things had unfolded as they were meant to. While he conjured sheets of invisible force to protect the young Space Marine, Sachiel and the others had followed the patterns laid out for them and taken things to their conclusion. The actors were playing their parts, just as he had foreseen it.

The chambers Stele had taken as his living quarters were nearby, and as he approached he could already feel his strength starting to return; still, he would need to take a resting trance in order to be ready for the next progression. He allowed himself a smile. That was the beauty of his plan, the inquisitor considered, the perfection of all the best schemes. It was not that Stele forced these men to veer from their chosen path by sheer brute coercion. Such a performance lacked subtlety and elan. No, Stele's skills came in the gentle push, the honeyed word in the doubting ear. His expertise was in gently guiding the righteous and honourable into places where it became easy for them to make questionable choices. Men like Arkio and Sachiel. The inquisitor would lead them over one moral line, then another and another, until they were set on a path to damnation.

He had done it many times; he was good at it. But this would be his greatest work. Before it had been men, sometimes nations, that he led astray. Arkio, Sachiel, the Blood Angels... to turn a Chapter of the Emperor's most loyal Marines would be his crowning glory.

The door to his chambers opened under his hand, but Stele hesitated. He felt a presence close by. Inwardly he frowned. Someone was shadowing him, following him through the dim halls of the fortress. Had he been recovered, at his full capacity, he would have sensed the watcher automatically, but his wearied mind still buzzed with fatigue. Careful to ensure he gave no sign of awareness to his observer, he entered the room and allowed the door to remain open behind him.

THE HAND OF *Chaos hides here*. The words turned over and over in Rafen's mind as he kept pace with Stele, careful to keep out of the inquisitor's line of sight. He had seen the way that Vode had stared at Stele in the chapel, the momentary look of pure revulsion on his face. What had the Librarian seen? Rafen's gut crawled at the thought of the mind-witchery that passed between the two men. As much as he disliked the arrogant Sachiel, Rafen could not bring himself to believe that the Sanguinary Priest would ally himself with the Ruinous Powers, and for all the changes that had been wrought on Arkio, his sibling refused to consider him a traitor.

Stele. He lurked in the background, concealed and yet visible, always there with a word or deed when a choice presented itself. Sergeant Koris had died cursing him, and once again Rafen found himself wondering what insight his old mentor had gained in the throes of the deadly red thirst.

The Blood Angel saw the open door and slipped through it. Inside, the room was muted. The last fading streaks of thin, watery daylight managed to push through thick brocade curtains to illuminate a suite of rooms, dissipating as the sun dropped below the industrial horizon. This had once been the domain of Shenlong's governor, and Stele had claimed it as his planetside residence in the days after the death of the Dark Apostle Iskavan. Rafen hovered close to an array of tall tapestries that depicted the history of the forge-world, from its discovery in the distant past to the consecration of the planet as a weapons manufactory.

'Don't stand on ceremony, Rafen.' Stele's voice seemed to come from everywhere at once. 'Come in.'

The Marine's face twisted in a scowl, but he did as he was bid. Stele emerged from a pool of shadows on the far side of the wide room. The light from the window rendered him in shades of grey, like a charcoal sketch on dull paper.

'Have you come to kill me, Rafen?' he asked conversationally. 'Do you wish my death?'

Rafen scanned the room for any signs of the inquisitor's hovering servo-skulls and found them humming quietly in the eaves, crystal eyes intent. The needles of small-bore lasguns tracked him as he moved. 'Would your murder end this madness, inquisitor?' he replied.

'Madness?' Stele repeated, taking a seat in a large chair. 'Is that what you see in the plans of the Blessed?' He covered his exhaustion well as he sat.

'Not since the Horus Heresy has Astartes turned upon Astartes, yet I saw the same crime unfold in the chapel.' Rafen's jaw hardened with anger. 'You did nothing to stop it.'

Stele cocked his head and gave a shallow nod without speaking. Slowly, carefully, he began to gather in what remained of his mental fortitude.

Rafen did not notice. 'Is it not the code of the Ordo Hereticus to seek out and purge that which falls from the Emperor's Light?'

'Are you suggesting that Arkio is a heretic, Rafen?'

'I…' The Marine faltered at the question, unwilling to voice such a thing. 'His path… It will lead only to darkness and death.'

The inquisitor made a noise of dismissal. 'Consider this, Rafen. Perhaps it is not Arkio who is the apostate, but Dante.'

Rafen's eyes flared with bright fury. 'You dare to profane the lord commander's name?' His hands bunched into fists. 'Perhaps it is *you* who is the agent of disorder here.'

He expected the inquisitor to become enraged, but instead Stele fixed him with a strong, unwavering gaze. There was a look in his eyes that might almost have been pity. 'Comrade brother,' he began, in a fatherly voice, 'we are at a juncture of history, you and I. It is no dishonour to be awed by events such as those that have taken place in recent weeks. Your brother's rise to ascendancy on Cybele, the Emergence that you were witness to in the manufactorium… Lesser men would be broken under the weight of such things.'

Rafen felt his words of reply dying in his throat, his anger fading.

'But you, Rafen, you are at a different crossroads. Your choice is one that no other Blood Angel faces. You cannot go forward without first resolving it.' Stele's voice never rose in volume, but seemed to grow to fill the room, pressing in on the young Blood Angel from all sides. 'You are filled with questions and confusion,' the inquisitor continued.

Unbidden, Rafen nodded to himself. The doubts, the unending distrust that he had carried since the battle for Cybele returned to him all at once. Like a black, suffocating coil, the dark thoughts unfolded from the deeps of his soul. Rafen staggered back a step; suddenly, he felt the consequence of them like a physical force.

'Why do you continue to question your brother?' Stele urged. 'Is it because you truly doubt what he has become, or is it because you are jealous of your younger sibling?'

'No…' Rafen forced the words out of his mouth. 'Father… He…'

Stele's presence seemed to permeate Rafen's perception. 'You look upon him and you feel rejected, yes?' He pointed a sharp finger at the Marine, his voice rising. 'You see him resplendent in the golden armour of the Great Angel and cry out *it should have been me!*'

'Yes.' The reply came from nowhere, startling Rafen even as he said it. 'No. I do not… Arkio is not ready!' He staggered backward, his hands coming up to press against his face. Every single doubt and misgiving that had ever plagued Rafen was welling up inside him like a foul surge tide. Clinging wreaths of despair enshrouded him. *I am Adeptus Astartes*, his mind cried out, *I will not submit!*

'But you must,' Stele answered, the inquisitor's voice humming in his very bones. 'You must give up your life for Arkio – don't you understand? It is you that holds him back from true greatness, your influence that ties him down! You always treated him as the lesser, the unready youth, but in truth it was you that feared him.' Rafen was on his knees now, and Stele's tall form arched over him, towering and monstrous. 'You could never admit that his success would be your failure.'

In the canyons of Rafen's mind, he relived the moment when he was rejected at Angel's Fall, when he walked out into the deserts to die an ignoble death rather than face his tribe with his inadequacy.

Stele saw the memory and honed it into a blade, cutting into Rafen's will with all the psychic force he could muster. 'You should have died that day. You should have let him go alone on to achieve his destiny…'

'Yes.' Rafen choked on the word, staggering to his feet under the weight of the suicidal gloom enveloping him. 'Father, I failed you…'

Stele could barely contain the cold smile that threatened to break across his thin lips. With one final effort, he rammed home a black psy-knife of pure misery into Rafen's troubled soul. 'You can still save him, Rafen.'

Save him save him save him save him save him save him save him. The words echoed through his sensorium. 'How?' he wailed.

'Die.' Stele's voice cracked like thunder. 'Die for your brother, Rafen. End your life and free him.'

Free him free him free him free him free him free him free him free him. 'No… no… no!' Suddenly Rafen was running, the corridors flashing past him, the city beyond, crashing through the streets, heedless and broken. *You must die*, said the voice in his head, *betrayer of blood, you must die*.

'I must die,' he wept, falling to his knees.

STELE'S VISION TUNNELLED and he gasped for breath. The rush of his blood and the thumping of his heart sounded in his ears as he struggled to the chair. The effort of pushing Rafen had left him dry, his psionic will draining the very life force from him to maintain the pressure. He fell to the floor in a heap, a guttural, harsh laugh escaping from his lips. 'Rafen must die,' he said aloud, and then sank into unconsciousness.

CHAPTER FIVE

RAFEN RAN.

The streets of the city, most of them still without power after the Chaos invasion, opened up before him. Warrens of twisting stone canyons deep with shadows drew the Blood Angel in. He crossed rooftops in shuddering leaps, blundering through bombed-out pits where workshops had once stood. He stumbled through voids cut in the city by lance fire and sites where Word Bearers had been put to death.

He ran to escape the pain, the black miasma of despair that snapped at his heels, tentacles of darkness always at his back, hungry for him. He was a heedless engine of motion, mind swept clean of nothing but misery.

He could not stop. If he stopped, the melancholy would engulf him and he would be lost, destroyed by the flood of guilt unleashed from his own psyche. What he had witnessed tore at him like a storm of razors. The transformation of his brother, the deaths of his battle-brothers on Cybele and again on Shenlong, all these things weighed and beat him down. The sheer anguish suffocated him. Rafen watched his comrades die around him, unable to stop it. His mind reeled as he remembered every soul he had known extinguished. He wished that it had been him instead of them.

Mother, perished in childbirth. Omeg, his childhood friend dead from shellsnakes. Toph the aspirant, torn open by fire scorpions. Crucius, shot on Ixion. Simeon, boiled alive by plasma. Koris, lost to the thirst. Gallio, gunned down…

Faces, voices, screams, a torrent of them whirled around him. There was some distant part of him calling, some last inviolate corner of Rafen's soul still begging him to have strength and resist, but moment by moment the voice became fainter and fainter. The touch of Inquisitor Stele's psychic force had broken open the place inside the Space Marine where he kept his blackest regrets, and now they were free, boiling through Rafen, drowning him in his own remorse.

Uncontrolled, the Blood Angel found himself falling, tumbling into a steel door. The hatch parted under his weight and Rafen crashed through in a tangle of armour and limbs. Hands clasping his head, he rolled to his knees. Through misted eyes he saw the place where he had come to rest, and a dart of surprise took him for a moment. Around him was a metal-walled chamber, dim and thick with chemical scent. Against one wall, a brass idol of the God-Emperor lay watching him.

'How?' he asked the cloying air. Perhaps it was the hand of the Emperor that had guided him here; perhaps blind chance or some animalistic muscle-memory, but Rafen's headlong flight from the Ikari fortress had returned him to the makeshift meditation cell he had created for himself in the ruins.

Rafen reached out a trembling hand and ran his fingers over the icon; the yellowed metal felt blood-warm to his touch. Under the unblinking eyes of the Emperor, the crushing weight of his guilt came all at once and he let out a moan of anguish, an echoing, feral cry.

'Holy Master, I have failed you. My life… means nothing. I am broken and defeated, my sorrow unbound…'

The Marine's hand closed around the hilt of his combat knife, drawing the bright steel of the fractal-edged blade from its sheath. His limbs seemed to be working on their own, unwillingly following the suicidal compulsion laid into Rafen's mind by Stele's dark influence. The tip of the weapon touched the belly of his torso armour as it dipped downward, the blade inexorably drawn to his flesh.

It was someone else working him now; Rafen was a hollow puppet, woodenly moving through actions that the black power of suggestion forced on him. The knife kissed the red ceramite of his chest plate and scratched a course across the armour as his hand drew it upward.

'I am ended…' Rafen's blade was at his neck, the serrated edge dipping into the meat of his throat. Blood pooled in the lee of the knife as the wound opened, running down the gutter of the weapon, across his bare knuckles and wrist.

Pain came then, pain, and the smell of his own vital fluid. The sensations pierced the shroud of despair gathered about Rafen's soul, punching through the fog of his mind. He gasped – and in that moment everything changed.

A trembling sensation came upon the Blood Angel, every muscle in his body throbbing like a struck chord. The dual pulse-beat of his twin hearts rumbled in Rafen's ears, the racing thunder of blood through his arteries suddenly a roaring torrent. Adrenaline heat surged out from his chest to fill his hollow core. He was an empty vessel abruptly filled with molten energy. Saliva flooded the Marine's mouth at the thought of rich vitae on his lips. His vision, clouded moments before with morose shadows, was darkened by a red mist of passion.

Rafen shook with the raw power that welled up inside him, letting it wash away the insidious venom of melancholy. He knew this sensation well: it was the precursor to the black rage. The Blood Angel threw back his head, the brilliant white darts of his fangs baring. The red thirst was upon him, warring with the psychic toxins left behind by Stele's potent mind-witchery.

And still his knife was at his throat, the metal cleaving flesh and threatening to sever arteries. One small jerk of the wrist would be enough. A war was being fought inside the Marine: rage facing despair, fury versus misery, white-hot wrath crashing against cold, soul-numbing anguish.

'I… will… not… *die.*' Rafen screamed. He had come too far, fought too hard to be felled by his own inner fears. 'I am Adeptus Astartes,' he roared. 'I am the Emperor's Chosen.' Rich blood tricked down his torso armour, staining the white metal wings surrounding the ruby droplet sigil. '*Sanguinius, hear me! I am a Blood Angel!*'

His sight grew hazy as prickles of gold-white light unfolded out of the air around him. Rafen's words choked off in a gasp as a pressure rose inside his skull, pushing at the edges of his perception. He glimpsed a halo of honeyed illumination glitter about the brass icon in the seconds before the light overwhelmed him. Radiance touched his bare skin with delicate warmth, like the kiss of a perfect summer day. Rafen's heart swelled, the pain, the blood, the misery all swept away from him.

His vision collapsed to a single point: a face, a figure, a shape opening there in the void before him, coalescing from the fines of dust in the air itself. It towered over him, made him childlike in comparison; it filled the room even though the chamber could never have contained it. The golden form accreted and took on features – eyes, nose, mouth. Rafen gasped, the thought of it thrilling at his lips.

'Sanguinius…'

This was no pretender, no Reborn Angel, no mere changed man before him. The mellifluent, achingly perfect face of the Blood Angels primarch bore down on Rafen, a vision of the Great Progenitor of his Chapter invoked from the very matter of the blood surging in his veins. Every battle-brother carried an iota of the Pure One inside him. Since the foundation of the Blood Angels, the conclaves of the Chapter's

Sanguinary Priests had kept the living vitae of their long-dead master in the sacred Red Grail, and on their induction into the Chapter initiates would drink from a holy cup that held a philtre of this hallowed fluid. Rafen felt that blood within his blood sing out as like touched like. The Crimson Angel ran a hand over Rafen's face and, with infinite tenderness, drew away the bloody knife. Suddenly the blade seemed his again, his body responding to his commands once more and not the suggestions of another.

Rafen lowered his face to the flat of the knife and licked his own blood; the rich coppery taste was strong and heady. The violence within, the clawing feral might of the red thirst ebbed as he drank, receding – and with it went the vision, the gold aura about him disintegrating. Rafen's hand stabbed outward, fingers reaching for his primarch. 'Lord, help me!' he cried. 'What must I do?'

The crystal blue eyes of Sanguinius took on a sad distance, glancing down at the stained weapon in Rafen's hand, then back to meet the gaze of the Blood Angel. Rafen mimicked his master's action, studying the weapon in his grip.

When he glanced up, he was alone. Rafen sat there until sunrise, weighing his knife in his hand and wondering.

THERE CAME A heavy pounding on the sturdy nyawood doors and it insinuated itself into the mind of Ramius Stele, dragging him unwillingly from a deep, healing slumber. The noise had been going on for quite some time, so it seemed.

Stele turned where he lay on the floor, a dried patch of dark blood from his mouth and nose sticky on his cheek where it pressed to the careworn stone tiles. Swearing a curse beneath his breath, he pulled himself from the ground to a semblance of standing, the sickly weakness in his stomach making him wince. Energy had returned to him, but he still felt lethargic with the effort of his psionic exertions. He gave a slow shake of the head, forcing away such thoughts. It was time for a communion once again, and it would not do for him to show fragility.

Stele strode to the door, wiping away the caked matter from his face, and opened it. A Blood Angels serf reacted with shock as he did so; the servant had been about to knock again and his hand was raised as if to strike the inquisitor. The serf backed off a step, bowing contritely. 'Forgive me, Lord Stele, but I was afraid you did not hear me…'

Stele held up a hand to silence him. 'I was detained with another matter.' If the helot saw any indication of fatigue in his face, then he gave no sign. 'Where is it?'

The Chapter serf tugged at something behind him in the shadows of the corridor, and, with atonal footsteps, a crooked woman came forward, led into the wan light by a rope about her neck. Stele pulled a ragged cloth sack from her head to reveal her face and the serf recoiled at the sight, nauseated. The woman had no eyes; the Word Bearers had taken them. Her ears and nostrils had also been sewn shut, and there on her forehead in a parody of Stele's Imperial aquila electro-tattoo was an eight-pointed star.

The inquisitor nodded. This would be an acceptable vessel. He snatched the rope from the serf and dismissed him. 'Go now. I will send for you later to dispose of the remains.'

The poor unfortunate had not been asked to take the mark of Chaos Undivided willingly. More than likely, she had probably expected to die in the Word Bearers attack. Instead, some subordinate cohort of the Castellan Falkir, the corrupted invader who had taken Shenlong before the Blood Angels arrived, had picked her to serve as a messenger-slave. There were many of these poor wretches still alive in the warrens of the manufactories. Most had been put to death as a mercy soon after their Chaos masters had been routed, but some had escaped into the industrial zones. Locals had taken to hunting the remainder and bringing them to the fortress as some sort of offering, in the way a feline pet might present its master with half-dead prey. When they brought ones that were relatively intact, Stele arranged for them to be quietly kept in the dungeons below the stronghold. Innocents spoiled by the touch of Chaos; their profaned bodies offered much in the way of arcane potential, if correctly harnessed.

Stele released the rope and let the woman wander blindly across the vast room. It amused him to see panic grow on her face, her hands stabbing out in anxious motions, desperately searching for walls that were nowhere nearby. He watched the slave reach the centre of the room and blunder into the ornate table he had placed there. The jar of ichor sitting atop it upended and spilt on her fingers. A quizzical look on her ruined face, she held up a hand dirty with the matter and touched it to her lips – the only sense she still possessed.

Stele smiled; the concoction brewed from dead Word Bearers hearts stung her throat and she choked off a strangulated scream. The slave dropped to the floor and began to melt like hot wax. Bones and organs, bunches of nerves, raw muscle, all of it shifted and changed, shimmering wetly in the light of photon candles as a whispering metamorphosis took place. Presently, the slave stood, and in the dead sockets it grew new eyes with which to look at the inquisitor.

Stele made a theatrical bow. He had seen this parlour trick too many times to be affected by it. An ephemeral, potent splinter of monstrous psionic will was now inhabiting the helot, turning it into a mouthpiece for his hellish cohort full light years distant from Shenlong. 'Warmaster Garand. So nice to see you again.'

The tiny piece of the Chaos warlord's essence examined itself, the molten skin and mealy matter of the messenger. 'A poor frame for such a force as I. It will not last for long.' Even as Garand spoke through a broken throat, the Witch Prince's energy was burning up the life of the slave woman. 'Perhaps for the better.'

'How so?' Stele asked, approaching the possessed form.

'It means we can forgo your usual tedious prattle.' Garand bubbled blood. 'You have been on this blighted sphere for over a solar month, and yet you seem to have made little progress.'

A nerve in Stele's jaw jumped. 'What do you know of it?' he snapped, his fatigue briefly allowing his annoyance to surface. 'Your blunt intellect has little comprehension of the subtlety of my enterprises.' He made a dismissive motion at the helot. 'These communions I am forced to take with you do nothing but divert my attention from the tasks ahead.'

Garand's fleshy avatar gave him a sideways look. 'Indeed?' it mocked. 'And yet it was my, what did you call it, "blunt intellect" that allowed you to cement your position of authority with these boneless human cattle.' The proxy padded over to him, the psionic stink of Garand's mind-spoor clouding Stele's telepathic senses. 'I broke the sacred compact of the Word Bearers codex in order to lay the path for your scheme, man-filth! I sacrificed an entire host for this endeavour. Never forget that!'

Stele's face soured. 'Don't make it sound like such a hardship, Warmaster. You yourself would have taken the head of Iskavan the Hated if he had not died here. He and his ninth host were of no value to the Ruinous Powers.'

Garand made a negative noise. 'But still… I have fulfilled my part of the bargain. You are tardy with yours.' It spat a globule of necrotic flesh on to the floor. 'There are larger plans at work, Stele. Larger than the turning of these mewling Blood Whelps… If you cannot fulfil your responsibilities–'

'I need more time,' Stele snapped. 'Already, events gather their own momentum. Arkio's powers are still unfolding, the faith of his followers grows stronger by the day–'

'You waste your breath explaining it to me,' Garand said, and nodded to the shadows. 'It is not I you must justify your dilatory manner to–'

Stele's breath caught in his throat as something dark and cold fell across the room like a psychic eclipse. A foetor that could only exist in the unreality of the warp entered the chamber; for miles around, plates of food suddenly spoiled, wine turned to vinegar in corked bottles, births came stillborn. In high orbit aboard the *Bellus*, Ulan's blind eyes wept tears of thin blood.

'No,' said Stele, the denial puny, minuscule. The word fell against a black curtain of shapes that hissed and whirred about him.

From every dark corner came insects, not in mad swarms or crazed armies, but in careful, quiet and orderly ranks. There were flies of every size and colour, spiders and beetles by their hundreds of thousands. They came together into a formless mass, and in moments they became an unholy daemon-shape, united by a single hideous intent.

'Malfallax,' Stele spoke the warp-lord's name and bowed his head. 'I had not expected to greet your magnificence.'

'Better this way,' it said, in breathy tones that were chitin wings rubbing against each other. 'Unexpected.' It bent down and licked absently at the dry patch of blood.

Garand's avatar dropped to the floor in genuflection. 'Great Malfallax, Changer and Monarch of Spite. Your presence honours us.'

The daemon did not acknowledge the Word Bearer. 'Sssssssstele.' It savoured the name. 'Our long-held bargain comes to its fruition, but you tarry. Why?'

The sheer psychic presence of the daemon beat at Stele. 'They... cannot be forced, lord. To guide these Astartes from the corpse-god's will to the way of eight requires time and guileful purpose.'

'A luxury you no longer possess,' the creature replied. 'In the Eye, time changes and shifts as all things do. You must accelerate your plans.'

Stele frowned. 'Lord, if we move too quickly, all I have done may become unravelled. Garand's offering will be forfeit...'

On the mention of his name, the Warmaster's avatar interposed itself. Parts of the flesh-form were alight now, crisping and burning. 'He has spoken. You proceed too slowly. You will move forward at once or I will have this world ended and you along with it.'

BAAL. THE PLANET had been green once, hundreds of thousands of years ago, back before the Imperium had existed.

Once, lush forests and oceans rich with life had covered the world, but those were forgotten myths now. Their legacy remained in fossil records as the planet moved on, catastrophic forces scouring the surface until it was a fierce sphere of blood-red rock and sand. The name of the world came from the depths of human history, a cognomen that men had once given to a daemonic beast king. Like its namesake, Baal was an unforgiving master, a place that would destroy the unwary and the faithless.

Fitting, then, that the Blood Angels had come here and turned it to their own purpose. Commander Dante crossed the battlements of the fortress-monastery, the constant desert wind tugging lightly at the hems of his robes. Above the horizon he could see the shapes of Baal's moons in the evening sky, their surfaces glittering.

The constant storms of rusty fines in Baal's upper atmosphere made the skies shimmer with a faint pink glow. Dante's eyes ranged down over the landscape, tracing the lines of the Great Chasm Rift to the north and the towing caps of the Chalice Mountains. After millennia, the warrior was still touched by the sight. Baal lived in his heart, as it did in all of his battle-brothers. In the *Book of the Lords*, there was a passage that talked of the planet's birth, as a place created by the God-Emperor to test the faithful. If that were truly the purpose of Baal, then the Blood Angels had succeeded here. They had taken a world that threw death at anything which dared to stride across its surface, and made it their home. Baal would never be tamed – that was a thing for gods to do, not for men – but it had been taught to respect its masters. The harsh environment lived in harmony with its people. It was only here, in the inner sanctums of the fortress, that the ancient and long-passed character of the planet could still be found.

Dante passed through an ornate airlock made of brass and synthetic diamond plates, and into the arboretum. The air was warm and moist, quite unlike the rasping dryness outside; the slightly sweet smell of rich loam reached his nostrils. From soft soil of dun-coloured earth, trees and plants grew toward a domed ceiling made of oval lenses. Each pane was as large as a leviathan's eye, forged by some process lost to the depths of history. Perhaps, in the beginning, the diamond windows had been clear, but now they were scarred white by untold centuries of scouring sand, shedding only a milky, indistinct light across the vast garden.

The Blood Angel walked with care through the riot of foliage, picking his way around the boles of tawny trees. Some of his brethren questioned the value of this place; they asked why it was that valuable servitors be maintained in order to keep the arboretum alive. Dante suspected that they saw the place as some eccentricity of his, a personal diversion for the master of the Blood Angels. Perhaps it was all of those things, but it was also a vital link to Baal's past. Every plant that grew and thrived here was extinct in the wilderness outside. The garden was a portal into deep time, a reminder of how things could thrive, only to become dust as the future encroached upon them. It was a living reminder of life's struggle against the weight of history.

'Calistarius,' Dante said gently as he approached a clearing. Before him, a man in simple prayer robes knelt on one knee, tracing his fingers across the petals of a bed of white flowers.

'My lord,' said Mephiston, glancing up at him. 'I have not heard that name spoken in many years.' The Chief Librarian of the Blood Angels gazed at Dante with hooded eyes, the burning gaze that so transfixed the minds of his enemies at rest. 'I have not been Brother Calistarius for an age.'

The commander studied the face of his friend and comrade. Dante had been there on planet Armageddon on the night that he had emerged from the rubble of Hades Hive, reborn as Mephiston, Lord of Death. Calistarius had been lost to the red thirst and buried alive, thought dead until a vision of their primarch had guided him back to life. 'Forgive me,' said Dante. 'For a moment, my mind took me back to days past. To simpler times.'

'In this place it is easy to lose one's self in ancient history. Others may doubt the merit of this garden, but not I.'

Dante gave a slight nod; the psyker had picked up on his thoughts. 'You sent word you wished to speak with me.'

'Yes, lord. I thought it best we talk alone, less incautious ears or minds catch wind of what I must tell you.' He gestured around. 'I often come here to meditate, commander. The tranquillity of Baal's past smoothes the path into the empyrean.'

Dante's face became grave. He could tell from his old cohort's tone that Mephiston's news would not be good. 'What have you to tell me?'

'Vode's mind was silenced, Great One. Even as I rested here and projected my thoughts into the void, I felt the edge of a ripple from his psychic shriek.'

'Killed?'

'Aye,' Mephiston said grimly, 'and Gallio along with him. Every man we sent to Shenlong, ended in a blink of fire.'

'You are certain of this?' Dante asked.

'The ways of the warp are never fixed,' replied Mephiston. 'Like desert sand, the real slips through my fingers. But on my sword, I tell you. Those men are dead.'

A cold, sickening familiarity touched Dante, one he had known a million times over since his first command as a Blood Angel warrior. He felt the death of each battle-brother as keenly as he had the very first to die under his stewardship. 'How?'

'I can only guess,' the psyker added, 'but if this Arkio is touched by the ways of Chaos—'

'There must be another explanation,' snapped the commander. 'An accident perhaps, an attack by enemy forces…'

Dante's old comrade gave a slow shake of his head. 'No, lord,' he said, with grim finality.

'You would suggest our own kind have drawn blood against us?' Dante growled. 'I pray you are mistaken.'

'As do I,' Mephiston agreed. He was silent for a moment before he spoke again. 'The *Amareo*'s mission will not remain concealed from our brothers forever, commander. Despite my best efforts, word of it spreads among the men. Soon, questions will be asked.'

Dante shook his head. 'I will not reveal news of this "transformation" until we know the truth behind it. If talk of a second coming of the Great Angel grows, dissension in the ranks will follow.'

'And a schism is something we cannot risk.' He met Dante's gaze. 'My doubts are gone, lord. I believe this boy Arkio is a false messiah. Only out of fear would he have killed Gallio's party.'

'But you said that you cannot be sure that is what took place.'

Mephiston frowned. 'Dark threads gather out there. They knit together in a web of deceit and we are caught in them. Shrouded forces, hatreds incarnate are at work manipulating events. This Arkio is at the hub of them, commander.'

'We can only be sure by facing him in person,' said Dante. 'Until then, he remains an unknown, a tarot card unturned.'

The psyker fell silent again, studying the delicate plants at his feet. 'You know this flower, commander?'

'Redkin,' Dante replied. 'It has not existed on this planet in the wild since the thirty-eighth millennium.'

Mephiston ran a bare finger over the tough, rubbery petals of the white flower, the serrated edge of it drawing blood. Instantly, capillaries in the petiole began to absorb the fluid, turning the plant scarlet. 'The flower's roots mesh with those of the others that surround it,' the Librarian said, 'it shares the bounty it gathers.' In a bloom of crimson, the coloration spread across each of the plants in the cluster. Mephiston's fingers closed around the flower in his hand and crushed it, spilling a trickle of his own vitae on the rusty soil. 'Like us, one gives strength to all. But if that unity is broken...' He paused, cocking his head. 'We have company.'

Dante turned at the sound of the airlock opening. A spindly messenger servitor ambled over on clanking mechanical feet. Once it had been a human being; now it was a device in service to the Imperium, mind wiped of any personality, a featureless automaton made of flesh and implanted steel. Its blank face swung left and right, finally locating the Blood Angels commander. 'With your permission, Lord Dante. A message from Shenlong arrives. Your attention only.'

'Speak,' he demanded.

'Via the astropathic duct Ulan aboard the battle barge *Bellus*, Brother-Captain Ideon commanding, protocol omnis octo,' it recited, relaying the trance-speech from the monastery's own psychic communicators. 'The Sanguinary High Priest Brother Sachiel, chosen of the Blessed Arkio, requests an audience with the Lord Commander Dante on the shrine world of Sabien in nine solar days, on behalf of the Reborn Angel.'

'The Reborn Angel,' Mephiston repeated the title with a sneer on his lips. 'This whelp has no need for modesty, it seems.'

Dante was lost in thought for a moment. 'Sabien. I know it well. There was a Blood Angels garrison there, in the worst days of the Phaedra Campaign.' He frowned. 'Many of our kindred shed blood for every metre of that blighted planet.'

'An abandoned monument world,' said the psyker. 'An ideal location for an ambush.' He got to his feet, fire dancing in his eyes. 'Lord, this is so transparent a trap.'

'Of that, we may be certain,' Dante agreed. 'But this priest Sachiel, if he truly speaks for Arkio, knows only too well that I am forced to agree to the meeting.'

Mephiston's eyes narrowed. 'Commander, you cannot think to accept this so-called "request"? If Arkio wishes to meet, he should come here to Baal.'

'He will not,' Dante retorted, 'and I will not risk more lives to bring him under force of arms. No, we must seek the truth about Arkio and determine if he truly is Sanguinius reborn or an impostor.'

'To do that, I would need to turn my gaze upon him, lord.'

Dante nodded. 'And so you will. You will attend me at Sabien and I will have this Arkio answer for his deeds.'

Mephiston shook his head. 'I cannot allow that.'

The Blood Angel gave the Librarian a sharp look. 'Do you defy me now as well?'

'Forgive me, great Dante, but you are the sworn commander of this Chapter. Your place is here, at the throne of Baal. I shall meet with this Arkio, alone. As your second, I cannot allow you to place yourself in such danger.'

Dante went red with annoyance. 'In eleven hundred years I have led my men from the front! Now some child presumes to the godhead over my Chapter and you demand I stay behind?'

Mephiston's iron-hard gaze never wavered. 'If it pleases the lord commander, I am best suited for this endeavour. For all your greatness, you do not possess the warp-sight as I do. My vision will see the heart of this pretender as plainly as day, and I will not flinch from his execution when the moment comes.' He placed a hand on Dante's shoulder, a gesture of familiarity that no other Blood Angel alive would ever have dared to make. 'My lord, when the men learn of this Arkio there will be questions. They will look to you for guidance.'

'And so I must be here to answer those questions.' Dante frowned. After a long moment, he spoke again. 'Very well. Your counsel has never failed me yet, Mephiston, and I will accept it now. On my orders, assemble a force of your most senior brothers and take command of the battle barge *Europae*. I grant you full power to speak on my behalf and that of the Blood Angels.'

The Lord of Death tapped his balled fist to his chest and bowed his head in salute. 'For Sanguinius and the Emperor,' he said.

'For Sanguinius and the Emperor,' repeated Dante.

RAFEN ENTERED THE chapel unseen and moved from the shadows to the altar. He had barely taken a step when Arkio's crystal-clear voice called to him. 'Rafen. I see you.' His sibling stood up from prayer and beckoned him forward. 'Come now. We are alone.'

The Marine walked into the dimly lit transept. 'They say that tomorrow Sachiel will choose the thousand and consecrate the Blood Crusade.' His voice was tight with emotion.

Arkio nodded. 'It shall be thus.'

'And how many will die?' Rafen demanded. 'How many more Blood Angels and innocents will perish?'

'Only those who stand against the will of Sanguinius.'

Rafen faltered for a moment. 'Brother, I beg of you. Go no further. I implore you, in our father's name, do not do this! You will lead the Blood Angels into self-destruction.'

At any moment, he expected Arkio to turn on him in anger, to strike him down for his presumption, but instead the golden figure gave him a sorrowful, pitying gaze. 'No, my kinsman. I will free them. With your help, and Sachiel, Stele, all of us, we will begin a new era for our battle-brothers.'

'Arkio,' Rafen felt his voice catch. 'Can you not see the bloodshed that lies ahead?'

His brother turned away, returning to his prayer stance, dismissing him like some irrelevant vassal. 'I am the eye of the infinite, the Deus Sanguinius. If there is blood to spill, then it shall be spilt in my name.'

Rafen found no more words and fell silent. He turned his back on Arkio and walked away.

CHAPTER SIX

IN THE CONFINES of the makeshift arena, their war had
raged for days and nights without respite. Some of them
had been soldiers in the Shenlong Planetary Defence Force,
desperate to regain a little honour after failing so miserably
against the Chaos invaders, others were just citizens, dispossessed by the Word Bearers, lost and purposeless in the
ashes of their city. All of them had spirits that were wanting, great voids in their hearts that could only be filled by
one who could offer them hope.

This Blessed Arkio did; the Shenlongi had believed
themselves abandoned by the might of the Imperium.
Their prayers for salvation had gone unanswered, and as
the Traitor Marines subjugated them, the vile demagogues of the Word Bearers cult mocked them for their
loyalty to an Emperor that had turned his back on them.
Those were the darkest days. Some had broken under the
yoke of oppression and taken their own lives, others
casting off their fealty to Terra and embracing the
bloody way of the archenemy. The people had faced

their fate with gloom, convinced that rescue would never come.

Arkio changed all that. On wings of sacred fire, he fell from the skies and smote the Word Bearers with his Holy Lance. In less than a day, the Reborn Angel and his cohorts swept Shenlong clean of the enemy and liberated her people. They were all too willing to cast aside whatever devotion they had given to a distant ghost atop a throne a million light-years away; all too willing to bend their knee for a god that walked like a man, passing among them in a vision of golden light. Arkio was their rescuer, and they loved him for it.

When the Blessed's priest Sachiel gave word that Arkio was to draw an army from the people, untold numbers of men and women rose to the call. They would be proud to lay down their lives for their new saviour, taking any chance to stand a little closer to his magnificence. There would be a choosing, Sachiel said, the conscription of a thousand souls to join Arkio on his Blood Crusade. Those so ordained would become the Warriors of the Reborn, and for their hearts and souls the reward of life anew was theirs. The penitents spoke in whispers of the far-off world of Baal, the birthplace of the Blessed, where legends said normal men could be transformed into avatars almost as great as he – the Adeptus Astartes. There was no shortage of volunteers.

In the great plaza on the steps of the Ikari fortress they fashioned an arena from fallen buildings, and inside those who dared to aspire to warriorhood took up arms against one another. Only the strongest, the most ruthless would be selected for the thousand. They began their little war, corralled there beneath the mountainous tower, and they fought and fought. Life by life, hour by hour, their numbers dwindled, the survivors nearing the thousandfold as day followed night followed day.

ALACTUS AND TURCIO opened the gate as the Sanguinary High Priest approached, the dawn light gleaming off the

white gold on his armour. Within the arena, the melee had
grown quieter and more infrequent as the massed battles of
the early days had given way to attrition. Hundreds of commoners had perished in those first confused free-for-alls,
gallons of shed blood turning the flagstones brown beneath
them. Some of the weapons were crude – clubs, axes, huge
steel spanners stolen from the factory cathedrals – while
others were more deadly. A few of the applicants had pro-
jectile weapons, flamers, even lasers, the guns looted from
the corpses of war dead and brought here to turn against
one another.

As Turcio watched, the Blood Angel could see a firefight
in progress between two men, one barely able to carry the
heavy stubber in his hand, the other snapping shots back
with some sort of small-bore lasgun. The figure with the
stubber gave out a war cry and tried to rush his enemy, but
the weapon was too bulky, too heavy for an unarmoured
human to manage. He stumbled, and the figure with the
laser stitched him with hot fire. He sank to the ground, his
corpse catching alight.

Sachiel paused at the arena gate and spoke a whispered
command into his vox. In reply an air raid warning siren
keened from a high balcony somewhere on the side of the
fortress tower. The lowing shriek settled over the plaza and
silence fell after it. This was the pre-arranged signal; the trial
was over. All across the arena fights staggered to a halt and
weapons were lowered. Those who could still move emerged
from cover, into the open space in the centre of the battlefield. In the makeshift grandstands erected along the walls of
buildings bordering the arena, people boiled forward in
unrestrained eagerness to see who would be selected.

The siren shut off and Sachiel basked in the quiet. It
seemed as if every eye on Shenlong was set on him. The
Blessed had charged the priest with the task of making the
final choices, and it was a duty he was only too eager to
perform. He entered the arena, with Turcio and Alactus at
his sides. Sachiel's gaze ranged over the faces he saw
around him, all of them bloody and dirty with the effort of

fighting. In their eyes was an unquestioning readiness to do anything that he ordered, and the realisation of that made him swell with power. These men would follow Arkio into the jaws of hell and never question.

To think he had harboured doubts about the raising of this army; now it seemed ridiculous to him. Of course, these were only mere men, no match for the might of a Space Marine like him, but still this helot battalion would have its purpose on the field of conflict. The fact alone that commoners were willing to sacrifice their futures for Arkio spoke volumes for the power of the Blessed. When the Blood Crusade began in earnest, the ranks of the Warriors of the Reborn would swell to ten, twenty times this size. His shook off all thought of his previous hesitancy. Who was he to question the wisdom of the Blessed?

A movement caught his eye and looked down to see a straggle-haired female as she tried to rise to her feet. She could not do it; livid, weeping wounds along her side had opened her to the air. Sachiel studied the injury with a practiced eye. A Space Marine might have been able to survive such a cut, but a normal human would have no chance at all. The woman met his gaze, and there in her eyes was an entreaty so pure and heartfelt it gave the priest pause. He stooped over her.

'Who are you?' he asked.

'Muh-M-Mirris,' she coughed. 'Mirris Adryn.'

Sachiel noted the remains of a small pennant badge on her shoulder. The Shenlongi had a tradition whereby the cadre and rank of a citizen would be displayed through a set of knotted ribbons on their clothing. The woman wore the colours of a mother of three, a teacher. 'Mirris,' he said gently. 'Your children are proud of you.'

'Yes.' She forced a smile, tears streaming down her face. She knew death was coming, and that she would never fulfil the dream of joining Arkio's cohort.

'Let me give you a gift,' began Sachiel, and he drew his reductor from his belt. 'Do you desire the Blessed's Peace, Mirris Adryn?'

'Lord, the offering of the reductor is only for Astartes–' said Alactus, his face a grimace.

Sachiel silenced him with a look. 'All those who serve the Reborn Angel shall share in this.'

Mirris's eyes shone, accepting the benediction. 'Yes, lord. I wish it.'

He gave her a gracious nod and shot her in the heart. The blunt-headed titanium bolt was designed to punch through the hardened ceramite and plasteel of a Space Marine's power armour and pierce the bone cage projecting the organs within, it was the final, honourable solution for a battle-brother too close to death for recovery. Against normal, unenhanced flesh it blew a cavity in the teacher's chest as big as Sachiel's fist. With care, he closed Mirris's eyes and stood, wiping away the backwash of her blood from the device. 'Even in death, the thousand will serve the Blessed as a monument to his righteousness,' he said, his voice clear and hard as it carried across the arena.

Turcio stared at the dead woman, the faint smell of her cooling blood reaching his nostrils through the grille of his armoured helmet. The tang of the scent-taste touched a deep and primal chord inside him. Battle would be coming soon.

Sachiel stepped forward boldly, holstering the reductor and spreading his hands wide. He moved through the crowd of bedraggled and worn fighters, touching some on the shoulders, nodding to others. Each one that he indicated bowed in return, and those around them shrank back to see the greatness in their midst. Man by man, Sachiel chose the thousand. Those that fell short of the benediction watched in mute silence, others breaking into tears. Alactus saw two men place guns in their mouths and end their own lives rather than accept the failure.

In the middle of the arena was the gutted hulk of a Word Bearers Land Raider, a burnt box of warped metal and bony protrusions killed in the opening salvoes from the *Bellus*. He climbed atop the ruined vehicle to address the people before him.

'Your lives are over,' he told them. 'Whatever you were before this moment, whatever your words and deeds before this day, now they are nought but vapour. You are dead and you are reborn. You are the thousand.'

A ragged cheer erupted from the men in the arena, quickly picked up by the watchers in the stands and the streets beyond. The sound carried like a wave, and Sachiel fancied that he could hear the whole of the planet crying out. 'You are the first to bear the honour of the Warriors of the Reborn, the chosen of Arkio the Blessed, the servants of the New Blood Angel. Your names will be carved into history alongside the legions of Sanguinius, alongside the name of Arkio himself!'

The thousand rattled their weapons and sent shots into the sky, a clattering clarion of thanksgiving. 'Mark this day well,' he told them, 'for it shall never come again. In the ages, men will look back to Shenlong and see you all as a beacon of principle and loyalty. They will know you as I do – as heroes of the wars to come.'

The roar came again, and this time it split the air like rolling thunder.

A WRY SNEER formed on the inquisitor's lips as the noise penetrated the stained glass windows of the chapel. The shouting had such force that the ancient panels vibrated under each exultation, and the priest's rhetoric made the sound rise and fall like a conductor directing an orchestra. He considered Sachiel with cold amusement; all men bore weaknesses, even such preternatural superhumans as the Space Marines, and the key to manipulating them was to isolate and exploit those defects. For men such as the late Sergeant Koris, it had taken more application than others, and with Rafen the effort had almost killed him – but he fully expected to hear of Arkio's brother soon, perhaps to be found dead in some dingy corner of the city after taking his own life.

Stele had been forced to drive Rafen into the depths of his own despair to control him, but Sachiel was a different story. A supremely arrogant man among an arrogant breed, the priest's touchstone was his self-superiority. Stele discovered that in his youth, Sachiel had been born into the closest thing that Baal Primus had to aristocratic nobility. A highly-placed warrior tribe with many dominions on the First Moon, he viewed his ascension to the hallowed ranks of the Blood Angels as a matter of course, and Stele had no doubt that Sachiel imagined a future with his hand on the command of the Chapter in the centuries to come. Stele had worked carefully to cultivate Sachiel, over the years of the *Bellus*'s mission into ork space to recover the Spear of Telesto, teasing out the thread of vanity that lurked inside him, feeding it and nurturing his pretension. He had allowed Sachiel to advance quickly in rank and in turn gained a trusting ally. Combined with the priest's fanatical devotion to the cult of Sanguinius, Stele had an agent who would willingly further his plans without ever considering the true motives behind them. As long as Stele kept his purpose cloaked in the mantle of the primarch's rebirth, Sachiel would follow him unflinchingly.

He looked away from the window. Arkio was not present, and to his irritation, the honour guard stationed at the gate to the inner crypt refused to let the inquisitor enter. The young man was in there once again, communing with the Holy Lance. In truth, Arkio's affinity with the archeotech weapon was a source of some concern to Stele. He found himself wondering what secrets the device held, secrets that only someone with Astartes blood would ever be able to unlock. The Blood Angel was meditating in the sanctum, hoping to catch some fragment of his primogenitor's soul from the weapon Sanguinius had once called his own. Stele gave a silent entreaty to the Ruinous Powers that he would find no such thing. If Arkio began to exhibit signs of dangerous independence, all Stele's carefully-wrought plans would be for nothing.

Another lusty roar brought his attention back to the crowds below. Sachiel was building to a crescendo now, unleashing a blazing tirade.

* * *

IN HIS HAND the priest held the copper chalice that was the symbol of his high office. He thrust it aloft, and the dawn sun glittered off the replica of the great Red Grail. It held Sachiel's gaze for a moment. One day, he told himself, I will carry the true Red Grail itself, even if I have to wrestle it from Corbulo's dead fingers. The naked avarice in his thoughts sent a thrill through the priest. It was a hidden desire, something he would never have dared to speak of openly – and yet suddenly he felt empowered by it, the daring of such dissension making him bold. The thousand bowed their heads under the shape of the chalice.

'The Blood of ages flows through us all,' he said, phrases from the *Book of the Lords* bubbling up inside him without conscious thought. 'The Sons of Sanguinius will rise to take the galaxy from all those who oppose order and light.' They cheered him on, frenzied and wild. 'The Blessed lights the path, we must lead the way along it and welcome those who praise his name!'

'Arkio!'

'*Arkio!*'

'Praise him!'

Voices all around were raised in adulation. 'We bring light to those who see the truth, and all-consuming fire to those who deny.' Sachiel slammed the grail to his breast-plate, tapping it to his hearts. He was shaking with raw emotion. 'Heed me. I am the right hand of the Reborn Angel. I give you all his call to glory. Take up arms, Warriors of the Reborn, take up your weapons and make ready for war.' Sachiel threw back his head and bellowed to the sky. 'This day the old order dies. This day we are *all* reborn anew. This day we begin the Blood Crusade!'

'Arkio! Arkio! Arkio! Arkio!' The chant went on and on until it filled the air.

DESPITE THE BRIGHTNESS of the morning, Rafen could see only shadows. From the roof of the fortress he watched the priest continue his bombast, a tiny figure in red and white he could blot from his sight with the thick of his thumb.

There was no silencing his voice, though, every word Sachiel said was being broadcast through the vox network of the Blood Angels and the telegraphs of Shenlong's city-sprawls.

'Those men who seek to control us, we disavow them!' came the priest's cry in his ear-bead, the sound of his voice on the wind reaching him a split-second later. 'The Imperium is choked with petty bureaucrats and debased fools, weaklings who corral the destiny of mankind laid down by the Emperor. Sanguinius knew this. He died in the war with the arch-traitor Horus so the Emperor might live!' Rafen's lip curled in a sour sneer; Sachiel was warping the truth to suit his sermonising. The priest continued, working himself and his audience into a frenzy. 'But now the Pure One has returned to us, and his sight is unfailing. He came to us because this plague of deficiency has stretched across the stars, even to poison the very highest office of the Blood Angels themselves. We cannot stand by any longer and allow the will of our Chapter, our species to be dictated by impotent men. Now is the day for action, in Arkio's name!'

The crowd roared his brother's name, sending a shudder through the rock. Rafen glanced down at the knife in his hand, still stained with his own dried blood. Hours ago he had been within a heartbeat of taking his own life, and now he was again, but this time it was by his own choice.

'We abandon the rule of these so-called Adeptus Terra!' Sachiel bellowed. 'We deny the dominion of Dante. We find him wanting. From now on, we answer only to the command of the Blessed!' The crowd boiled around the priest and the thousand, demanded answers, begging him for a mandate. They wanted to be told what to do, they would not be complete without an edict to follow. 'Warriors, I charge you. You will stand as cohorts to the Blood Angels aboard the *Bellus*, the sacred flagship of the Blood Crusade. Together we will face Dante and excise him so that Arkio may take his rightful place as master of the Chapter!'

'Vandire's oath...' Rafen felt the impact of the words like a physical blow. He had never doubted that sooner or later he would hear such heresy uttered, but still when it came it made him feel like vomiting. Sachiel stood there advocating murder and sedition, and to Rafen's eternal shame there were battle-brothers who took up the call. All at once he felt tarnished and humiliated, ashamed to admit that he shared blood with these addled turncoats.

'Baal shall come to our fold,' Sachiel roared, reaching a climax. 'All Blood Angels and successors will bend the knee to Great Arkio, or face oblivion.' The answering cry blotted out everything, and Rafen's hot shame cooled into an icy anger. *Could none of these blind fools see it?* As clear as the day, it was there before them, masquerading in comrade's clothes, appealing to their baser natures, their fears and secret hopes.

'Chaos.' Rafen spat the word from his mouth. The hand of the eightfold star moved Sachiel and the others like mindless pawns across a vast game board, marshalling them for ill deeds so huge they were beyond the reckoning of these blinkered, misguided fools. 'Curse me, but I will *not* let this go any further.'

'Brother?' said a voice behind him, and Rafen spun about abruptly. He was caught unawares, his own dark thoughts and the rage of the crowds distracting him. Lucion approached him, a questioning look on the upper half of his face where it protruded over the half-mask of his breather plate. The Blood Angels Techmarine paused, his arms at his sides but the mechanical servo-limb on his back still twitching with concern. 'What did you say?'

Rafen glanced from the knife in his hand, back to Lucion in his armour of red ceramite and cog-tooth gunmetal trim. 'Arkio is no messiah,' he told the Blood Angels Techpriest. 'My poor brother is an oblivious catspaw.'

Lucion's face went white with shock. 'How can you say such a thing? You, of all men, the sibling of the Blessed.'

'How?' Rafen repeated, advancing on the Techmarine. 'I say it because I am the only one on this desperate world with eyes still clear enough to see.'

Brother Lucion backed away toward the service platform running the height of the Ikari fortress. 'No, no,' he waved all three of his limbs in the air before his face, as if he could banish Rafen's utterance like a nagging insect. 'You are mad.'

Rafen produced his bolter and aimed it squarely at Lucion's forehead. 'On the contrary,' he told him. 'I fear I am the last sane man.' The black tunnel of the weapon's maw never wavered. The Space Marine felt an odd kind of calm sweep over him as the final parts of his plan fell into place. Since the day this madness had begun there on Cybele, a slow-burning certainty had been building in Rafen's soul. In the marrow of his bones he knew the rightness of it, and now it had come to a head. The fear, the constant dark fear that it would be by his hand that Arkio would perish was swept away. As he studied the confused face of the Techmarine, Rafen decided that he would take his own life, and that of every wayward mortal and deceiver that had strayed from the path of light. 'The beating heart of this fortress, the core. You have spoken with its machine-spirit.'

Lucion gave a slow, wary nod. 'Only in the most cursory fashion. I do not fully understand the ways of the reactor-spirit, but–'

He gestured toward the elevator platform with the gun. 'You will take me to it, or I will kill you where you stand.'

THEY DESCENDED THROUGH the interior of the conical tower in the open metal cage of the lift. Lucion whispered a quick litany over the controls and, with a squeak of iron on iron, the platform began a controlled fall past level after level. Rafen kept the Techmarine in his sights, never allowing his bolter to shift from a point targeted at Lucion's skull.

A memory flashed through Rafen's mind, of a similar elevator in the planetary defence bunker on Cybele. He and Lucion had been there as well, Arkio and Sachiel too, dropping into the dark with vengeance on their minds. It seemed like so long ago, as if years and not weeks had passed between then and now. For a moment, the weight of his weariness threatened to come upon him like a heavy cloak, but Rafen shook it away with an angry blink of his eyes.

Lucion was talking to himself. At first Rafen thought he was praying, or worse, using his vox to call for help. 'It's a test,' the Techmarine was saying aloud, giving voice to his thoughts, 'This is a loyalty test. The Blessed is testing my devotion.'

'Would you do anything he asked?' said Rafen.

'Of course,' Lucion replied instantly, as if the answer were as plain as the service stud on his brow. 'He is the Blessed.'

Part of Rafen felt hate and antipathy for his battle-brother as he listened to Lucion's answer. Perhaps, in the weaker minds of ordinary men, it was unsurprising that the commoners took up the cause of Arkio's supposed divinity, but to see it so readily accepted by the rank and file of his own Chapter sickened him. 'Has it ever occurred to you, brother, that you make a grievous error in venerating him?'

'Why would I think such a thing?' Lucion retorted. 'By the grace of the Omnissiah, Sanguinius has been restored to us.'

All the anger that had been building in Rafen for weeks suddenly found an outlet and he snarled at the Techmarine. 'He sprouts wings and suddenly he is a god-prince? Are you so credulous that you cannot see past the glitter of the gold armour?'

They had been travelling down in near darkness for several minutes, and so Rafen could only see glimpses of Lucion's face. Conflicting emotions danced there for a moment before he nodded to himself. 'A test,' he repeated. 'I will not be found lacking, you may carry my word of that to the Reborn Angel himself.'

With a clatter of metal, the elevator halted. 'Fool,' Rafen said under his breath, and motioned to the door. Unconcerned that he still had a gun trained on him, Lucion opened the wire-mesh and walked forward into the sub-level of the fortress. A spotlight mounted on his shoulder snapped on, and Rafen followed the bobbing blob of sodium-white glare.

The Techmarine carefully removed a ring of prayer beads from a rotary lock and powered open a series of thick steel hatches. Inside, there were consoles and panels of such diversity and intricate workings that Rafen was instantly reminded of the *Bellus*'s bridge deck. 'A question,' he said to Lucion. 'Which one of these does the machine-spirit for the power core inhabit?'

Lucion frowned, then pointed at a large, ornate module. 'Here. Although the spirit-programme extends itself out through the entire reactor system, tending to the fusion heart, the cooling factors, the regulatarium…'

Rafen didn't understand most of the tech-priest's terminology, but he grasped enough for his purposes. He drew in a breath. 'The power-spirit. I want you to kill it.'

Lucion blinked. 'Did I mis hear you? Rafen, perhaps you are taking this test too far, but I cannot–'

He shook his head, raising the bolter. 'No test, priest. Do as I say.'

The Techmarine's face drained of colour. 'What you ask is madness, brother. Even if I could, such a deed would enrage the fusion core. It would reach critical potentiality in moments and detonate with enough force to punch a hole in this planet. We would all be destroyed!'

'Arkio, too?'

At last Lucion understood what Rafen's intentions were. 'Oh, Holy Terra, no. Brother, please! I will have no part of this.'

He began to babble and Rafen tuned him out; the tech-priest would not assist him any further. He nodded at the console. 'This one, yes?' Without waiting for confirmation, Rafen raised his gun and unloaded a full clip of bolt-rounds into the device. Lucion screamed, his voice lost in a sudden clarion of whooping sirens.

The Techmarine staggered forward, shaking his head. 'Wha-what have you done? What have you done?'

Rafen reloaded his weapon, slamming a fresh clip home. He was trying to find an answer for the priest when the rush of metal-shod feet signalled the arrival of more men. Figures in red armour appeared at a hatch on the opposite side of the room, visible through the smoke from the console and the strobes of warning lanterns.

'We heard gunfire–' one of them shouted.

'Traitor!' howled Lucion. 'Rafen has turned against us!'

The automatic reaction of the Marines was to raise their weapons and fire. Rafen wheeled away, letting off a trio of wild shots as he went through a tuck-and-roll out of the access hatch to the lift shaft. Stabbing streaks of tracer cut through the control chamber and Lucion was hit in the crossfire. He spun in place and stumbled against the wrecked console.

Rafen made it to the metal cage as the other Space Marines dived out of the hatch after him, bolters chattering. Pushing away all thoughts that his targets were fellow Blood Angels, he fired back. Return fire blazed over his head and struck part of the lift's cabling, severing it in a blare of noise. Rafen expected the cage to drop suddenly into the stygian dark at the bottom of the shaft, but the opposite happened, the bolts cut into the counterweight control, and suddenly the lift platform shot upward, trailing streamers of sparks. The acceleration threw Rafen to the deck and pinned him there as the lift raced headlong toward the circle of light above him.

Inside the chamber, Lucion inched himself forward, using one hand to keep his intestines and preomnor organ from spilling out of his belly wound. Here, surrounded by the lights and sounds of the Omnissiah's most holy creations, the Techmarine felt alive even as his blood leaked from him in brilliant red runnels. He took his other hand and tossed away his gauntlet, so that his last sensation would be the touch of his flesh against the sacred technology. Lucion gripped the thick switch rod beneath the rune that read: 'Emerg. Scram.' in the old tongue and turned it. With a sullen flicker, the lights inside the fortress winked out as Lucion cut off the fusion reaction before it could become critical.

'No victory for you, turncoat,' he gasped, 'no victory...'

THE TECH-PRIESTS insisted on re-consecrating the room before they would set to work in it, and that took the better part of the day, but as Shenlong's feeble sun began to dip beneath the horizon, the Ikari fortress and the district around it erupted with light and power once again, and the people cheered for Arkio's beneficence in saving them from the darkness and cold.

Their idol did not hear their thanksgiving through the veil of rage that shrouded him. 'Answers!' he thundered at Sachiel, the sheer momentum of his anger rocking the priest back on his heels. 'I demand answers. What warpspawn filth could it be that would dare to enter my fortress and render it impotent? Tell me.'

Stele smoothed his formal robes as he entered, giving a cursory bow. 'I shall do so, Great Arkio, but I must warn you. The news is hard.'

'Hard?' he spat, turning from Sachiel to stalk across to the inquisitor. 'You think me some child you must keep insulated from the ills of the world? Tell me, Stele, or I'll rip it from you.'

The force of the youth's words actually made Stele stumble for a brief moment. The awful light of the black rage danced in Arkio's eyes, turning the patrician, handsome face into that of a fanged, angered god. Arkio's aspect mirrored the sacred tapestry of Sanguinius in his blood-thirst that hung in the cloisters on Baal. 'Lord, I have prepared a shuttle to take us both to *Bellus*. It is not safe here on Shenlong for you any more,' Stele began, recovering his poise. 'You will understand my reluctance when I explain myself.' He gestured at the photon candles around the room. 'The cowardly saboteur in our midst, the viper at our breast attempted to smother the will of the machines that empower this edifice. Had he succeeded, he might have caused a catastrophe.'

'Explain, lord inquisitor,' Sachiel ventured, earning himself a leaden look from Arkio.

Stele continued, finding the meter of his performance. 'Were it not for the selfless courage and sacrifice of Brother Lucion, the machine-spirit would have become turbulent, perhaps to unleash the fire of the atom from its heart.' He took a calculated pause. 'The Ikari fortress and all living things for six kilometres in every direction would have been immolated in a nuclear firestorm.'

'Who did this?' Arkio hissed. 'A rogue Word Bearer? One of Iskavan's host that escaped the net of our execution squads?'

The inquisitor bowed his head sadly. 'No, Blessed. It sickens me to say that a Blood Angel was the culprit.'

Arkio froze like a statue, his wings snapping rigid. Behind him, Sachiel took a cautious step closer. 'And his name, Lord Stele?' asked the priest.

'I suspected there was an apostate in our midst when the mind-witch Vode arrived with Gallio and his other assassins,' Stele sneered. 'I have since learned that the vox of the late Brother-Sergeant Koris was used to send a message to Baal to summon them. They came only because the betrayer in our midst called out to that fool Dante, and bid him send killers to end you, Great Arkio.'

'A man still loyal to Dante, to the old order, here?' Arkio's voice wavered, incredulous, so sure of his own majesty. 'After all the miracles I have enacted?'

Stele nodded. 'But graver still is his identity, Blessed.'

'Name him.' Sachiel snapped. 'Name this treacherous bastard and I will have my personal honour guard hunt him down and tear him apart like a prey beast.'

The inquisitor wanted so badly to smile; but that would have spoiled the act. 'My lord, the traitor is your brother. The traitor is Rafen.'

The roar of inchoate anger that erupted from Arkio's throat struck like an elemental force, echoing across the city zones in baleful thunder.

CHAPTER SEVEN

THE STREET WAS alive with gunfire, shots clipping at Rafen's heels, whining off the cobbles to punch craters in the walls. The Blood Angel made a daring move, leaping off a low wall to launch himself behind the cover of a cargo pod. He snap-fired a burst at his pursuers, not expecting to do any more than make them keep their heads down.

Rafen glimpsed them as fleeting images, the red of their armour matching his, the brilliant gold of their helmets catching the light. Sachiel's honour guard had caught him in the alleys and he had led them on a merry dance through the warehouse district. Each time they tried to box him in, he found a route out of their closing net, but each escape was becoming more difficult than the last.

He checked the sickle magazine on his bolter, half-empty. Rafen frowned. The gold-helmeted troopers were wearing him down, making him waste precious ammunition. There were simply more of them than there were of him, and sooner or later Rafen would become too fatigued or too distracted to fight them all. There would have been a time when would have relished the chance to fight against the elite of the Blood Angels, testing his skills against them in a wargame – but this was no exercise, and the battle-brothers who dogged him did not bear harmless marker shells in their guns. The honour guard had been given one order – to capture him, dead or alive.

Rafen chanced a quick look around. In this part of the factory city ponderous monorail haulers carried crates of shells and warheads back and forth between store yards and assembly lines. Tall construction towers climbed into the dirty sky, dwarfing the blunt wedges of the fabrication barns. He considered his options – unless he could find a way to escape Sachiel's men, they would run him into the ground. It was taking all his effort just to stay one step ahead of them, and a single error on his part would turn everything against Rafen's escape. Shots rang off the exterior of the cargo module as the honour guards found his range. A surge of heat pressed at his back as a plasma blast burnt a wide hole in the metal. He had seconds to make a decision.

Rafen's eyes fell on an enclosure surrounded by racks of missile tubes. The building was dark and silent, probably serving as a temporary storehouse for the munitions. It would do. The Blood Angel took his last smoke grenade and flicked off the pin with his thumb. Dropping the metal egg, he launched himself from cover and into a full-tilt run. He heard shots cracking after him, and then the hollow crump of displaced air as the grenade exploded. A thick veil of metallic haze full of complex chemical strings emerged and filled the canyon of the street. The honour guard came on, moving slowly through the smoke, the visibility of their helmet optics curtailed sharply by the discharge. Their heads bobbed in silent conversation, messages flickering between them on an encoded frequency that Rafen's vox could not read.

Beyond them, Rafen threw his shoulder into a wooden doorway and it splintered under his weight. He dashed inside to be greeted by a forest of warheads ranging back through the building. Hellstrikes built for the wing roots of Lightning fighters and Marauder bombers were bound like cordwood. There were the fat cigars of Manticore missiles, mounted on wooden stays ready to be loaded on firing platforms. The shells of incomplete Atlas-class megaton bombs stood vertically on their aerofoil fins, the unfinished warheads almost scraping the supports holding up the corrugated iron roof. Rafen shouldered his bolter and wove through the inert steel trunks, slipping deeper inside.

Sachiel would never stop hunting him, that much was certain. Rafen had taken his chance to end this madness once and for all in the reactor core, but his spur-of-the-moment plan had collapsed. He had stood for long seconds on the roof of the Ikari fortress, waiting for the eruption of fusion fire to consume him, but it never came. Once again, he found himself running, and this time there was an entire planet of zealots at his heels. Rafen needed to gather his wits, to plan his next move, but as long as the golden-helmed troopers chased him he would be forced to stay on the defensive. Sachiel would only rest when Rafen was dead – and so he would have to find a way to die… for the moment.

There was a rattle of metal above, and the Blood Angel froze, for a moment believing that the honour guard were coming across the roof for him; but then the sound grew into a rushing, chattering roar and he realised it was the rains. Shenlong's rust-brown skies opened, releasing a downpour of polluted water that clattered off the metal roof of the manufactorum. Runnels of thin, russet liquid penetrated through breaches in the corrugated iron, pooling on the stone floor. Rafen caught the noise of heavy boots splashing through shallow puddles.

Sachiel's men followed him into the warehouse, holstering their guns as they entered. A gesture from the veteran sergeant commanding them was the only order they required, and as one they drew their close combat weapons and spread out to search the building. None of the Blood Angels would dare to discharge a bolt or beam in here. A single stray round could end all their lives in a heartbeat if it struck a live warhead.

Rafen moved. On a raised catwalk he located a set of unfinished and skeletal Manticores on a cradle. With a rough jerk, he ripped free the metal petals protecting the inner detonator unit, exposing it to the air. Like most of the other missiles in the store yard, the half-built Manticore munitions were empty of their volatile promethium fuel and still lacked the dense explosive matrix that would give them their murderous power – but the detonator rods were in place, and those alone were the equal of a dozen krak shells. Rafen tore fibrous wires from the missile's innards and used them to tie a quartet of frag grenades in place. His makeshift bomb was almost complete when the drumming of the rain was joined by a new sound – the ripping snarl of a chainsword.

Rafen reacted instantly, barely dodging the blow from the melee weapon. The honour guard's strike flashed past him with a blare of tungsten-alloy teeth, cleaving the wood of the cradle into a whirlwind of spitting splinters. He rolled back as the Space Marine struck out again, rebounding off a stanchion. In the confines of the catwalk gantry, Rafen had little room to manoeuvre and the tip of the chainsword blade cut into his armour, skittering off the chest plate and away. The blow left a finger-wide channel in his wargear.

'Filthy apostate.' snarled a voice from inside the gold helmet, 'You'll bleed for your perfidy against the Blessed!' Rafen parried a third lunge with an ironwood rod he snatched from the cradle, but the shimmering chain-blade bisected his substitute weapon. The Blood Angel pressed his free hand to his helmet, initiating a vox link to the other hunters in the warehouse. 'I have him. Form on me–'

Rafen sprang forward before he could finish the sentence, hands clawing into the shoulder pads of his opponent. With a sudden downward motion, Rafen butted the honour guard across the bridge of his helmet's nose, cracking the optic lenses. The shock of the blow staggered the Marine; Rafen was too close for the attacker to turn the sword on him, and he stumbled backwards. The honour guard's right foot slipped back along the decking and into space where the gantry ended. His balance fled and the Blood Angel fell away from Rafen with an angry howl, the chainsword tumbling from his fingers.

The other Marine collided with a nest of tool racks and slammed into the stone floor with a flat crash of sound. Winded, he still had enough impetus to draw and fire his bolt pistol, sending a spray of shots back up at the catwalk, in his fury ignoring the risk of a ricochet. Rafen recoiled and grabbed at a knife-switch set on the gantry, yanking it downwards without conscious thought. The release opened a set of clamps holding a drum of Hellstrikes above them, and the canister fell the height of the warehouse, flattening the honour guard beneath it like the blow of a steam hammer.

Rafen shook off a dizzy, sick sensation as he watched the Space Marine twitch and die under the tonnage. It had all happened so fast. 'Primarch forgive me,' he whispered, his blood running cold. 'I have killed a battle-brother…' He had always known this moment would come, from the very instant that he had heard Sachiel decry Dante and exhort the Blood Angels to turn on their heritage, but nothing had prepared him for the physical shock it brought with it. The blood of a Blood Angel was on his hands. And *he will not be the last*, Rafen admitted to himself.

A voice cried out from below him, and Rafen glimpsed red armour and gold masks flashing between the featureless greys of the rocket fuselages. 'There!' came the shout, 'Above. Close in on the traitor and take him.'

Traitor. Rafen felt dislocated from reality to have that hated brand turned on him, but in his beating heart he knew the reverse was true. He stooped, dialling the fuse setting on his grenades, and yanked the firing pin. Bolt-rounds hissed past his shoulders; the honour guards had clearly thrown caution to the wind after he killed one of their number.

Rafen ducked behind one of the inert Atlas bombs and pressed his shoulder into it, rocking the tubular fuselage on its pallet. The tall metal pipe wallowed and shifted dangerously. He threw himself at it again and the weight of the Atlas shifted suddenly, tilting away from him. Rafen staggered back along the gantry as the hollow tube fell against another of its kind, in turn knocking another off its base. The Atlas hulls rang like bells as they impacted each other, and they tottered like giant ninepins, ripping through stanchions and scattering Sachiel's men beneath them.

In the confusion, Rafen grabbed a chain dangling from the support beams and swarmed down it, swinging to land in a ready stance on the stone floor. He threw a last look at the gantry where his jury-rigged time bomb lay counting down the seconds and sank to his knees. There was a circular grate in the floor, surrounded by small rivers of rainwater pooling from every part of the building. Digging his fingers in the metal grid, Rafen let out a cry of effort and pulled at it. Aged bolts gave way in snaps like breaking bone.

Any moment now. Tossing the grate aside, Rafen pitched forward into the murk of the drainage channel, where fast-flowing floods the colour of tilled earth raced by, swelled by the sudden downpour. He fell into the grip of the sewer water and let it drag him away, scraping his armour across muck-encrusted walls.

The honour guards were reaching for him even as the igniters in the frag grenades burnt down to nothing. The explosives blew apart in a ball of orange thunder, catching the detonators inside the Manticores in sympathetic annihilation. In a tenth of a second, the missiles detonated, rippling fire into cases of battle-ready rockets. Flame set flame, fire birthed explosion, and the entire manufactorum ripped itself to pieces in a blood-red hellstorm.

Kilometres away in the Ikari fortress, a wall of noise cracked the ancient glass of the chapel window in a dozen places.

* * *

SACHIEL PRESSED ON through the corridors of the *Bellus*, his stride never slowing as Chapter serfs scrambled amongst themselves to get out of his way. The news boiled inside him; the Sanguinary High Priest was wound so tight with the message he carried that he thought he would blurt it out at any second. Space Marines came to parade ground attention as he passed, mailed fists tapping their chest plates in salute, while servitors and serfs bowed low.

There had been a time when Sachiel would have chastised himself for enjoying the veneration of the faithful. In the *Credo Vitae* there were edicts and oaths the Sanguinary Priests were required to avow, dedicating themselves to the sacred Blood of the Chapter, foreswearing any glory for themselves, but those old, weak words seemed so distant and removed now. Sachiel's heart swelled at the notion.

Since Arkio's Ascendance a moment had not passed where the priest did not think himself blessed to bear witness to such a miracle – and more, to be called by the Reborn Angel to serve as his adjutant and loyal commander. A smile crept across Sachiel's face as he entered the cavernous cathedral deck, making his way through the cloisters toward the inner sanctums. Since his youth, he had never doubted that he was touched by greatness. Many of his contemporaries had called him arrogant for daring to voice such notions. Let them have their petty jealousies, he thought, because he had been proven right. Great Sanguinius, to whom Sachiel had dedicated his life, had rewarded the priest beyond his wildest dreams. To be present at an event of such magnitude showed the lie of all those who had upbraided him. Sachiel was no mere priest now; he was the hand of the Blessed, and it was glorious!

His fingers fell to the velvet bag at his belt, and the replica of the Blood Angels chalice he carried there. Not for the first time, Sachiel imagined the moment when he would take the true Red Grail in his hands and accept the role of High Priest over the entire Chapter. The thought of it made his blood rush. Power, naked and beautiful, was within his reach.

The priest walked on alone into the sanctum sanctorum, where only the chosen of Arkio were allowed to tread. Normally there would have been Marines on guard here but the devastation wrought by the traitorous Rafen had required the recall of all available troops to the planet. A brief flicker of displeasure crossed his thoughts, but he banished it. Sachiel had hoped that he would be able to present his news to the Blessed in person, but Captain Ideon had informed him their high lord was at rest in his chambers. Sachiel accepted this with a nod, even a god-prince rich with a primarch's potency would need repose on some occasions. Instead, Sachiel would attend Inquisitor Stele and reveal what had taken place on Shenlong. The explosion of the missile store yard had obliterated six square blocks around it. Some of the priest's most loyal men had been turned to ashes in the conflagration, but their sacrifice had been worth it to end the life of the thorn in his side, the faithless and deceitful Rafen. He would swear upon it; nothing could have survived the catastrophic blast.

'You are dead, Rafen,' Sachiel said to the cool, still air of the cloister. Just uttering the words lifted a huge weight from the priest's heart. Ever since they had first laid eyes upon one another, Sachiel and Rafen had brought the worst traits in each other's character to the fore. Now the Blessed's brother was dead, the last tie holding Arkio and his loyalists to the old codes of the Blood Angels was gone, and with it Sachiel's hated antagonist. He could admit it now and release the feeling that had built up inside him. Sachiel loathed Rafen's quiet strength, the manner in which he would sneer at every utterance from the priest's mouth as if *he* were the holder of ordained office, not the priest. He hated the easy way that Rafen had earned the respect of men he served with, while Sachiel remained aloof and indifferent to the Space Marines he outranked. The pleasure he would take in announcing Rafen's end would be as sweet as a fine amasec liqueur.

The Sanguinary Priest paused before a stained glass window showing Sanguinius at the Conclave of Blood, and something in the turn of the primogenitor's face suddenly brought Rafen's final words back to him. *Piety alone will blind you.*

'Fool.' Sachiel spat out the insult automatically, but even as he did there came a nagging irritation in his mind. He hated himself for admitting it, but the deserter had stirred up doubts with that damning utterance. Sachiel looked into the eyes of the primarch, searching for clarity, and allowed himself the indulgence of hesitation. Arkio's path had broken with the tradition of his Chapter, shattering old codes of conduct that before had seemed inviolate. As the Reborn Angel had said himself, they were now writing a new chapter in the history of the Sons of Sanguinius, and the laws laid down by aged and passionless warriors like Dante were too confining, too limiting. On some deep level, the indoctrination of decades of Blood Angels dogma and training rebelled at the thought of Arkio's Blood Crusade and his Emergence – but Sachiel had seen Arkio's divinity shine through, he had felt the divine radiance of the Spear of Telesto upon him. This was proof, not the dusty words of long-perished men from millennia past.

His moment of weakness gone, Sachiel resumed his passage to Stele's quarters. Brother Solus had informed him that the inquisitor had left orders that he was not to be disturbed, but Sachiel waved him away. Such commands did not apply to the High Priest of the Reborn, and besides, Sachiel knew that Stele would be as pleased as he was to hear of Rafen's death. That his body had yet to be found was merely a formality; after such a detonation, all that would remain of Arkio's brother would barely be enough to fill a drinking goblet.

Stepping past the empty sentry alcoves, as Sachiel approached the door to Stele's chambers he tasted something strange in the air. A faint, almost undetectable whiff of brimstone and dead skin. Shaking the sensation away, the priest opened the doors and stepped inside. The atmosphere within felt thick and greasy with dark potency. He heard voices; some seemed to be coming from an impossible distance, others made up of rustling and whispering sibilance. Amid all of them he heard the inquisitor murmuring a gruff entreaty. Without waiting to announce himself, the priest pushed through the voluminous folds of black curtains enveloping the doorway and emerged in the chamber.

What he saw there made a wordless cry of shock erupt from his lips, and Sachiel groped for his pistol in self-defence.

Stele's sanctum was an arched chamber big enough to house a Thunderhawk dropship with its wings at full spread. Stands of photon candles gave weak, yellowish light that died fighting the heavy shadows that wreathed the room. There were a few biolume globes drifting about on anti-grav impellers, but they too were strangled by the arcane, liquid dark that enveloped everything. To one side was a twitching, steaming sculpture cut out of fast-decaying human flesh. Sachiel knew the smell of putrefaction all too well from hundreds of battlegrounds. It was misshapen and ugly as sin, a parody of life warped by the hand of some crazed sculptor. Bones and cartilage in the body had been reordered to present the shape of a hunched, muscular form. It bore the most striking resemblance to the armour of the Word Bearers that they had executed on Shenlong. The flesh-thing opened a wet orifice in its head and let out an angry moan; and with his back to the door, Stele craned his neck around to spy the stunned priest there behind him. The inquisitor was pale and damp with perspiration, the normally hard and unyielding lines of his granite face soft and pallid.

The priest was only aware of them in the most peripheral of ways, however, his gaze was captured by the thing that towered over all of them, writhing and fluttering in an immaterial breeze. It looked like a pict-print of a hurricane, a frozen tower of wind and storm wreckage that had somehow taken on the aspect of a living creature. His mouth agape, Sachiel understood all at once that the shape was made of paper. All about the walls of Stele's chamber, books lay open, spines broken and covers discarded, their pages torn free to make up the matter of the daemonic creature that rustled and crackled like dead leaves.

'What is this?' Irritation bubbled out of the fleshy avatar, steam popping from blisters all across its skin.

Stele gulped air and turned to face Sachiel, shrugging out of the restricting cloak about his neck. 'You conceited imbecile,' he hissed, the effort of anger trying him to the limit. 'I said no interruptions.'

Sachiel tried to make his mouth work, but nothing seemed to come. He could not look away from the intricate folds of parchment across the daemon's heartless, monstrous face. In a crushing blow of realisation, the priest suddenly understood what he had stumbled into – Stele, the trusted servant of Arkio, was in league with the Ruinous Powers. The thought galvanised him into action. He had to escape, to get away and warn the Reborn Angel that a viper far more venomous than his errant brother lay in their midst…

'Kill it,' rippled the daemon, the words hidden in the sound of fanning pages.

'No,' Stele grunted. 'I need him alive… He is useful to me.'

The priest brought his gun to bear and his finger tightened on the trigger, but he made the mistake of meeting Stele's baleful gaze and abruptly all function in his muscles ceased. 'Nnnnnn–' Sachiel's mind flashed to the moment on Cybele, when the inquisitor had held a Word Bearers sniper in a similar mind-lock. With every gramme of his will, the priest pushed against the pressure in his mind.

'Ah,' Stele managed, eyes watering. The effort was hard on him, coming so soon after spending his abilities on the Blood Angels mere days earlier. He wavered, and felt the phantom grip begin to slacken.

Pages of ancient dogma, documents filled with arcane scripture and illuminated proofs, rustled past him, shifting and reforming into shapes that might have been men, might have been beasts. 'You wish to preserve this manling?' asked the creature, breaths of polluted air gusting through its manifested form.

'Yes, great Malfallax,' Stele bit out. 'We need him.'

'Very well,' said the daemon, and the papers spun around Stele in a narrow typhoon, their edges slicing hundreds of tiny cuts in his bare skin. From its beating heart still floating in the depths of the empyrean, Malfallax projected a concentrated portion of itself into the open gate of Stele's corrupted mind. A black pearl of raw warp briefly entered the inquisitor – and suddenly all his weakness and fatigue melted away, replaced by a giddy psychic head-rush. 'A gift,' the creature whispered.

Colour returned to Stele's face and his teeth bared. 'You are most gracious, Spiteful One.' His eyes bored into Sachiel's, flaying his mind open to the psyker's dark will. 'Kneel, priest,' he commanded.

Sachiel found he had no resistance within him, and he did as he was ordered, the reductor in his hand falling to the tiled floor. His head swam with a sickening roil of recall, as his recent memories replayed in flash-frame blinks of pain – Stele spun though the Sanguinary Priest's thoughts as easily as he might the pages of a book.

Stele gave a grunt of laughter, reading his intent. 'You came to tell me Rafen was dead? Such trivia is hardly worth my notice.'

It was as if Sachiel were kneeling on the edge of a bottomless abyss. The priest's mind fluttered like an insect caught in setting amber, teetering on the brink of a horrific realisation. *Stele is tainted by Chaos, and if that is so then everything he has touched has also been sullied by corruption. By the blood of the primarch, what have we done? I am tainted. The Warriors of the Reborn too? The Spear? Even the Blessed Arkio…*

Stele shook his head. 'Cease,' he said, halting Sachiel's thoughts with a gesture. 'No, priest. I cannot have you venture down that road. Your role is yet to be completed.' His eyes glittered, and the inquisitor threw an ephemeral dart into the Blood Angel's mind. Sachiel screamed as Stele unfolded his psyche and deftly excised his memories, painting blackness over them from the moment he had entered the sanctum. A drool of fluid issued out of the corner of Sachiel's mouth.

'Frail little men-beasts,' Garand's latest avatar said with a grimace, flakes of dead flesh falling from it with each word. 'Its mind may break beneath your ministrations.'

'I think not,' retorted Stele, withdrawing the needle of his psychic power from a blank-eyed Sachiel. 'He will remember nothing of what he saw.'

Rough laughter crackled through the singed papers. 'Ah, Stele. You grow ever distant to your human roots and closer to us with every one of your gestures.'

'It pleases me to hear you say that,' Stele said, with a forced smile. In his mind's eye, Malfallax's dark seed of potency was lodged in his soul, glistening with the eight-fold star upon its surface. 'And while it gratifies me to accept your mark, Great Changer, perhaps it might be better for you to withdraw it for now–'

The pages gave an angry wasp-swarm vibration. 'Keep it, my friend. It will be important in the days to come.'

'We shall begin, then,' grated Garand. With a shrug of broken bones, the Word Bearers Warmaster withdrew from his mouthpiece and let it die.

Gently, the ripped shreds of paper began to drift apart as Malfallax retreated from the material realm, leaving the inquisitor with only a decaying corpse and the silent priest for company. Stele watched the pages settle, at once refreshed and newly afraid of the boon his monstrous master had given him.

THE DOCK WAS alive with noise and motion, men swarming like ants around the iron wharves and gantries. Dozens of ugly, bullet-shaped orbital tenders waited at rest on vertical rails, plumes of vaporised liquid oxygen hissing white clouds into the air. Cargo pods, normally crammed full of munitions crates and warheads, were being loaded with human freight instead. Hundreds and hundreds of men, a rag-tag army clad in cloaks and scavenged armour, filed solemnly into the modules. Here and there, tall figures in red armour could be seen, calling out orders and directing the erstwhile soldiers to their departure points.

Rafen watched from his vantage point in a burnt-out building, studying the ebb and flow of the crowds, watching the ordered procession with a practiced eye. He kept his vox on the same channel as the Blood Angels on the docks, listening to their terse communications as he rested, tending to his injuries. In the sewers, the explosion of the warehouse had forced a plug of filthy water into a floodhead and carried Rafen along with it, tossing him like a piece of debris. Sealed inside the airtight frame of his power armour, the Space Marine was forced to ride out the shock wave as each impact against the tunnel walls threw him closer to unconsciousness. The headlong surge along the pipes was a blur of rushing noise and blunt pain, but eventually the flood spent itself and deposited him in an overflow chamber on the lower levels of the factory city. Rafen flexed his arm, grimacing. His skin was marred with broad purple-black bruises where he had suffered impact after impact and the limb was slack where it had been dislocated. Carefully, he gripped his wrist and tugged; with a dull click of cartilage, the joint popped back into place. He shrugged off the pain that came with it.

Using an abandoned chimney stack, Rafen had climbed until he found his current hide. He took stock of his situation, examining his weapons and what little he had in the way of supplies. The Blood Angel considered himself behind enemy lines now, and conducted his battle drill accordingly. He had no idea how long he would be able to go unnoticed; certainly it might be days before the rubble of the store yard was picked through and the bodies of the dead men counted. He had a window of opportunity, but it would close quickly.

A roar of rocket exhaust drew his attention back to the dock. With a clang of steel on steel, a launch gantry fell away and one of the tenders threw itself into the dull sky on a plume of yellow flame. Fins folded out of the craft as it ascended and Rafen watched it go, disappearing into a sickly glow as it vanished through the low cloud cover. Another fifty or more men for Arkio's helot army were on their way to *Bellus*. There was a flurry of orders over the vox. The next launches were almost fuelled and ready to lift off. Legions of zealots, all of them adorned with the crude halo-and-spear symbol of the Warriors of the Reborn, shifted back and forth, eager to board the ships that would take them to be with their messiah.

Arkio was aboard the battle barge; Rafen had caught a cursory mention of 'the Blessed' and pieced together the meaning. With his brother on the *Bellus* and the army Sachiel had raised from the Shenlongi joining him in their droves, the situation was clear. The Blood Crusade was beginning, and soon the massive warship would be departing. Rafen replaced the gauntlet about his arm and re-sealed his wargear's links. Twice now he failed to bring this travesty of the Emperor's will to an end. Alone with Arkio in the fortress, it had been his own weakness that had stopped him from ending his sibling's life; and in the reactor core, blind chance had prevented the destruction of the tower. If *Bellus* left without Rafen, then Stele would be free to manipulate Sachiel and Arkio to whatever ends the inquisitor chose. The Marine's mind returned to the vision he had seen in his makeshift retreat, as it had many times in the past few days. He held his combat knife in his hand once more, then slammed it into his boot sheath with grim finality.

BENEATH THE DOCK platform was a web of supports extending into the dry mud of the riverbed. Orange knots of rust clustered at every giant bolt and weld, releasing rains of ruddy fines with each rumbling blast of exhaust from the tenders launching above. Rafen made his way through broken catwalks and bent spars and selected a pad on the southern edge of the dock where spindly Sentinel walkers had just completed the loading of a brace of cargo pods. The Blood Angel emerged directly beneath the gaping maws of the ship's engine bells, which twitched and hissed as the pilot-servitor in the nosecone ran through the final countdown sequence. The modules packed with soldiers were sealed shut – they would only be opened when the tender had safely landed in an airtight bay on *Bellus* – so Rafen could not enter there. The cockpit, high above him at the tip of the rocket, would not suffice either. Too small, too filled with arcane machinery and Adeptus Mechanicus complexity.

There would be only one route for a fugitive to board the battle barge. He could not chance accompanying other Blood Angels aboard a shuttle or Thunderhawk. Even with the dirt smeared across his armour, he could be seen and recognised. Once aboard *Bellus*, it would be a different story, the vast starship had many places for a careful soul to conceal itself. Rafen grabbed a maintenance ladder and hauled himself up it, into the nest of pipes and feed channels that poured promethium fuel to the engines. As the rockets hummed into life about him, he pushed his broad form into the open framework and found a vee-shaped stanchion that would accommodate his armour. The thunder of the engines built into a deafening crescendo, even through the noise-dampening protection of his helmet. Rafen gave a last look at the life-support monitor gauge on his wrist; all the vacuum seals on his armour were intact. With effort, he dug his ceramite-hardened fingers into the girders and wedged himself in place. Rafen closed his eyes and began a prayer to Sanguinius as gravity laid into him.

Clinging to the underside of the tender, Rafen hung on in grim determination, as the dock, the city and then the cloud-shrouded landscape of Shenlong fell away beneath him.

CHAPTER EIGHT

IN THE DARKENED corners of the landing bay, where only the blind rat-hunter servitors would dare to venture, Rafen was concealed. With care, he rubbed away the thin patina of ice that had formed on the outer shell of his armour, the rimes of frost tinkling as his gauntlet brushed them away. The twin beats of the Blood Angel's dual hearts were loud in his ears as the organs worked to supply additional oxygen to his bloodstream, counteracting the lingering side-effects of the trip through hard vacuum. Rafen's armour had protected him well, but still the incredible cold of space had leached the heat from him, and the Marine's muscles were tense. Typically, a Space Marine would have luxury of a chemical sacrament before venturing into the void. The philtre granted by the Chapter priests stimulated the Astartes mucranoid gland, turning their sweat into a complex compound to protect the skin against such punishing extremes of temperature. Rafen had no such defence, however, and the kiss of the airless dark had touched him with its full force.

The machines and men in the landing bay moved in synchrony as each new transport arrived. The shuttles paused just long enough to disgorge their loads of helot troopers before overhead gantries lifted the ships into refuelling sockets or directed them back out to be launched on a return course to Shenlong. Each new group of Arkio's zealots was herded away toward the bilge decks by a clattering servitor or a Chapter serf. The serfs held shock-staves to keep the more curious members of the Warriors of the Reborn in check. Rafen used the magnification functions of his helmet optics to watch the motion of the bondsmen; now and then a battle-brother would intervene, overseeing the activity.

Inwardly, Rafen felt uncomfortable and conflicted. He was in every sense past the point of no return. It felt wrong, *alien*, to be in the midst of his brethren yet also in the thick of his adversaries. Every fibre of his being rebelled against the unwelcome, gut-sick sensation. Like all his kind, Rafen had come to know the camaraderie of his fellow Blood Angels as an extended family, a brotherhood in all senses of the world. By rights, *Bellus* was supposed to be a sanctuary, a place where he should have felt safe and content – instead, it was a danger zone as lethal as any field of melta mines or bio-web. As long as Sachiel thought him dead, then surprise was on his side, but he had to be careful not to squander his only advantage. Too many men aboard this ship knew his face, so to go unhooded would be an instant death sentence. Even with his armour sealed, if he freely moved among the other Astartes it would only be a matter of time before someone questioned him. Rafen needed to find somewhere that his presence would not be challenged.

He shook off the chill as another cargo lighter rumbled past him, the bullet-shaped vessel settling into a landing cradle with a heavy bump and a shower of orange sparks. The brass and cast-iron rig folded up around the transport like a gripping hand and turned the vessel to present it to a debarkation ramp. Rafen moved out of his cover and balanced on the balls of his feet. As with many starships in the service of the Empire, the *Bellus*'s tech-priests encouraged the battle barge's machine-spirit to lower the gravity in the docking bays so that cargo could be manipulated more easily. Rafen felt light here, and he prepared himself for the necessary change in his gait. A cloud of white vapour belched from the lighter's dorsal vents, momentarily occluding the ramp and the cradle. Rafen sprang out of his hiding place, using the mist to cover him. In the long, loping steps that he had been taught, the Marine crossed beneath the slow-moving ship and emerged at the foot of the ramp, as if he had been meant to be there all along. The cargo transporter touched the ramp edge with a hollow thud, and all across its hull gull-wing hatches opened.

Men boiled out of the ship in a ragged wave, all of them shivering and trembling, some from the cold and others from awe. Rafen saw a couple of them drop to their knees. At first he thought they might have been injured, but then he realised that they were kissing the deck, genuflecting in honour of the ship they saw as Arkio's sacred vessel. All of the conscripts had weapons, after a fashion. Some had guns, others swords, spears and other bladed things that had a makeshift look to them. Many of them wore armour fashioned from metal junk, although a few sported dark ballistic mesh tunics. Planetary Defence Force hardware, Rafen noted; the wearers were either former members of Shenlong's PDF that had survived the Word Bearers invasion, or else they were opportunists who had looted the bodies of the dead. The Space Marine's expression soured. Either way, they were not worthy to set foot on a fighting ship like *Bellus* – even the lowliest of the Chapter serfs were nobler than this rabble.

The warriors came to a stumbling halt as they saw the Blood Angel standing there before them, cowed by his presence as much as by the incredible sight of the cavernous starship interior. Rafen would warrant that hardly any of these men had ever left their birthworld before today. He scanned their faces and found some with the vacant, transported look of a true fanatic, while others were brutal and crude, the most vicious of Shenlong's dregs. Why Sachiel had selected these men was beyond Rafen's understanding; none of them would ever measure up to the standards of the Chapter. All they were good for would be to die on the point of an enemy's weapon and clog the muzzles of guns with their corpses. He suppressed the urge to sneer. Such tactics were base and ignoble, better suited to the traitor-kin of Chaos than to the Sons of Sanguinius.

'Lord?' A serf approached him with a questioning look on his face. 'How may I assist you?'

Rafen glanced at the bondsman. 'You are to escort these men below, correct?'

'Yes, lord. Is there some problem?'

He shook his head. 'No. The priest Sachiel has ordered that I accompany this party... He wishes me to oversee the transfer.'

The serf nodded. 'As you command, lord.' With a wave of his shock-stave, the servant directed the soldiers from the ramp.

The shabby figures filed past him, some of them averting their eyes, others studying him with a bald mix of hate and fear. Among the men, a single face suddenly leapt out at Rafen – a sallow, drawn complexion atop the remains of a PDF officer's uniform. The man bowed his head as he passed and Rafen watched him go. He had last seen the soldier inside the Ikari fortress, after Sachiel's honour guards had gunned down a group of innocents as repudiation. The man had actually thanked him for the 'murdergift' given to his sister who died in the crossfire, as if it were some great blessing. He seemed drained of all spirit now, a hollow shell stained with blood and driven only by belief in Arkio's divinity.

Rafen followed the group along the echoing corridors of the ship and into the open caverns of the dark lower levels. To call them 'decks' would have been a misnomer: the hull spaces resembled a stygian canyon with plates of fungal growth extending from the steep walls. Sections of decking jutted out here and there, never broad enough to meet the vast skeletal ribs of the ship's inner hull. Webs of cable, nets and rope-bridges looped them together. The warriors made themselves places to live and sleep from jury-rigged hammocks and discarded cargo pods. It was like a series of broken bridges arching over a valley so far below that the floor was lost in utter blackness.

The new arrivals were greeted with a welcome of cold-eyed glares and veiled threats. He lost sight of the PDF officer as the men wandered into the junkyard community, the law of the wild taking precedence as figures among the groups tussled for places to bed down. Rafen left the Chapter serf behind and walked through the encampment, picking his way along creaking gangplanks and between sagging trestles cut from salvage. There were loudhailers dotted about the place, each connected to the ship's primary vox network with knots of wires, the hasty work of servitors under the direction of Inquisitor Stele. Spitting with reverb and interference, data-slate recordings of Sachiel's speeches from the victory on Shenlong were playing, interspersed with snatches of Imperial hymnals. Conscripts clustered around some of the speaker rigs, joining in with the broadcasts. Everywhere the symbol of the Reborn Angel was daubed. Rafen paused at one such display and ran a finger over the still-wet marking. He raised his glove to his breather grille and sniffed: it was human blood.

The Marine peered over the edge of the gantry he stood on, wondering how many of Arkio's chosen had already met their end in the darkness below. For all Sachiel's high words and oratory, the thousand-strong army seemed to be filled only by the most heartless or the most fervid of Shenlong's populace. To cast them as men in service to the glory of Sanguinius was an insult to the Great Angel.

Rafen moved deeper into the decks, losing himself in the dimly lit spaces. Down here, there would be no man that knew his face and no one to call attention to him. He would hide in plain sight and prepare; when the Warriors of the Reborn were called to arms, he would be there to stop his brother – or to die in the attempt.

'THE LAST GROUP of lighters is docking now,' Solus announced in his sombre, level voice. 'Engineseers report power to drives is optimal. All rites of passage are complete and *Bellus* is free to make sail.'

'Proceed.' The static-choked order issued out of the vocoder implant in Brother-Captain Ideon's neck, his face immobile. 'Make preparation for warp transit the moment we reach the translation point co-ordinates.'

Solus hesitated; another man might not have noticed it, but Ideon had served with the Blood Angel as his aide-de-camp for decades and the man's moods were as clear to the starship captain as the temperaments of his vessel's machine-spirit. 'Was there something else?' Ideon prompted.

As *Bellus* moved away from Shenlong, the planet slipped from the forward viewport, and with it the wreckage of the *Amareo*, some of it still burning as it tumbled in a higher orbit. Solus glanced at the fragment and then away. 'Lord, I–'

The brass leaves of the bridge iris retracted into the walls with a well oiled hiss of hydraulics, and Sachiel entered, his ubiquitous honour guards two steps behind him. Ideon watched him approach through his own eyes and those of the bridge's sentry servitors, the data flowing into his brain through the complex forest of mechadendrites connecting him to his command throne. Solus fell silent, his words swallowed.

The Sanguinary High Priest seemed fatigued, there were dark circles beneath his eyes and his face was paler than usual. Through the infrared monitors Ideon registered a slightly higher skin temperature for Sachiel. Still, he seemed no less animated than usual, and the brightness in his eyes was a strong as ever.

The priest threw a nod to the captain. 'Brother Ideon, what is the disposition of the Blessed's battle barge?'

'Fully prepared, Sachiel,' he replied. 'The navigator assures me that the prayer-computations for the course to Sabien have been completed. *Bellus* will enter the empyrean as scheduled.'

'Excellent. Great Arkio demands nothing less than total efficiency.' Sachiel's voice rose at the end of the sentence and he blinked, as if the effort of the words were difficult for him. His eyes ranged around the bridge, over the hunched chorus of servitors ministering to cogitator consoles, until he found Solus at the wide oval observation window. He homed in on the Blood Angel. 'Brother?' Sachiel began innocently. 'You seem distracted. What can it be that vexes you?'

Solus looked up, not at Sachiel, but to Ideon. The captain remained – as ever – an unmoving statue on the raised command dais. Solus turned to the priest after a long moment. 'Sachiel, I would have you answer a question for me.'

'Name it,' the priest snapped back, a little too quickly.

'What enemy do we go to face, brother?'

Sachiel nodded again. 'Ah, I see. The matter of the *Amareo*'s destruction, yes? It troubled you to give the firing command on a Chapter vessel, did it not?' When Solus did not answer, he pressed on. 'Brother, listen to me. The men aboard that ship were assassins, sent to murder the Reborn Angel and purge anyone who gave fealty to him. That truth is self-evident.' He came closer and touched Solus's arm. 'You did the only thing you could – you helped save the Blessed's life.'

Solus would not meet his gaze. 'I… I have taken the oath for Arkio and the Holy Lance, Sachiel, and I would not flinch against its demands but this…' He glanced out the window at the stars. 'Those men were our battle-brothers, we fought alongside some of them. That we were forced to exterminate them like some common heretics turns my gut.'

The priest's voice was low, but it carried across the room. 'Solus, friend Solus. I understand your feelings. At prayer, I too confessed my mis...' He halted, his face colouring. Sachiel ran a finger over his twitching eye, as if he were banishing some inner pain. After a moment he continued as if nothing had happened. 'Misgivings, yes. To Lord... Lord Stele.' He smiled. 'But I realised, those men had ignored the path of the primarch. That they came here with murder in their hearts made them our enemies.'

'We could have talked to them,' Solus blurted out, 'reasoned with them. Perhaps they would have thought differently if they had understood Arkio's great miracle–'

'No, Solus, no.' Sachiel's expression became one of deep sadness. 'They were lost to us before they even reached Shenlong. Like those who fell from the Emperor's grace in the dark years, those men had chosen a path that pitted them against us. It was their choice, brother, not yours. You and I, all of us remain true to the Pure One.' He nodded at the distant wreckage of the strike cruiser. 'They forced our hand. Those deaths are on their own heads.'

'Yes,' Solus said finally. 'Forgive me my outburst, priest. These past days have tested my faith.'

'As they should,' Ideon's voice buzzed and rumbled from his vox-implant. 'Arkio brings us a new lease of life, and *Bellus* will be the chariot that carries it to the ends of the galaxy.'

Sachiel's head bobbed. 'So shall it be.'

BY THE POWER of forces that dwarfed human understanding, the fabric of space began to writhe and shift around the prow of the *Bellus*. From the places where thought and energy became a unified melange, the raw mind-stuff of the warp spilled into the reality of matter, slicing open a raw, bleeding gate in the void. It was a violent miniature supernova in the blackness, a whirlpool into which the battle barge threw itself. Time, elastic and flowing like molten wax, enveloped the ship and projected it across vast distances. *Bellus* vanished from the realm of men and was gone, cast to the wild currents and energy storms of the immaterium.

In another place and time, the same unthinkable inversion of natural laws was occurring. A leviathan ship emerged from the phantasm of the warp in a violent burst of exotic radiation, coruscating colours and sickly hues of lightning trembling across the vast iron hull. Space itself seemed unwilling to let the vessel exist within its body, as if the vast craft were some metallic cancer growing and polluting the void with its presence. Shedding energy in sheaves of arcane power, the battleship fell from the empyrean realm and reverted to steady, obdurate reality. Engine maws, their exhaust bells as big as volcanoes, took on bloody glows as thrust spewed forth from ancient fusion drives, and with deadly purpose the warship *Misericorde* made speed toward its destination.

She was a horrific sight, an engine of torture almost a mile in length, and on *Misericorde*'s guns many mewling human worlds had been broken just as men had been broken on the racks of her dungeon decks. In aspect, the battleship was a broad dagger, a serrated arrowhead forming her prow, a haft of razors growing backwards to present the dorsal castle of her bridge, and below the plunging knives of skeletal stabiliser vanes. Guns protruded from every shadowed corner of the craft, punching through the red skin of the hull like broken ribs. The ship was adorned with skulls by the thousand. The largest were made from bones, ravaged from the bodies of dead enemies and fused into shape as badges of victory. At the very bow of the vessel, a design had been shaped out of broken pieces of hull metal and ceramite; centred on an eight-pointed star was the screaming face of a toothed, horned daemon, shouting defiance and black hate at all of *Misericorde*'s foes. Like the skulls, the sigil was constructed from war salvage, but instead of bone, the monstrous face was cut from the ships and armour of Adeptus Astartes unlucky enough to fall before the vessel.

In the command sanctum atop the bridge citadel, figures moved in a precise, careful ballet around the presence of the Warmaster Garand. The flayed shapes of servitors passed to and fro, clawed metal feet scratching across the decks as they went about their business. There was no speech except for the low, bubbling bursts of machine code between the slaves. The sound reminded Garand of the chattering predator insects on his Chapter's blighted forge-world, Ghalmek.

Before him, he could see the *Misericorde*'s hololithic display presenting their destination – the shrine planet Sabien. It resembled a ball of age-worn iron, like the warshots spat from cannon on primitive pre-nuclear planets, it made Garand think instantly of Fortrea Quintus. Recall of the planet sent the Chaos warlord's mind back through the veil of memory, thousands of years dropping away in an instant.

The Warmaster's thin tongue slipped out of his lips to lick absently at his chin barbs. Yes, the similarity was quite marked, and the connection brought a glow of anticipation of the commander's dark heart. Although ages had passed since the day Garand had set foot on Quintus, his memory of the glorious campaign there was still as vibrant and sensuous as ever.

The scent of spilt blood came to his nostrils and he closed his eyes, allowing himself to wallow in the luxury of it for a moment. Garand had been the second-in-command to Brother-Captain Jarulck in those days, when outwardly the Word Bearers still paid lip service to the corpse-god of men. He smiled. Even then, the Chapter had already embraced the perfection of the eightfold path, and the blind fools of the other Legion Astartes had been too pathetic to see the touch of Chaos in their midst. Great Lorgar, primarch of the Word Bearers, had personally charged two thousand men to the subjugation of the planet, and they had taken to it with battle-lust in their eyes. Garand recalled Jarulck's fiery oratory to the Quintian natives, the words of power that had drawn the commoners to their banner in their droves. When they marched on their enemy's stronghold in the last days of the conflict, their hordes of followers had perished in the thousands while the Word Bearers lost little of their original number, the bodies of the zealots forming the ramps that Garand's troops used to ford the battlements. Fortrea Quintus fell, but not for the Emperor. With Jarulck's blessing, Garand had been charged with the indoctrination of the locals. He ensured that although the world outwardly paid fealty to Terra, its secret face would forever be turned toward Chaos.

When Horus rose on his great jihad against the weak men-filth, Garand had swelled with pride to learn that the Quintians slaughtered every Emperor-fearing lackey on their homeworld within hours. For his part, Garand cemented his place on the path to high command of a Word Bearers Legion with the blessing of Great Lorgar, but Fortrea Quintus had always remained close to his black heart as the site of his first great victory. Now the smile on Garand's horned and twisted face fell away, his aspect becoming crooked with ill temper.

The Quintus Conversion was at once the source of the Warmaster's pride and his enmity – for it had not been soon after the death of Horus, when the Legions of Chaos were in disarray and scattered, that his prized victory was rendered into ashes by the supercilious Blood Angels. Garand and his hosts had been distant, fighting running battles toward their nest-worlds in the Maelstrom. The Word Bearers had been cut off from the planets they had turned; they had not been there to resist the so-called 'cleansing' by the corpse-god's legions.

Garand listened in impotent anger to the screamed transmissions of astropaths as the Blood Angels swept across Fortrea Quintus and left nothing alive in their path. The prized achievement of his youth was burnt to ashes, kindling within him a dense, diamond-hard hate for the Sons of Sanguinius. Centuries had come and gone since then, but the rancour had never dulled. In a world of warriors who nurtured their hate like keen knives, Garand honed his loathing of the Blood Angels into something utterly murderous and unyielding in its purity.

Sabien filled the shimmering holoscreen and beyond it, the real planet was visible as an occluded disc eclipsed by a swollen, red-orange sun. The Warmaster was almost salivating in anticipation of the battle to come. He loved the impotent screams of idiot piety his enemies released whenever a Word Bearers host made planetfall on one of their pathetic 'holy worlds', how they wailed and wept to learn that the legions of Chaos had sullied their ridiculous worship of that dead freak they so revered. As the *Book of Lorgar* commanded, the Word Bearers were unique among the apostate Legions of the Chaos Marines. They alone retained the priests and dogma that their Chapters had kept during their fealty to Earth, but once they had bent their knee to the Ruinous Powers, their soothsayers and psykers embraced the mark of Chaos Undivided, the Blasphemous Hex. Now, when worlds fell beneath their might, the Word Bearers would erect massive monuments to the dark gods of the Maelstrom, they would profane the human churches and ritually deconsecrate anything that purported to glory the name of the Imperium. This and much more was precisely what Garand intended for Sabien.

The planet was a shrine world for the Blood Angels; the Warmaster knew little of the reasons that the Astartes whelps had named it thus, and he cared even less. It had been the site of some great conflict and in their asinine, maudlin way, the Blood Angels had isolated the planet and made it a place of pilgrimage. Sabien had absolutely no tactical value. It had no bases, no minerals waiting to be exploited, not even a population to be tormented and killed – but for the Word Bearers to set foot here would be as much a blow to the Astartes Legion's honour as a spit in the eye of their precious Sanguinius.

'Great Witch Prince,' a servitor addressed him from the control pit at his feet. 'We will achieve orbit momentarily. The assault force awaits your blessing for deployment.'

Garand did not grace the slave with eye contact. 'Send them. Have my personal shuttle prepared. I will attend once the troops have begun their concealment.'

As much as he detested the turncoat Stele, he was forced to admit that the human had provided exactly what was needed. With the galactic co-ordinates of Sabien – a world whose location was hidden from all but the most secret Blood Angels star charts – it had been easy for the swift *Misericorde* to reach the planet before the other players in Stele's little drama arrived. He found the inquisitor an unctuous, arrogant sort, far too enamoured with his own intellect. Had circumstances been altered, Garand would have been only too pleased to have torn the psyker's throat from his neck – *and perhaps I may still have that opportunity*, he told himself – but it was the High Beast Malfallax's wish that Stele be the tool they would use against the enemy.

He frowned; the eye of the mighty Abaddon was upon their endeavour here, and it would not go well if it came to nothing. Garand had given much of his Legion to the scheme, allowing that fool Iskavan to be sacrificed for the sake of Stele's complex gambits, but he could not have anything but cold dislike for the inquisitor. After all, a traitor to his own species was still a traitor, and who could know if he would not turncoat again? Of course, there were those in the Imperium that called Garand and his kinsmen traitor too, but like most of the Emperor's sheep, they did not understand. No Chaos Marine was a traitor. If anything, they were the most loyal of them all, casting aside everything that made them weak to give fealty to the most ruthless forces in all creation.

Garand's reverie fell away as he studied the thick ring of asteroids girdling Sabien in a wide elliptical belt. He imagined they were all that remained of some moon, no doubt obliterated in the conflict that made Sabien the blighted sphere it was today. Repeaters from the battleship's machine-spirit confirmed that the shaggy cloud of stones was rich in dense, sensor-opaque ores that would adequately mask the *Misericorde*'s presence. He glanced up, and saw the twinkle of lights swarming away from the vessel's hull. The Warmaster's clawed hand tightened around the blackened iron railing before him in rapt expectancy. The grand plan of his daemon lord Malfallax had moved one step closer to its deadly conclusion. This day would end with the Blood Angels throwing off their allegiance to the Emperor and embracing Chaos, or it would end with their bones joining those of their brethren already perished in Sabien's crypt-yards.

THE DREAM.

At first it had been a minor irritation, some piece of his past life impinging on the changes that fate had wrought upon him. It came in those moments when he was at rest, the brief periods of repose now less and less necessary as the wonders of his new body revealed themselves to him. In the beginning, it was only when Arkio slept that the dream came to him – but now, as the Blood Crusade took its first steps, the apparition had begun to infiltrate his waking moments. Whenever his mind began to drift from the matters at hand, it was there.

Arkio knelt before the vast frieze of Sanguinius in the grand chamber, the majestic face looking down upon him, mirroring his own in its lines of jaw and chin, in the nobility of mouth and eye. His silver-white wings moved of their own accord, gently unfolding in a whisper of sound, the tips of them drooping to pool around the golden shoulders of his artificer armour like a cloak of snow. At rest there on the altar of red Baalite sandstone was the sanctified metal cylinder that held the Holy Lance. Arkio opened the case so the honey-coloured light from the ancient weapon could be free to illuminate him. As he laid eyes on the Spear of Telesto, so once again Arkio felt the hum of unchained power in his veins. The preternatural potency of the Blood Angel bloodline ran strong in him.

Arkio bowed his head; none of the Chaplains in their black armour and skull-mask helmets had dared to approach him when he entered, and without any spoken orders from him, they had sealed the chamber closed. He could not see them, but he knew they had gathered at the far end of the cathedral's aisle, watching him in awe-struck silence. Arkio made the sign of the aquila, the reflexive gesture soothing him.

'Pure One, hear me. Grant me guidance. I am your vessel and your messenger. I will know the way of Sanguinius so I will make it my own. Grant me understanding of this vision that haunts me…'

Arkio closed his eyes and let the dream unfold in his mind. For days now as the *Bellus* raced through the warp, he had been holding it back, resisting the pull of it. The touch of the empyrean seemed to nurture it and strengthen its influence.

It begins on Baal, as it ever does. At the head of a throng of men and Space Marines a million souls strong, Arkio marches towards the gates of the fortress-monastery. At his shoulders are Astartes in armour all shades of crimson – not just Blood Angels, but warriors from the Flesh Tearers Chapter, the Blood Drinkers, the Angels Vermilion and more. There are men in the black of the Death Company, their greaves crossed with the red saltires that mark them as fallen to the rage, but they walk with him as tranquil as their battle-brothers at rest. His presence alone is enough to calm them.

The wind-scoured gates open before Arkio and the monastery presents itself to him and his crusaders. Every figure within, Marine and Apothecary, tech-priest and Chapter serf alike, all of them drop to one knee and bow their heads as they pass. There is none of the rough clamour and bellowed shouts that the people of Shenlong poured forth for him – here on Baal, only the wind is heard, and the silence of these faithful marks their devotion to him. None shall chance to speak in the presence of the Reborn Angel, such is their reverence.

Through the silent cloister and into the grand hall. He sees the faces of the greatest Blood Angels as they salute him, fist to chest as he strides past. Argastes. Corbulo. Lemartes. Moriar. Vermento. Even the honoured dead are here to greet him, Tycho standing shoulder to shoulder with Lestrallio, and for a moment, he spies Koris among them, his aspect a flicker, then shadows.

At the altar beneath the towering statues of Sanguinius and the Emperor stand Dante and Mephiston. There is a moment when both men meet his gaze and Arkio fears that he will be forced to draw the Spear upon them; but then both the high commander and the Lord of Death bow to him. Then, and only then, are the voices of his warriors raised, and they shake the pillars of heaven as they call his name.

But from the shadowed corners, something dark and foetid approaches.

'LORD INQUISITOR, WHAT are we to make of this?' said Delos, his voice barely concealing an edge of fearful concern. 'See, the light that falls from the Blessed.'

Stele's face soured as he watched the play of yellow-white colours over Arkio's golden form at the other end of the grand chamber. The hot glow of the Spear of Telesto crackled around him like summer lighting. 'Yes, Chaplain, you were correct to summon me. This… This is a manifestation of the Reborn Angel's will. He prays for guidance in our coming battles…' The lie tripped easily off his tongue.

Delos exchanged glances with his fellow priests. 'But his face… It shifts and moves, Lord Stele. I have not seen the like before… And his cries. I would swear that Arkio is in pain–'

'No!' Stele snapped, 'You cannot fathom the ways of the Holy Lance, priest. Arkio communes with the blood within him, no more. He must… He must be given solace to do this alone.'

'But we cannot–'

'You must leave,' the inquisitor thundered. 'I will stand sentinel for the Blessed.' When Delos hesitated, he stabbed a finger at the chapel doors. 'Out!' Stele's voice became a roar. 'By Sanguinius's name, I command it.'

The moment the wooden doors rumbled shut, Stele broke into a run toward the altar. There was a stench in the air, and it was as familiar to the inquisitor as the sound of his own breathing; dead flesh, hot blood, cold iron.

Chaos.

CHAPTER NINE

THE DREAM COLOURS and darkens. It becomes a nightmare.

And now all transforms into ashes.

In the moment of his greatest triumph, as every Blood Angel living and dead pays fealty to Arkio's name, the shadows gathering in the corners of his vision flood into sight. A wash of aged blood sweeps over everything, turning the men around him into rotting corpses, their bodies flayed under the tide, ceramite turning to paper, skin curdling over greying bones. The stone walls crack and crumble, ageing aeons in seconds. Baal itself cries out in agony at the pollution spilling across it. The dead are a tide about him, oceans of clawed skeletal fingers scoring into his golden armour. Dante and Mephiston clutch at him, screaming in pain, shrivelling eyes begging him for the reason that he has forsaken them.

Arkio's mouth will not form the words, and he does not have an answer for them. All he knows is that this great decay is his fault.

The wave of ruin reaches his boots and climbs him like fast-growing fungus. The golden armour turns to tarnished brass,

*then dull rust, then crumbling dust. Arkio's voice finds him in
time for a soul-shattering scream.*

THE SOUND THAT left Arkio's lips made Stele pause as he
skidded to a halt at the foot of the altar. The cry hammered
at the walls of the grand chamber, vibrating the stands of
photon candles and the censers that dangled from chains
high above. He threw a nervous glance to the doors – they
remained closed. At least the Chaplain had taken his order
to heart. It would not go well if Delos and his battle-brothers observed what was about to transpire. Stele grimaced as
he stepped into the halo cast by the Spear. The touch of the
weapon churned up complex, heady emotions inside the
inquisitor, and he forced them to the back of his mind. He
would need all his ability to concentrate on the here and
now.

Arkio was trembling, his skin white and wet with perspiration. Shapes seemed to be moving beneath the
surface of his elegant face, thin, worm-like cilia pushing at
the curve of his cheekbones and his jaw. Stele swore a
curse; the young fool had brought this on himself. Unwilling to simply leave the Holy Lance alone, Arkio had spent
too much time in the radiance of the device, and now the
architects of his change were in danger of spoiling. Dark
lesions, hard and black like rare pearls, were appearing
over his neck and forehead. Some of them had opened
like eyes.

'Too soon,' Stele snapped. 'It's too soon. The mutation
was stable, I made sure of it.'

He shrugged off his coat and placed his hands about the
sides of Arkio's head. Biting back a sudden urge to throw
up, the inquisitor marshalled his strength and let his psychic senses extend through the skin contact. Gently, his
fingers began to melt into the matter of Arkio's face.

THE WORST OF *the horrors is left for the last.*

*Everywhere his battle-brothers have fallen, a new and mon-
strous shape takes form, rebuilding itself from the debris of bone*

and armour. Things come. Unhallowed creatures in sick paro-
dies of Blood Angels nobility, their crimson armour stained with
the blood of innocents, the white wings of the Chapter sigil now
bones and blades, the red teardrop wet with gore. Horns and
teeth sprout from them; their abhorrence outpaces even that of
the traitorous Word Bearers. Everywhere, his twisted brethren
paint eightfold crosses, throwing back their heads to call Chaos
to their midst.

Air thickens about Arkio like quicksand. He reaches for the
Holy Lance, the last beacon of purity, even as the skin sloughs
off his bones. His fingers touch the warm, yielding metal...

ARKIO'S ARM JERKED, a marionette pulled by a careless pup-
peteer, and his fingertips brushed the Holy Lance.

Hot air sizzled around the two men and Arkio was
shoved backward.

The murky infections across his skin bubbled and
popped. Out of sight beneath his armoured chest plate,
more cancerous growths erupted across Arkio's flawless
body and spat yellow pus. Bony juts of distorted matter
pressed at the cage of his skin. The flesh of the young
Space Marine, so perfect and magnificent, was rotting
inside.

'No!' snapped Stele. 'Not yet. I will not permit it.' Moving through his flesh, the inquisitor's fingers buried
themselves in Arkio's spine, probing and feeling for the
ebony egg of corruption that had been planted there so
many months earlier.

...AND THE SPEAR of Telesto rejects him.

Pain, great stabbing swords of agony more powerful than
mortals could comprehend surge into Arkio. He recoils and his
body shifts; the flash-burned hand knots and writhes. It
become a nest of tentacles and claws. He touches his face and
finds an orchard of spines and barbs there, black flapping
tongues and runny flesh. The black tide is in him now, rewrit-
ing his soul. He sees it there, cutting the mark of Chaos
Undivided into him.

And there is a roaring beast within him, the hateful heart of the red thirst, that welcomes it. Arkio teeters and falls.

He has become the Unblessed.

THERE. THERE IT was, clasping the bones of Arkio's spinal column like a nesting spider. Thin lines of liquid darkness issued out of the egg-form, thousands of feelers infiltrating every organ and element of the Blood Angel's body. So delicate, so subtle were they that only by flaying him open or ripping up his mind on a psyker-rack would anyone discover the lurking poison inside Arkio. It was a black heart of raw, undistilled Chaos. The object was glassy and hard, a piece of some decayed thought-form created by the Malfallax. The Monarch of Spite had made it from himself, granting the seed to Stele on the day that this intricate plan had become a reality. There was not a part of Arkio that was not touched by the mutations the egg created. Its cilia had infiltrated all of him, warping the youth's flesh; it had been this that granted him the gift of his wings, his change, his Emergence.

Stele cooed to the egg, stroked it and calmed the malignant parasite. He had to be careful now, while the mutation progressed slowly and subtly, the taint in Arkio's body would lay undetected – but the foolish whelp's obsession with the Spear of Telesto had aroused the seed. Unless he could quiet it, all these carefully laid plans would unravel.

BEFORE, HERE WAS *where the vision ended, but now it went on.*

Something comes. A man in crimson ceramite, untouched by the mutation and corruption about him. The tides of foulness retreat about his footfalls. Arkio's traitor-self spits and loathes.

There is a blink of yellow light; suddenly the Holy Lance crosses the room and settles into the hands of the new arrival. Arkio, lisping through manifold mouths crowded with the buds of crooked new fangs, speaks his name.

'Raaaaaafffffffffennnn.'

His brother does not know him. Rafen turns the Spear of Telesto on Arkio and plunges it into his heart.

Betrayed, mutated, changed and discarded, Arkio dies screaming.

ARKIO SAGGED AND dropped to the stone floor of the grand chamber, his breath coming in ragged gasps. Deftly, Stele withdrew himself from the flesh of the Marine's neck, the skin sealing over like the surface of a pond. A few small rivulets of blood clung to the inquisitor's fingers and he wiped them away with a silk kerchief.

The figure in gold moaned. 'Rafen… No…'

Stele grimaced at the mention of Arkio's brother, watching the lesions on the Blessed's face shrink back to nothing, the raw mouths of weeping sores retreating into the folds of his skin. Once again, Arkio was perfect, an alabaster ideal of the Pure One. His eyes fluttered open.

'Stele?' he asked. 'My friend? What happened to me?'

The inquisitor displayed a mask of concern that hid his genuine annoyance. 'Blessed, praise Sanguinius that you are well. I feared the worst…'

Arkio got to his feet, his wings furling behind him. 'I saw… a terrible vision, inquisitor. A victory snatched away by the tide of Chaos.'

Stele's face remained utterly impassive. 'You must be mistaken, Blessed.'

He looked down at his hands, then to the humming form of the Spear. 'The lance…' Arkio began, his voice catching, 'it turned against me.'

'Impossible,' said Stele, his tone soothing. 'Such a thing could never happen.' He approached the Spear on the altar. 'Look here, Great One. The Holy Lance is yours alone. Touch it.'

Hesitantly, Arkio extended a hand to the weapon, fingers tracing the shape of a hooded figure on the haft of the lance. The Spear of Telesto glowed beneath his caress. Relief crossed the Marine's face.

'You see?' Stele smiled. 'It was no vision, Arkio. Just the weight of days preying upon you. The Holy Lance is yours,' he repeated. Inwardly, the inquisitor was relieved. His ministrations had been enough, and the mutations had been suppressed so that the Telesto weapon would not react to them – for the moment.

'It was so real,' Arkio was saying. 'I could feel the hand of the warp inside me…'

'Your mind changes as does your body and spirit, Blessed,' said Stele. 'Only you can know what purpose Sanguinius holds for you. Perhaps this… vision was something of a warning…'

'Explain yourself,' Arkio demanded, his hesitance falling away as his lordly manner returned.

'Perhaps… perhaps the Great Angel is showing you what will transpire if we fail him…'

'Yes…' Arkio turned away. 'That shall never happen, Stele. With your counsel, the Blood Crusade will ignite the stars with its righteous fire.'

The inquisitor gave himself a nod of self-approval. The crisis was passed. 'Indeed it will, Blessed. And we will begin with planet Sabien.'

Arkio nodded and walked on into the transept alone. Stele watched the feathers on his wings flicker as he moved. It would only be a matter of time before the taint of mutation made itself visible again – but if all went to plan, by the time that happened Arkio and his Blood Angels would be glorying in the name of Chaos, and they would welcome it like the gift that it was.

JETS OF SPENT thruster discharge vented from the underside of the Thunderhawk as it settled under the gravity of Sabien. From the deployment ramp at the ship's prow there was a scramble of quick, controlled movement. Four Blood Angels, each grasping a bolter in battle-ready postures, fanned out and stepped into a wedge formation. Their eyes and their guns never stopped scanning the landscape for any sign of movement.

Behind them came a figure towering like a dreadnought, striding with cool purpose across the deck. Two more Marines, one a grizzled veteran, the other a tech-priest, followed at his heels. 'Deploy scouts,' he said, his voice carrying over the rumble of engines as a second and third Thunderhawk landed nearby. 'I want a secure perimeter established, brother-sergeant. We may appear to be the first arrivals, but appearances can be deceptive.'

'By your command, lord.' The veteran saluted and broke into a run, growling out commands to a cadre of lightly armoured Space Marine outriders.

The other warrior paused, listening to a voice in his vox. 'Message from the *Europae*, lord. The ship has attained a geostationary orbit above this location. Awaiting your orders.'

Mephiston stepped on to the surface of Sabien and took a lungful of air. Hundreds of scents assailed his heightened sense receptors, his brain quickly processing the smells into familiar categories. *Death. This planet smells of death.*

'Lord Mephiston?' asked the Techmarine, hesitant around the Chief Librarian. Even among the members of his own Chapter, the supreme psyker of the Blood Angels was feared as much as he was respected.

'The *Europae* is to remain at maximum battle readiness,' replied Mephiston, studying the landing zone. 'What of the sporadic sensor contact in the debris belt?' He glanced up. Above, a ghostly white shimmer could be seen bisecting the blue-orange sky – the thick band of rocks and captured asteroids ringing Sabien, the remnants of the planet's largest moon.

'No further detections,' replied the Marine. 'Cogitator reports conclude the contact may have been solar refraction from ice crystals or possible thermal outgassing.'

Mephiston curled his lip at that assessment. 'We shall see.' He left the tech-priest behind and walked out, the squad of tactical warriors moving with him. He eschewed the use of the more typical honour guard Marines on planetside missions; he preferred the company of line trooper Blood Angels, better to see first hand the disposition of the men that Lord Dante commanded, better to watch for signs of dissent or corruption.

This was not the first time Mephiston had set foot on Sabien. Once before, several lifetimes ago, he had stood in the same place, breathed the same air. He had been a different man then: Brother Calistarius, a mere codicer centuries away from the events at Hades Hive that would remake him as Mephiston, Lord of Death. Yet, as much as he had changed in the intervening years, Sabien had not altered at all. The shrine world remained as it was, as it had been for hundreds of years after the smoke and ashes of the brutal Phaedra Campaign had cleared. At that time, Sabien had seen the largest loss of life to the Blood Angels Chapter since the battles of the Horus Heresy, and when the world had finally been pacified at the cost of untold expended lives, the Imperial Church had awarded custody of the planet to the Sons of Sanguinius. The site of their desperate last stand against the enemies of mankind became a place of pilgrimage, and it had been on such a journey that the psyker had first come to Sabien.

Mephiston's piercing gaze crossed the broken ridges of the skyline. The Thunderhawks had landed in the city square, in the place where the last great engagement of the campaign had taken place. The open space was littered with fallen masonry as far as the eye could see, shattered spars of rusted iron laid down upon the crumbling remains of columns. The remnants of architecture created in the ancient styles of Old Terra were everywhere. Long halls and cloisters mingled with cathedral towers that once had cut the sky with their magnificence. Now, Sabien's streets were filled with drifts of fallen stone and the towers were humbled. Only a single construction still remained in the middle of the echoing square. Canted at an angle by eruptions of some long-silenced shell fire, a statue on a stone plinth kept watch on the dead city. Somehow, the figure of an angel had never once been struck in all the madness of the fight for Sabien. It remained here now, its features worn to vague shapes, as a symbol of human will.

The Librarian rested one hand on the hilt of his sheathed force sword and closed his eyes. Gently, he summoned the energy of the Quickening that coiled inside his mind, moulding it and absorbing it into his senses. The exhilarating rush of potency ran through him in a shiver, and Mephiston allowed his mind to slip free of its sheath of meat and bone. Gentle blue glows hovered around the horned skulls that decorated his psychic hood and the Lord of Death reached out, searching for life. The ghost of his psy-self slipped through the ravaged streets, a breath of mental power shifting and flowing in a gust of wind.

The dead had left their mark on the psychic landscape of Sabien. In the ruined city there was no place where the scars of violent death could not be found. Anguish and raw pain were burnt into the stonework, as clear to Mephiston's senses as the scorched shadows of human figures left by a nuclear flare. The faded screams of Blood Angels hung about the edges of his esper perceptions, the phantoms crowding him. A nerve twitched in the Lord of Death's jaw. Even for a Librarian of his awesome discipline, it was difficult to sift through the white noise of the haunted city and search beyond. He frowned. There seemed to be something out there at the very edge of his mind-sight, but it was ephemeral, hidden in the clutter of the war dead. Perhaps...

Mephiston's head jerked around in a swift motion, and the Techmarine froze, startled by the action. The Blood Angels psyker looked up into the sky. Evening stars were slowly emerging from the darkening blue, and one steady dot of brightness showed the position of the *Europae*. 'They're coming,' he whispered to himself, his voice too low for anyone else to hear. Like a new constellation flaring into life, Mephiston's inner sight could see the cluster of glowing minds approaching the planet at high speed, and among them he could read the strange flickers of a mentality like none he had ever encountered before.

There was a mumbling crackle of communication from the Techmarine's helmet vox, and he glanced up at

Mephiston. 'My lord, word from the *Europae*. The battle barge *Bellus* has arrived.'

He nodded. 'I know. I can taste him.'

BELLUS PRESENTED HER hammerhead bow to her sister ship as she slowed. The vessels were almost mirror images of one another, the huge slab-like hulls beweaponed with cannons and missile tubes. Each displayed a huge disk with the Chapter sigil beneath a golden crest of the Imperial aquila, but the similarities ended at the surface. Across the gulf of Sabien's orbit, the crews of both ships eyed one another with suspicion and doubt. It was a rare sight to see two ships of this class in the same place. Such deployments were usually the prelude to war on a huge scale, and there were many Blood Angels aboard *Bellus* and *Europae* that wondered if war was what would soon follow.

On the command deck, Captain Ideon scrutinised the other vessel with all the tactical acumen he would have given an enemy warship. 'Solus,' he crackled. 'Detector pallets on the port forward quarter read what looks like a fluctuation in her drive coils.'

Ideon's aide nodded from his post at the primary cogitator. 'Agreed, captain.'

'Log that information with the gunnery servitors. It may prove useful if we are required to engage.'

At the observation window, Stele turned away from his conversation with Sachiel to face the captain. 'It saddens me that such precautions must be taken, but after the *Amareo* incident...'

'You may rest assured, the crew of the *Europae* are planning the same for us,' Arkio snapped. He was wound tight with tension, and in long strides he pushed his way past the Sanguinary Priest to face the command dais. 'Ideon. Do you detect any other starships in the area?'

The captain blinked as he addressed the eyes and ears of *Bellus*. 'No, Blessed,' he answered after a moment. 'No contacts at this time.'

'It appears that Dante kept his word,' said Sachiel. The priest seemed muted, his usual bluster quieted. 'Perhaps we may yet see a peaceful path out of this cha–' He stumbled over the word. 'This... This disorder.'

Stele threw him an arch glance. 'Indeed. But I respectfully suggest that our watchword should be vigilance. If Commander Dante decides–'

'Dante is not here,' Arkio broke in, steel in his voice. 'I know it in my bones. He has sent his second, the psyker Mephiston.' The golden-armoured Space Marine looked Stele in the eye. 'Do you not sense him, inquisitor?'

Gingerly, Stele extended the smallest of mental feelers toward Sabien's surface, and just as quickly he jerked it back, like a hand too close to a naked flame. 'The Blessed is correct. The Lord of Death awaits us.' For the briefest of instants, a glimmer of concern crossed the Hereticus agent's face.

Arkio approached Ideon and nodded a command to him. 'Set war conditions throughout the ship, captain. These are my orders – the Warriors of the Reborn will attend me on Sabien. Launch transports and Thunderhawks. I will meet Mephiston at the head of my multitude.'

'I have selected a company of Marines, Blessed,' added Sachiel. 'Your army will truly be a glorious sight.'

Arkio nodded. 'Attend me, priest – and you as well, inquisitor. We go to make history.'

Stele gave a shallow bow and followed the Reborn Angel from the room. Entering the echoing corridors, he hung back a few steps and spoke urgently into a concealed vox in his collar. 'Ulan, listen to me. Come to the landing bay and prepare for planetfall. I will have need of you on the surface.'

'Mephiston?' came the reply.

'With haste,' he retorted, quickening his pace.

ELSEWHERE ABOARD THE *Bellus*, the cargo lighters were accepting their loads, each of the bullet-shaped ships sealing shut with a warshot of armed, zealous men. Ideon's orders crackled through the air on every deck of the ship, calling the vessel to arms and preparing the troops for a landing. In the days that had passed between their departure from Shenlong and the arrival here, the Warriors of the Reborn had grown restless and impatient for release. Each group was wired with anticipation as they filed into the transports, their eagerness to prove their worth to Arkio far outweighing their fears.

Rafen carefully joined the rear of a trailing group of helots, keeping as far as he could from the other Space Marines herding the rag-tag army into their troopships. Hidden in the lower decks, the journey had passed quickly for the Blood Angel as he dipped in and out of trance-sleep, his brain's catelepsean node keeping one half of his brain awake while the other slumbered. Rafen was thankful for the capability of the implant. He suspected that the dreams true slumber brought would not have pleased him.

The slave-soldiers marched up the boarding ramp in a loose, undisciplined group, the very antithesis of the finely drilled formations of the Adeptus Astartes. As they entered the cargo lighter's interior, a figure pushed through them, giving out terse orders. Another Marine.

Rafen licked dry lips; this would be the moment of truth. If his subterfuge failed now, he would never make it down to the planet alive. He gave the other Blood Angel a cursory nod as if nothing were amiss, and strode past him, up the ramp toward the ship.

'Brother,' said the Marine. 'You are overseeing this group? I thought that I was to accompany...' His voice drifted off, confusion in his tone. Rafen recognised him as he stepped into the light, the biolume glow illuminating his face. *Alactus*.

Rafen kept walking, and made an off-hand grunt that he hoped would be enough.

'Wait,' Alactus continued. 'I know you, do I not?' His brow furrowed. 'What is your name?'

How could he not know me, Rafen asked himself. We have served the Chapter together for decades.

'Brother!' The shout halted Rafen at the top of the ramp and he half-turned to glance over his shoulder. Alactus had his hand at the grip of his bolt pistol. 'I asked you a question.' The Marine stepped closer, suspicion clear on his face. 'Take off your helmet.'

He glanced at the transport; the helots were secure inside now, and none of them could see what was going on outside. Rafen turned to face the wary Alactus. There were no other men around this high on the launch cradles, just the two Blood Angels.

'Take off your helmet,' Alactus repeated, and the bolter was in his hand. 'I will not ask you again.' The warning in his voice was needle-sharp, the Marine would shoot Rafen dead if he did not respond.

Rafen nodded and descended the ramp, unlatching the connector ring on his headgear as he did so. He halted in front of Alactus and turned the helmet off his head. When he met his battle-brother's eyes he saw shock there.

'Rafen!' husked Alactus, 'but you're dead…'

'No,' he replied, and in a single sharp movement, Rafen swung his helmet at the other Space Marine, rushing at him. He smothered the sick feeling in his gut that welled up as he assaulted his former comrade; to do such a thing made Rafen feel soiled, but he knew that there was no choice here. If he did not kill Alactus, then he would perish in his stead.

Alactus was caught by the surprise attack, and the ceramite helmet struck him hard, knocking the pistol from his hands. The gun clattered away as Rafen hit out again, knocking the other Marine to his haunches.

'Traitor!' spat Alactus, whipping his combat blade from its sheath. 'Sachiel told us what you did, what you tried to do. You murdered Lucion.'

'I didn't want to–'

'Liar! You craven wretch, you turned on your own brethren. You tried to destroy the fortress – you would have killed us all, you would have murdered the Reborn Angel.'

Anger boiled up inside Rafen. 'You fool. It is not I who is the turncoat, it is you. You and everyone who follows Arkio's misguided insanity!'

'No.' Alactus shook his head, 'I will not hear your false-hoods! He is the Pure One returned–'

'He is nothing of the kind,' Rafen retorted. 'Open your eyes, man. Open your eyes and see the truth, Arkio is just a pawn. Stele is behind this, that ordos mind-witch is cloud-ing everything for his own ends.'

'Lies!' Alactus dived at him, the blade glinting. Rafen blocked, but the knife bit down and cut into his armour. 'To think I trusted you,' hissed the other Marine. 'To think we fought together in the Emperor's name when all along you were an agent of Chaos.' He forced the blade deeper and Rafen bit off a cry of pain. 'I will kill you as a gift for the Blessed.'

Rafen's hands snapped up and found Alactus's neck. Ceramite-encased fingers bit into his skin and squeezed. 'Forgive me…' he hissed, the two of them locked together in a death-grip. Rafen felt the knife slashing and cutting, but still he would not release. Blood bubbled from his battle-brother's lips and bone in his throat cracked.

'Damn… you…' Alactus choked and died in his arms, his body turning limp.

Rafen dropped him to the deck and tore the knife from his wound, snarling at the pain of it. He stared at his hands; blood coated them with thick, accusing stains. He remembered the Word Bearer he had killed on Cybele in the same manner, his breath catching in his chest. 'San-guinius,' he asked aloud. 'Where will this madness end?'

But no answer came to him. Carefully, Rafen replaced his helmet, pausing to recover the bolt pistol before he marched aboard the transport ship. The hatch slammed shut behind him, leaving his comrade's corpse to vent to the void as the shuttle shot away toward Sabien.

'THE SCOUTS REPORT no contact along the outer perimeter,' said the sergeant, 'the landing zone is devoid of life.'

The hint of a sneer tugged at the corner of Mephiston's thin lips. 'Just because they have not found anything does not mean that it isn't there. Be watchful, sergeant.'

The Blood Angel gave a grave nod and pointed into the sky. 'Look there, lord. Ships.'

A rain of transports and cargo craft descended, touching down on the clearer part of the square in the north-west corner. 'Prepare yourself,' Mephiston told his men. 'Be ready for anything.'

Figures in shabby, makeshift uniforms emerged from the shuttles along with the red dots of Blood Angels. The sergeant frowned, scrutinising the warriors with his long-range optics. 'What's this?' he said in a low voice. 'The pretender has brought an army of commoners with him?'

Through an ornate set of magnoculars the Librarian watched the figures moving into a poor approximation of a parade line. 'Ah,' he said after a moment. 'Their eyes, sergeant. Look at their eyes. Tell me what you see.'

The Blood Angel did as he was told. 'They seem... manic, perhaps.'

'Yes. Those men have the fire of belief kindled in them. And those of their number who do not have ill-temper enough to compensate.' Mephiston's fingers drummed on the grip of his plasma pistol. 'Watch them. Their kind are unpredictable, given the right circumstances.'

The sergeant pointed again. 'There, lord, do you see him? I can't be sure–'

The Lord of Death did not need to be told where to look; floating like a mellifluent seraph among a throng of vagrants, Arkio approached them. His armour caught the red-orange glow of Sabien's setting sun and it glimmered off the gold ceramite like liquid fire. Broad white wings formed arcs above his shoulders.

'Emperor's blood...' breathed the sergeant. 'He could almost be–'

'He is not,' Mephiston grated harshly. 'Allow yourself to believe that and you are useless to me.'

'Forgive me, lord, it's just that… I have never seen the like.'

The Librarian could sense the same thoughts on the surface of the minds of all the Blood Angels in his guard. He set his jaw hard and lightly touched the psychic reservoir of his Quickening. Gently, Mephiston used the power to reinforce the will of his men, erasing any germ of doubt before it could grow larger.

RAFEN USED ROUGH gestures with the bolter to make the slave-soldiers go where he wanted. Hidden in the mass of the procession, he was far enough apart from Arkio's loyalist Marines that he would not be recognised again. He frowned beneath the visor of his helmet. There, a way ahead of him, marched his brother, and at his side the priest Sachiel, Stele and the inquisitor's retinue. He saw the shambling lexmechanic, the floating shapes of Stele's servo-skulls and a hooded female whose features were invisible beneath a voluminous cloak. Rafen elected to bide his time. His plan, such as it was, was taking shape on the fly. Perhaps, if the opportunity presented itself, he could approach Arkio unseen, and then – would he dare to shed the blood of a brother again? And this time, the blood of his own kinsman? He had been unable to do it back on Shenlong, and as he searched his feelings, Rafen could not be sure if he would do it now.

At the foot of a Thunderhawk, Rafen could see another figure, an unmistakeable form that seemed cut from a history book. He recognised Dante's Chief Librarian immediately, the most powerful psyker in the entire Chapter – and some said, the whole of the Legion Astartes – watching the approach. Rafen recalled his stony aspect from a statue in the cloisters of Angel's Fall: Mephiston, the Lord of Death. His name was well-earned, for it had been he alone that had looked into the unknowable void of the Blood Angels gene-curse and survived. Only through an incredible force of will had Mephiston passed through the punishing trials of the maddening red thirst and lived to tell of it. Men said that to look the Lord of Death in the eye was to see a window to the black rage and the dark places that waited beyond the realm of life. Mephiston's burning gaze had been known to stop enemies in their tracks and leave them broken and weeping.

As befitting a man of such stature, the psyker wore a crimson cloak inlaid with a profusion of bone skulls, the death-head symbol large on his shoulder pads. The twin rails of a powerful psychic hood extended above his head, and the armour across his torso resembled skinned flesh, glistening red bunches of muscle crossed with death marks and jewelled blood droplets. He was the darkest end of the spectrum when compared to Arkio's golden, mirror-bright form.

'LORD MEPHISTON,' ARKIO said, inclining his head in greeting, 'you honour me with your presence here. Thank you for coming.'

The psyker studied the youth. The sergeant had been correct, Arkio's resemblance to the Great Angel was uncanny. It was almost as if a statue of Sanguinius had shaken off its coating of stone and stepped down from a chapel plinth. Yet, as much as the image matched the legends that had shaped his devotion for so many years, Mephiston could already sense the taint of something foul and corrupt in the air, lingering like spent tabac smoke. He was very careful not to give even the slightest hint of obeisance to the man in the gold armour. This was the one who had ordered Mephiston's protégé Vode destroyed and Captain Gallio's crew executed in cold blood, something the Librarian would not soon forget.

But still… There was some small voice inside Mephiston's mind, some last fragment of his old self as Brother Calistarius, that was awed by what Arkio had become, this perfect living avatar of great Sanguinius. He silenced the discord within him and drew his psy-essence into a single place.

'You are the one they call the Blessed Arkio.' It was not a question. 'You claim that you are the vessel for the Angelic Sovereign.'

'I claim nothing,' Arkio said. 'I simply *am*.'

For the first time, their eyes met, and from within the dark pits of Mephiston's soul, he turned his transfixing glare upon the youth; the sheer force of the mental charge between them set other men staggering upon their feet.

'We shall see,' intoned the Lord of Death, turning his baleful sight on Arkio's very soul.

CHAPTER TEN

DARKNESS COILED FROM the evening sky and crossed the horizon with deep, inky shadows. Some of the Warriors of the Reborn shifted nervously and muttered, weapons rattling as they gripped them harder, afraid of what was to come next. Rafen moved forward through the ranks of men, better to observe the confrontation between Arkio's and Mephiston's titanic wills. He tasted the thick, greasy texture on the chill air, the same oily aroma that he had encountered before when Stele had brought his psychic powers to bear – but this time the magnitude was a hundred times greater, and the thickness of the atmosphere about him made Rafen feel like he was wading through a marshy bog. He could see the hellfire glow from beneath the Lord of Death's brow, his eyes twin embers of controlled menace like distant beacons.

The stink of mind-magick was all about him, and Rafen felt bile rise in his gorge. To be so near to such a naked show of psyker force made him feel soiled and unclean.

He was closer now; he could see Stele's bald head, the glint of the silver purity stud in his ear. The inquisitor appeared to be in distress, as if the effort of standing in Mephiston's aura was almost too much for him. At his side, Stele's woman trembled beneath her hood. Rafen swore he could see thin wisps of smoke issuing from her nostrils. The Space Marine kneaded the grip of the bolt pistol and forced himself to move nearer still.

The Gaze was a lens that opened up the hidden world to Mephiston's perception. The power burning inside him shone through the gates of his vision like the beam of a devout searchlight, pinning the weak and the unhallowed as it fell upon them. His sight-beyond-sight stripped away the illusions of reality and bared souls so that the Lord of Death could examine their pale, naked truths. He saw Arkio as if he were an anatomical sketch drawn from some textbook of the magus biologis, layers of skin, bone, muscle and nerve visible to him. The boy was glass, and Mephiston's gaze shone into him, illuminating every corner of his spirit as searing sunlight falling through a prism.

There. It was concealed well, buried beneath levels of wards and mind-baffles, the matter of it worked into the bone and meat of the Space Marine's body, but the taint could not hide from the unblinking eye of Mephiston's powers. The black ellipse floated among the perfection of Arkio's Astartes physiology, ruining the sacred organic design of the Blood Angel. The seed of Chaos glittered and pulsed.

In a faint way, he was slightly disappointed. Perhaps there was a part of him, however tiny, that had hoped Arkio's story might be true; but instead Mephiston found himself confronted by a dupe, a mutant ignorant of his own poisoned nature. Other men might have felt pity then; but not he.

The Lord of Death marvelled at the perfection and ingenuity of the taint – it was truly a work of psionic art, the construct of a maker both genius and madman. It bore the unmistakable fingerprints of the Changer of Ways across every aspect of its form. He traced thin thought-filaments from the infection, tracking the lines of their mutations, the reordering of fleshy matter that had altered the boy from a Marine to the simulacra he was now. Faint glints of contact danced in Arkio's aura, bending like flowers seeking the sun, all of them turning toward one man.

Stele. Mephiston could smell his emotions like spilled blood, a cocktail of arrogance warring with controlled fear, desire and avarice raging beneath the thin veneer of his icy civility. But the inquisitor was not the puppet master here; like a mirror within a mirror, Stele in turn was being directed by some other intelligence. He let his vision slip over the woman. She was like oil on water, repelling it instantly. Mephiston's sight could not hold purchase on her.

'Tell me, lord,' said Arkio. 'Now you have looked into my soul, what do you see?' The tension in the square came to a knife-edge on his words. 'Will you deny the work of the Great Angel upon me? Or will you accept that I am the incarnation of the Deus Sanguinius?'

Mephiston drew back with a grim sneer on his lips. 'If only your divinity matched the scope of your arrogance, lad, you might be what you appear.'

'How dare you!' blurted Sachiel, stepping forward. 'He is the Reborn Angel, the light of–'

'Silence, priest.' The psyker stilled him with a single glance, and Sachiel clasped at his throat, coughing.

The gracious expression on Arkio's face faded into a blank mask of neutrality. 'Mephiston, tread carefully. I offer you the chance to join my Blood Crusade. Do not be so quick to judge me. Come to my side, and I will welcome you as my battle-brother.'

He arched an eyebrow, gauging the moment. 'And if I do not?'

'It would go poorly for you, Lord of Death. The sands of your life have already run thin on borrowed time. If you test them again, you will not be so blessed as you were on Armageddon.'

A soft laugh escaped the psyker's lips; he decided to allow the boy to talk. 'Your presumption amuses me, Arkio. Tell me, this "crusade" of yours, what gives you the right to dictate such a thing? You speak as if it is your voice that leads our Chapter.'

'And so it will be,' Arkio replied. 'Your master Dante has lingered too long in command of the Blood Angels. He will step aside for me.'

The cold humour vanished from Mephiston's face in an instant. 'He will do no such thing for a pretender whelp like you.' The Librarian's voice was iron-hard and full of threat.

Arkio watched him carefully. 'Perhaps not. If he cannot release his petty fear of me then we will absolve him of his office. With all the due effort that may be required to do so.' The golden-armoured figure summoned a trio of Sachiel's honour guards and the men arrived with a titanium cylinder between them. Arkio opened the case and let the radiance of the Holy Lance light the darkening landscape. With a single swift motion, Arkio drew the ancient weapon and swept it up in a brilliant arc of light.

'The... the Spear of Telesto...' The words fell from the lips of the Techmarine in a humbled gasp.

Arkio pointed the spear at Mephiston, sighting down the length of the haft at him. 'I swear this by the blood of the primarch in my veins. Know me, Librarian. I am the Blood Angels incarnate. I am Sanguinius Reborn.' Gold lightning arced around the teardrop blade at the tip of the spear. 'Give me your fealty or perish. The choice is yours.'

For one dizzying, horrible moment, Mephiston felt his world lurch around him as the lance hove into view. *How can this be? He wields the sacred weapon!* A storm of chattering doubts engulfed the Lord of Death; it was impossible to think that some debased impostor would ever be able to lay hands on the spear, and yet Arkio held the Holy Lance like he was born to it. *Have I been mistaken? Could he really be the Reborn Angel? Who else could know the might of the Telesto artefact?* Mephiston shook the churn of thought away with a shake of his head, tiny darts of blue fire crackling along his crystalline psi-hood. 'No,' he growled. There was some magick at work here, a bewitchery so subtle and insidious that even a weapon forged by Holy Terra could be deceived by it. 'I am not cozened, pretender. Your parlour tricks mean nothing against my faith.' The Blood Angel's hand dropped to the hilt of his arcane force sword, the ancient mind-blade Vitarus. 'No true Son of Sanguinius will ever bend his knee to you, charlatan. You are false.'

A surge of anger thundered through the Warriors of the Reborn and cries of violence burst forth from Arkio's loyalists. Rafen let them jostle him forward.

Arkio shook his head in annoyance. 'Poor, old fool. You are infected with Dante's fear, just as Vode and Gallio before you, just as every misguided man who sits under Baal's sun and believes himself a true Blood Angel. I am the way.' He shouted, brandishing the spear, 'I am the truth reborn. Your blindness sickens me, mind-witch. I pity you.'

Mephiston's troops knotted together, breeches clattering on their bolters in a rush of noise. The Librarian drew himself to his full height, towering over Arkio's golden form and brilliant white wings. 'Save it for yourself, fool. You and your ordos accomplice, all of you are black with the stain of Chaos! It reeks from you…' He stabbed a copper-gloved finger at the inquisitor, who met his accusation with a sneer. 'This weakling is a lackey of the Ruinous Powers, and those who heed his words are equally disgraced with the stigma of heresy!' The psyker's words drew a chorus of denials and vicious retorts. 'Ramius Stele, I name you traitor. You conspire with dark powers and revel in corruption. You are the architect of this apostasy!'

'No!' roared the inquisitor, the shout slamming into the distant ruins like a thunderclap. 'The Blessed is right. You decry all that you fear! Your words are lies, Mephiston, lies. *Arkio is Sanguinius.*'

'Then he shall prove it,' the Lord of Death spat back. 'In the *Book of the Lords*, the Pure One was said to be the match of any warrior that lived. If this is so, then perhaps your so-called "Blessed" would be willing to face a true Blood Angel in single combat…' Mephiston bared his fangs. 'If he is the vessel for the will of the Angelic Sovereign, he will be victorious. If he is a mere pretender, he will die.'

He watched the consequence of his dare as it spread out among Arkio's loyalists, sensing the merge of anger and fear it engendered. He nodded to himself; exactly the reaction he had wanted. Playing the young fool into his hands, Mephiston had brought him to this moment, and now he would butcher the impostor like a prey beast. Such a brutal and very visible destruction of this golden figurehead was necessary – when Arkio died on the tip of Mephiston's force sword, his disciples and helots would break. Their confusion would make it easier for the Lord of Death to execute them. This insurrection had to be smashed in the most public and bloody way possible.

Men on both sides began to draw back, granting room for the coming duel, and Sachiel had found his voice once more. 'It's a trick,' he sputtered, the veins on his neck corded and tight with anger bordering on madness. 'You cannot accept, Blessed. The psyker is goading you.'

Arkio gave the priest a brief, beneficent smile. 'Sachiel, my friend. Your concern for my wellbeing is touching, but misplaced. I will not dismiss this challenge. If Mephiston wishes to see the might of the Red Angel enraged, then by the grail, I shall show it to him!' He stepped forward in a grim-faced swagger, the Holy Lance at rest beneath the curl of his wing. 'I will face any man here,' Arkio told the Librarian, 'and I will send him to the Emperor's grace knowing the truth of my divinity!' He made a show of opening his arms wide to the assembled men, Blood Angels, loyalists, slave-soldiers alike. 'Who here would take up arms to fight me? Which of you will shed your blood to prove the rightness of my decree?'

The sword Vitarus whispered as it drew free of its scabbard. 'Arkio,' growled Mephiston. 'It will be my–'

'*I will face him!*' The cry cut through the air and set heads turning, hands frozen on weapons.

'Who?' said the sergeant at Mephiston's flank. 'It came from over there.' The veteran indicated the mob of Arkio's men with the barrel of his bolter.

The psyker's perplexity increased as the crowd of ragged slave-troops parted to allow a single Blood Angel to come forward. His armour was that of a typical Tactical Marine, discoloured by bloodstains and a gouge in his chest plate. As Mephiston watched, the Marine stepped past Arkio's retinue and removed his helmet. For the first time, he saw an expression on the pretender's face that wasn't anger or arrogance, but pure, raw shock.

'RAFEN!' ARKIO CHOKED out the name. 'You survived…'

'Impossible,' Sachiel shrieked, grabbing at his gun. 'The factory was obliterated, he was inside, he could not have–'

'Quiet, you fool,' growled Stele, forcing the priest to lower his weapon. 'It appears that your news of his death was premature.'

Rafen and Arkio held each other's gaze for a long moment. 'Brother,' said the figure in gold, 'I did not think to lay eyes on you again.'

'I am a survivor,' Rafen replied, the weariness of all that had happened before in his voice, 'and now it has come to this.'

'You tried to destroy me, Rafen. You turned your back on me.' Arkio's words were thick with emotion, pain and fury.

He shook his head. 'I have not betrayed you, kindred. You have betrayed yourself. I warned you. I begged you to step back from the abyss.' Rafen looked away. 'You did not heed me.'

'And now it has come to this,' Arkio repeated. 'Very well, brother. If a son of Axan must die today, then die he will.'

The Lord of Death slammed his force weapon back into its sheath and beckoned Rafen closer. 'Come to me, brother. If you wish this, then let me know you.'

Rafen knelt before Mephiston and raised his head. 'Aye, I wish it.' The light behind the psyker's eyes glowed and burnt a path into Rafen's mind. He felt his body tense and

Mephiston's hand shot out, cupping his chin so he could not turn away.

The Librarian's powerful inner sight tore apart any defence of will that Rafen might have thought he had, slipping into the corridors of his psyche in a flood of power. His brain felt like hot magma, churning and boiling as storms of long-forgotten memory were dredged up and examined. Nothing that was Rafen escaped the gaze of Mephiston.

For a brief moment, their mentalities were unified as the Lord of Death sifted through the Marine's consciousness. Mephiston tasted Rafen's heart, the colours and shades of his soul – he saw pieces of the man that even Rafen himself could not comprehend. Duty and honour marbled his spirit, they were cut into Rafen like the age rings of a nya-wood tree. Once, there had been a time when this man was wilful and arrogant, when it was only his own glory that had occupied his mind; that Rafen was gone, a child grown into an adult with all the knowledge of life's hardest lessons. The Marine embodied the ideal of the Blood Angels. He was noble but humble, a warrior but not belligerent. *Among all these brothers who have lost their way, this one alone still walks the path of the Blood. There can be no better champion.*

Mephiston sensed something else, remaining only in fragments and splinters throughout Rafen's spirit. The touch of something higher, the marks where a force of being with powers far beyond the Lord of Death's had briefly influenced Rafen.

A vision…

The Librarian released him and withdrew, the fire in his eyes retreating. An unspoken moment of communication passed between the two men, a sadness at what Rafen had foreseen and what he knew had to be done. 'He is your blood kin,' said Mephiston.

'Aye, lord.'

He nodded. 'Rafen, you are true to our code. I stand aside to let you take my place in this challenge.' Mephiston gestured to the veteran nearby. 'Sergeant, give this man your power sword.'

The Marine drew the weapon and presented it to Rafen, who accepted it with a shallow bow. He turned the blade over in his hands, his fingers falling easily behind the spiked guard and into the knurled grip. The sword resonated with dormant threat, the polished silver blade catching the colour of the orange sky in its surface. Rafen traced the shape of a half-eagle cut into the hilt. 'A fine weapon,' he noted.

Mephiston stepped back to give him room. 'This matter will be decided,' he intoned. 'Brother against brother, with victory for the faithful.'

PERFECT.

Stele almost laughed out loud when Rafen took up the sword. This was ideal, he could have done no better himself at producing so exquisite a finale. Brother facing brother, with death alone the reward for Rafen's foolhardy presumption. Such a conflict would be a fitting end for that turbulent Marine, and at long last Stele would be rid of the irritant that had plagued him since they had first arrived among Cybele's war graves. It was regretful that Arkio's brother had proven so resistant to the cult that Stele had created among the Blood Angels – such a warrior with so defiant and unyielding a soul would have made a fine addition to the Reborn Angel's retinue. If only he had followed the route of his battle-brothers and truly accepted Arkio's new-found divinity, Rafen would be here now as a lord commander among the forces of the Blood Crusade; instead, he would be its first victim, and his vitae would be the wine of its consecration.

But no, Stele told himself, better that he dies. While he lived, Rafen was random chance, a wild card among the inquisitor's games of engineered plot and counterplot. It had been pure fluke that the Space Marine had been on Cybele when Garand sent the Word Bearers to attack it, but his presence had quickly grown from a minor diversion to the most serious nuisance. Rafen would never truly give his heart to his changed sibling – Stele had known that even when Arkio took his oath in the Ikari fortress's chapel – and so he had to be destroyed.

Rafen would die at his brother's own hand, and with that Arkio would be inexorably committed to a path from the Emperor's light for all time. Once the blood of his closest kinsman spattered that golden armour, once it hissed into steam from the burning blade of the Holy Lance, Arkio would have severed the last connection that still made him human. Once Rafen perished, Arkio would move ever further toward the eightfold way with nothing to hold him back. He would murder his conscience along with his brother.

Stele sensed Mephiston's attention upon him, and saw the Librarian from the corner of his sight, unwilling to meet his gaze directly. Perhaps the psyker sensed some measure of his thoughts, perhaps not. It mattered little, he would wait for the moment when the light died in Rafen's eyes, and then let loose a call for carnage. With Ulan's smothering mind-cloak to protect them, the loyalists would be upon the Lord of Death and his men in numbers so large that none of Dante's Space Marines would survive.

And if not, there was still one more card Stele could deal, one more player he could deliver to the field.

RAFEN BROUGHT THE power sword to arms and held it at his chest, the blade pointing at the sky. He gave his brother a grim salute.

In return, Arkio's eyes drew into narrow slits as he let the Spear of Telesto slide along his fingers to its full length. Sullen flickers of yellow-amber lightning crackled around the blade and the golden icon of Sanguinius carved in the hilt.

Both men stood for a moment; the battle balanced on a breath of silence as they watched for the sudden flood of muscle movement, the smallest telltale that would signify their opponent's actions. Warrior-to-warrior battles like this were commonplace in the wars of the Imperium, where conflicts were often fought with champions on either side engaging in single combat. Like every Adeptus Astartes, Rafen and Arkio were trained to fight alone, as an army of one; in years past, as initiates, the siblings had sparred on many occasions. Then, they had known each other well enough to counter every attack, neutralise every defence – but time had altered both of them.

Rafen surrendered himself to the moment, allowing his mind and spirit to flow together, merging into a single engine of action and movement. Arkio watched him, impassive and unmoving, a gold statue among the colourless debris of the city square. Rafen's focus narrowed until it was only his brother he saw before him, only the shape of a man. An enemy.

And suddenly he was in motion, a snarl ripping from his lips, fangs baring in fight rage. The power sword sizzled around him in a punishing arc of liquid silver. Arkio reacted, sweeping the spear down in a sharp gesture of defence, falling for Rafen's feint. With his other arm, Rafen brought up the blunt, brutish ingot of his bolt pistol and followed through with a three-round burst of shell fire.

Arkio recovered with frightening speed and turned the glowing lance like a propeller, the humming shaft making a gleaming disc in the air. The bolt rounds whined and screamed as they were shredded by the flickering shield. Rafen extended through his initial attack and spun on his boot, slashing down with a low cut of the sword. The blade sliced through air as Arkio slid away over loose-packed dirt. In a blur, he turned the spear back at Rafen.

His brother spied the infinitesimal loss of balance off Arkio's back foot and advanced, cutting a web of figure-eight lines toward him. The spear tip met the power sword and spat violently, bursts of fat, angry sparks hissing like fireworks as the weapons met and parted, met and parted, met again.

Arkio fell back step after step, unhurried and emotionless. The fan of light from the spinning lance was everywhere that Rafen's sword blade fell, halting its savage attacks, blunting each stab and cut with a flashing parry. To the untrained eye, it seemed as if the figure in the golden armour was on the defensive, fighting off an endless salvo of strikes. Some of the Warriors of the Reborn made harsh catcalls until the loyalist Marines commanding them gave out violent censures. Arkio let Rafen spend the energy of his assault in a flurry of blows, at the same time using the minimum amount of effort to counter. He had expected better from his brother.

Rafen was no fool. If he extended the attack a second longer, Arkio would turn it on him and strike back. He lunged forward, an easy move calculated to look like the action of a fighter frustrated and desperate. Arkio took it at face value and blocked the strike, opening a window of opportunity along his left side for an eye-blink. The winged Marine was powerful, undoubtedly, but he lacked the experience of his older brother. Rafen would never have fallen for the feint – but Arkio did.

The bolt gun came from nowhere, suddenly there in front of Arkio's face, the barrel still warm and hot with the stink of ozone discharge. Rafen's finger tightened on the trigger.

Arkio reacted with preternatural speed. His folded wings exploded open in a flare of brilliant white and he shot into the air, flashing out of Rafen's line of fire. The golden figure described a swift, graceful arc up and over his brother's head, spinning and turning toward the ground twenty feet distant. Rafen rotated in place, tracking Arkio with the gun. He fired a quartet of shots at the swooping shape, leading the target but missing with each bolt by the merest fraction.

The ground rumbled and rippled as Arkio touched down, the impact causing a shock wave in the centuries-old detritus around them. A grimace marred his perfect features as he whirled the spear to present the glowing teardrop blade to Rafen. Golden effulgence and sparkling particles gathered into a humming sphere of energy at the weapon's tip. Unable to dodge, Rafen saw it coming and raised his hands, gun and sword crossed over his face like some desperate invocation of the Imperial aquila.

The jet of unearthly power detached from the Holy Lance and ripped across the distance between the two men, splitting open and turning into a dancing fence of yellow flame. As it engulfed Rafen, he felt his skin searing; he remembered the Word Bearers, their bodies reduced to ash in the depths of the Shenlong manufactory. For one heart-stopping moment, Rafen thought his world was at an end, but then the flames flicked away, leaving him injured but still alive. He pawed at his face, shaking off a fine layer of ash where his epidermis had been flash-burnt.

'Sanguinius be praised,' he heard Mephiston's voice. 'The Spear of Telesto knows the soul of his Sons! He turns his holy fire from Rafen!'

The Marine nodded to himself – of course, the weapon was gene-coded. It could only be used by men who carried the genetic template of the primogenitor within them, and it would not harm those who bore the same mark in their blood. Rafen saw a brief glint of annoyance in Arkio's eyes – he would not be able to do away with him in such a showy display of power as he had the cursed Traitor Marines. It was fitting – the fight would be won or lost on martial prowess, not strength of arms. Snarling, Rafen threw himself at Arkio once more, leading into him with the hissing edge of the power sword's blade.

Arkio bit back an angry curse, rebuking himself for forgetting the weapon's gene-code failsafe. Instead, he dropped the haft of the spear into a two-handed grip, holding it like a quarterstaff. He blocked Rafen's attack, the sword blade bouncing as it struck off the unbreakable shaft of the weapon. He forced Rafen off-balance and shoved him back, reversing the ploy his brother had used only moments earlier.

Broken drifts of ferrocrete fragments and stone shifted beneath Rafen's feet and he dug in, refusing to let Arkio knock him back. Blade and spear came together, each weapon pressing back to the fighter's breastplates, hot flashes of light flickering over them. The brothers were toe-to-toe, pushing into one another with all the force they could muster.

'Yield, Rafen,' snarled Arkio. 'Yield to me and I will end it cleanly.'

'I will not yield to corruption,' he gasped. 'Brother, there must be something of the man I knew still in you, some piece of your soul that still remains pure?'

'I am purity itself.' Arkio's skin was taut across his face with anger, his fangs bared. 'Ignorant fool, you oppose your very lord. I am the Deus Sanguinius–'

'*You are a dupe!*' Rafen bellowed, howling the words, 'You're nothing but a clockwork toy for that ordos whore-son. He did this, warped you into this mutant obscenity.'

Arkio's threw back his head and roared. '*Liar. Traitor. Coward.*' With a massive, vicious surge of motion, the winged Marine brought the spear about and slammed the blunt end into the centre of Rafen's torso with a thunder-clap of force.

The impact struck the Blood Angel like a cannon shell and Rafen was blown backwards off his feet. He flew through the air, releasing snap-fire shots from his bolter that went wild, deflecting off broken rock and keening away from indirect hits on Arkio's armour. Rafen landed with a crash of rubble, sending a roil of brick dust up into the air. He struggled, his feet slipping below him.

Arkio became aware of his name on the wind, a heart-beat pulse of chanting from the Warriors of the Reborn as they sensed the end was near for his opponent. Blood as hot as molten iron engorged his body with murderous power, the unchained potential of the black rage unfold-ing to envelop him. Arkio let out a wordless scream of absolute and utter fury, throwing himself into the air on the great curves of his wings. The spear buzzed and hummed in his hands, twitching like a distressed mount, but he forced it to turn toward Rafen. The lance tried to face itself away from his target but in his ire Arkio would not allow it.

At the top of his arc of flight, Arkio spun about and raced back down into the arms of gravity, wings cupping the wind, diving like a hawk upon prey. The teardrop blade flashed in the dimness.

His bones still ringing with the impact, Rafen forced himself off the ground to confront the attack; the glittering gold shape blurred at him, the lance aimed at his heart. Rafen's eyes met Arkio's and the Marine leapt into the air to meet him early.

The instant stretched like melting tallow. Turning, spinning, the lance struck poorly and deflected off Rafen's shoulder in a sizzle of sparks. The Marine moved, slipping under Arkio's guard, the two of them passing in mid-air less than a hand-span apart. Rafen's sword led the way, and the crackling power blade found brief purchase. The weapon cut a wound in Arkio's wing, red blood exploding in a crimson blossom, stark white feathers raining about him like falling petals.

Both men landed hard, but only one bled. Rafen turned the sword so that he could see the fluid that kissed the blade. It was wine-dark and sluggish like tar, it was polluted.

'First blood!' shouted one of Mephiston's men, but the cry was lost in snarls and roars of Arkio's loyalists.

'No...' THE WORD was small and plaintive, a childlike denial of something the eye saw but refused to believe. Sachiel's hands came to his face and it was only then that he realised the voice had been his. A great splash of crimson disfigured Arkio's immaculate golden wargear and the sight of this offence burned into the priest's vision like a brand.

The sharp, tearing agony of the wound seemed to be instantly translated to every member of Arkio's retinue – the sheer shock of seeing their liege lord injured by a mere Marine hit them with a physical force. For a long second all of them were stuck dumb by the enormity of it.

Sachiel could smell the blood. As a Sanguinary High Priest, the scent of living vitae was as distinct as the bouquet of a fine wine or the aroma of a delicate flower. Sachiel had known blood all through his service as an Apothecary to the Chapter, and he had tasted a thousand strains and touched a thousand more in his duties. On battlefields he had seen great lakes of it shed by enemy and ally alike, he had witnessed it gushing in red fountains from the arteries of men screaming for the Emperor's peace. Sachiel knew the scent of his own blood, and that of Sanguinius himself as it lay captured and preserved in the Red Grail on Baal. The stench of what leaked from Arkio struck his senses like a mailed fist. He sensed corruption, black and ruinous, some foul seed of pollution swarming and writhing inside the Blessed's veins.

Sachiel's stomachs threatened to rebel and throw their contents on the ground. It was impossible. The priest scrambled inside himself for some explanation and found none – his senses had never betrayed him before and they did not betray him now. Sachiel turned away, blocking out the sight even though the smell was wrapped around him in invisible wreathes. His gaze fell on Stele; the inquisitor was growling some order at his hooded psy-witch. Stele caught his sight for a fractional instant and Sachiel saw him start.

'You,' Sachiel managed, the word bubbling up from a deep, hidden place. 'You...' Like glass breaking, the compulsions Stele had placed in Sachiel's psyche aboard the *Bellus* suddenly shattered. Perhaps it was the shock of Arkio's injury, perhaps some last fragment of Sachiel's honourable self rising to the surface, but in that instant the priest was freed of the psyker's hold on his will.

Sachiel's world, so perfect and so rationalised, so carefully assembled to serve his ego, came crashing down about him. Floodgates of denied, forgotten memories disintegrated and the priest was knocked to his knees by the force of them, wailing. Every line he had crossed, every choice he had made in order to aggrandise himself, and

Stele had been there to help him do it. Sachiel's gorge rose as the stink of mutation filled every pore of his skin, contaminating him and choking the air. 'Oh lord,' he wept, bitter tears falling from his face. 'What have I done?' He looked up at Stele and saw the inquisitor staring down at him, an expression of utter contempt on his cruel lips. 'What have you done to me?'

Stele knelt and whispered in his ear. 'I gave you the tools to destroy yourself.'

CHAPTER ELEVEN

THE RAINS CAME from the darkening sky, a whisper of falling droplets spattering across the grey landscape of the dead city-shrine. It hissed over the forms of the rag-tag warriors as they surged forward, rushing to Arkio's flanks.

Amid their lines, the priest and the inquisitor faced each other. Sachiel's tears were lost in the rush of the downpour, his fingers clenching clods of mud where he crouched on hands and knees. The chill, dirty rainwater washed over him and with it, it carried away the scales of willing blindness from the priest's eyes. Sachiel's perfidy was revealed to him with sudden, shattering clarity. No denials could assuage it, no words were strong enough to halt the tide of utter self-loathing that engulfed him. 'I… am… corrupted…' he breathed, damning himself with his own words.

Stele looked at him with complete disregard. Any familiarity or comradeship the inquisitor had shown to Sachiel now fell from his expression, and he understood that Stele had never, ever considered the priest as anything more than a tool. He was something to be used and discarded.

'I had intended to retain you for a while longer,' Stele's voice was low and only Sachiel could hear it, 'but it appears you have outlived your usefulness to me.'

The priest struggled to get to his feet, but his body felt like it weighed hundreds of tonnes. The burden of the sins he had committed were pressing him into the rubble. 'Does Arkio know? I would never have followed you...'

Stele laughed. 'How typical, priest. You think of your own reputation before the fate of your Chapter!'

'You did this to me!'

'You allowed me to. You secretly welcomed it, Sachiel, coveting the Red Grail, nurturing your resentments... You were ideal, your obsession with yourself blinding you to all the pacts you made!' He let out a harsh laugh. 'Fallen Angel, look how far you have tumbled from your perch.' Hellish light glinted in Stele's vision and the priest felt the sickening caress of his mind-touch. *You were not the first,* said the voice in his head, the hiss of snakeskin on bone, *and you will not be the last.*

The awful magnitude of the grand scheme of Chaos became clear in Sachiel's mind, and it turned his hearts to ice. 'No...'

'Oh, yes,' replied Stele, and through the open, bleeding wound self-inflicted on the priest's psyche, he sent a quicksilver hammer of mind-force.

Sachiel's scream merged into a howl of thunder and blood gushed from his nostrils, and wept in runnels from his eyes. *Die!* Stele ripped him apart within, breaking his mind like matchwood. *Perish, Sachiel. I compel you, die for me.*

The body in red and white ceramite collapsed in a puddle of thin pink fluids, death tearing away his last breath on the wind.

Stele masked his smile and fixed a disguise of righteous anger in its place. 'Murderer,' he bellowed, stabbing an accusing finger at Mephiston. 'See, the Librarian has killed our brother Sachiel. He burnt the will from him with his witch-sight.'

The fierce mood of the mob army and the loyalist Marines took voice and weapons were turned on Mephiston and his Blood Angels. They were on the verge of an adrenaline-fuelled frenzy, and all it would take would be one word from Stele to tip them over the edge.

He gave it. 'Attack. Destroy them all, in Arkio's name!'

THE RABBLE WAS a living, breathing entity, a war engine made from flesh and bone and ceramite and steel. It moved so fast that Rafen was caught off-guard, the figures in their red cloaks emblazoned with the spear and halo flooding around Arkio's imperious form in a headlong rush. There were loyalist Marines in the mass as well, bolters spitting hot fire.

Mephiston's men opened up into the Warriors of the Reborn, scything them down in gouts of crimson. Gunfire and screams merged into a symphony of destruction, raised high to the rattling fall of the rain. Rafen swung and parried with his sword as the mob reached him, cutting him off from his target. He lost sight of Arkio as the golden figure leapt into the sky and cut back toward the edge of the square, then he was fighting hard, his attention on the myriad adversaries upon him. His bolter pistol ran dry and he used it like a club, too far into the thick of the melee to spare the time to reload it. The power sword rose and fell, cutting a path through chattering men who died with the name of his sibling on their lips.

For the first time in what seemed like an age, Rafen felt the familiar tingle of battle lust inside him, the shadow of the black rage. He culled the zealots, losing count of the dead, but Arkio's thousand still had the weight of numbers on their side. Nearby, he caught the crackling hum of a force weapon. Blue lightning licked at the low clouds as the Lord of Death joined the fray.

* * *

ALL ABOUT HIM combat seethed and boiled, yet Stele stayed untouched, his lexmechanic whimpering in a cowering heap at Ulan's feet while the mutant psyker draped her nullifying power about them. The inquisitor examined the chalice in his hand; he had ripped it from Sachiel's belt as the light faded from the priest's eyes, flinging away the velvet bag to reveal the replica of the sacred Blood Angels artefact. He smiled. This simple trinket was the seed of Sachiel's undoing. The Apothecary had always dreamed of becoming the Keeper of the Red Grail, ascending to the highest office in the sanguinary clergy. He had nurtured bitterness toward Corbulo, the battle-brother that held the posting on Baal, and that had been Stele's gateway into manipulating him. With a shrug, he tossed the copper cup away. It was worthless litter now, with as little value to the inquisitor as Sachiel's cooling corpse. He nudged the dead priest with his boot-tip. Stele was glad to be rid of the self-important dullard, one less loose end to dispose of.

Ulan grunted in pain. 'Uh… difficult…' she said through gritted teeth. 'Mephiston's sight… stronger…' A line of purplish blood ran from her nostrils.

Stele made a dismissive gesture. 'In a moment. Where is Arkio?'

'Conflicted…' Ulan managed, nerves in her face jerking. 'He seeks… reassurance…'

'We cannot lose the momentum of the attack,' he growled. Already, things had deviated from Stele's carefully engineered plans with the sudden revelation of Rafen and Arkio's wound through a foolish moment of inattention. 'Attend me,' he demanded.

The thin, pale girl stumbled toward him, the lexmechanic mumbling fearfully in dozens of different tongues. 'Lord…' she said thickly. 'I… am at my limits…'

'Yes, yes,' he retorted, ignoring the agony that radiated off her aura. 'Here.' He grasped her face and let his fingers find the ghost-metal contacts under the polyflesh scabs on her skin. Ulan tensed as Stele corralled and used her haphazard power to augment his own warp-sight. At once he detected the hidden clusters of wild minds on the edges of his sensorium, visible only to him because he knew where to seek them. 'Garand,' he intoned, his voice slicing through the warp. 'It is time.' Stele released the woman with a jerk and her head lolled backward. Ulan's blind eyes showed only the bloodshot whites.

The inquisitor turned in place as he heard the first screams of rocket motors. From concealed hides scattered throughout the ruins, spat from beneath rubble and the protective sheathes of camo-cloaks, salvos of missiles looped in over the edges of the debris-choked square and fell on rods of orange smoke.

EVERY BLOOD ANGEL knew the sound, and they took cover – but the pressing knots of Arkio's zealots made rapid movement impossible. The warheads streaked into the square and struck a dozen points at once, throwing up red-black fireballs. Three of Mephiston's Thunderhawks were instantly crippled or destroyed, and a handful of men were blown apart when the rockets fell short and landed in the melee.

The Lord of Death raised his free hand to shield his eyes from the glare. Hot flame crackled as the rain sizzled into steam, the sudden glow underlighting the grey clouds. 'And so they spring their trap at last. I wondered how long we would have to wait.'

'Indirect fire from the south, west and east quadrants!' the Techmarine reported, fending off a zealot with a punch from his servo-arm. 'Weapon signature does not match Blood Angel munitions.'

'Of course,' Mephiston snapped, bringing up the sword Vitarus. 'And what new player has joined this sorry performance?'

The veteran sergeant nodded to the west as he slammed a fresh clip of ammunition into his bolter. 'I can smell them from here, lord. Horned braggarts by the cartload.'

Mephiston saw figures dropping from the upper tiers of ruined buildings or emerging from concealed trapdoors over rubble-filled basements. They wore armour in a stringent shade of ruby, bedecked with chains and smoking lanterns. Horns sprouted in riots from their helms and heads, and as they came on their voices were raised in blasphemous hymns. 'Word Bearers. The design of this infamy becomes clearer…'

'But the scouts,' said the Techmarine. 'The scouts reported no contacts.'

The Librarian threw the sergeant a grave look, and a grim understanding passed between them. 'Our scouts are all dead,' said the veteran.

From the instant he had spoken of traps and double-crosses to Commander Dante in the monastery's arboretum, Mephiston knew this moment would come; yet as it happened, his ire was not lessened. A guttural snarl bared his canines. 'Blood Angels!' he shouted. 'To arms!'

Vitarus sang high and drank deep from the enemy about the psyker.

'Confirmed,' droned the servitor. 'Multiple discharges on the planetary surface, evidence of small-arms fire and medium-yield tactical detonations. Vox traffic intercepts concur.'

Captain Ideon released a slow, metallic growl from his mechanical throat. 'More betrayal,' he snarled. 'Great Arkio was right to suspect the Lord of Death. He has eschewed the hand of peace in favour of attack.' Ideon made a grunt that was his immobile form's equivalent of a nod. 'So be it, then.'

Solus frowned. 'We cannot be sure who fired the first shot. It may have been a mistake…' The words seemed weak as they fell from his lips.

'Mistake?' Ideon rattled, his synthetic voice buzzing like hornets in a tin can. 'Mephiston does not make mistakes, Solus. This is a declaration of war!' The captain's stoic face twitched and the mechadendrites protruding from his skull whispered against one another. 'Prepare to engage the *Europae*.'

'*Europae* is turning,' called the sense-servitor, 'adopting battle stance. Detection transients indicate multiple weapon bay activations.'

'You see?' Ideon husked.

Solus found his words dying in his throat and he turned away. At the same moment, his eyes fell on the hololithic chart in the tacticarium. Warning glyphs were streaming through the ghostly green light. 'There's someone else out there,' he said aloud.

SABIEN'S DEBRIS RING was a mixture of broken stones as tall as mountains and great drifting lakes of frozen ice. Dense with heavy ores, to the eyes of a starship's machine-spirit the belt of asteroids was a confused swathe of garbled, reflected sensor returns. On the surface it seemed like the ideal place to hide a vessel, but no captain would ever have been so foolhardy to attempt such a thing. The blanket of confusion that seeded the ring also made navigation inside its confines virtually impossible. Both the *Bellus* and the *Europae* saw the belt as a natural hazard, just another element of the orbital environment. Neither vessel expected the chilling sight of a starship emerging from the shaggy morass of tumbling stones.

Under power from a hard thruster burn, the Desolator-class battleship extended out of the Sabien Belt like a red blade punched through a torso. The jagged prow dipped like the snout of a hunting predator, moving inexorably to bear on the *Europae*. Asteroids battered into the craft as it moved from the debris ring, punching rents in the hull; the captain of the vessel was willing to allow men on his outer decks to die so that the ship could complete its manoeuvre, weathering the damage. The crewmen aboard Mephiston's flagship sounded alerts and charged their torpedo tubes, gangs of Chapter serfs hoisting warheads as big as watchtowers into the open maws of launchers. The monstrous Chaos craft continued to turn, the target scanners of the bow guns briefly crossing the shape of the *Bellus*. Not one of the weapons released its warshot toward Arkio's battle barge; the battleship crew had their orders, on pain of lengthy and horrific torture, to concentrate all their initial attack on the *Europae*.

SOLUS SAW THE lance batteries wink at him like blinded eyes as the ship turned onward, coming to bear on Mephiston's vessel. 'They... they did not fire on us...' he breathed, hardly able to believe what he had seen.

'Aggressor identity confirmed,' the mechanical chatter of the servitor in the detection pit clattered forth. 'Vessel is the battlecruiser *Misericorde*, line warcraft in service to the Word Bearers Legion and the Ruinous Powers.'

'Vandire's oath!' spat Solus. 'What is this madness?' The Blood Angel's mind raced through the possibilities – could the Chaos ship be some sort of ally to the Lord of Death? Dare he believe that Mephiston, or even Dante himself was consorting with the scum of the Maelstrom?

'Status of *Misericorde*,' Ideon demanded. 'Are we their target?'

'Negative,' came the reply. 'All guns on the ship are coming to bear on the *Europae*.'

'A third force?'

There was a smile in Ideon's artificial voice as his eyes flicked at Solus. 'An unexpected piece of good fortune! The hand of Sanguinius protects us...'

'But we cannot simply ignore a Chaos capital ship!' Solus blurted out. 'It is our duty to–'

'You dare speak to me of duty?' Ideon snapped, his voice cracking about the bridge cloisters like thunder. 'I, who have served our Chapter for two hundred years from this very throne?' The captain's words dropped to a low rumble. 'Know this, my errant battle-brother, when fate's tarot deals a hand of swords, use them. You know the oath we take.'

Solus repeated the litany by automatic rote. 'To the ship, the Chapter, the primarch and the Emperor.'

'Yes, and while the *Misericorde* is the enemy of the Emperor, the *Europae* is the enemy of our primarch and our Chapter. Mephiston's extermination takes precedence.' In response to a mental command, pict-screens at Solus's station flickered to display long range images of the fighting on Sabien. 'You only have to view the battle unfolding below us to know the truth of that.'

'*Misericorde* is firing,' said the sense-servitor. '*Europae*'s void shields are holding.'

'Let's show those corrupted fools how it is done, eh?' said Ideon. 'The order is, target the *Europae* and fire.'

Solus hesitated.

'Did you not understand the command, Solus?' There was a razor-keen warning in the captain's manner.

'Open fire,' said Solus, in a dead, toneless voice.

THE SQUARE WAS a cauldron of inferno as figures in shades of red clashed across the rubble and the stones. Arkio's thousand-strong helot army in their terracotta robes and the loyalist Space Marines who fought with them clashed with Mephiston's Blood Angels, and they drew fire and laid weapons to bear upon the Word Bearers swarming into the broken arena. There was no plan of battle here, no careful tactics to rout and defeat the enemy – instead each side engaged in the grisly attrition of hand-to-hand fighting. The square became a mass of fire and screams as men and traitors came together to kill or be killed.

In the thick of it, Rafen was a whirlwind of destruction, the power sword running hot in his hand as he tore apart zealots and ripped open Chaos Marines. In equal measure the dark glamour of the battle repelled and excited him, the burning flood of adrenaline coming upon him like some ghostly caress. The raging fight was already spilling over the cracked and fallen walls of the plaza, into the surrounding streets. Some of Mephiston's men – veteran assault troops with their characteristic helmets of sunburst yellow – bobbed up on jump packs. They carried plasma weapons and heavy flamers, seeking out the missile shooters still hiding in the ruins and dousing them in liquid fire. On the winds came the smell of cooked meat and the bone-snap of superheated ceramite.

Daggers and work implements turned into clubs rang noisily against Rafen's power armour as a cluster of Arkio's warriors tried to surround him and beat the Marine to the ground. Rafen let out a cruel laugh at their idiocy; he pitied these fools, willingly blinded by the dogma spouted by Sachiel. In quick and economical moves, he used every part of the sword to dispatch them, breaking skulls with the flat of the blade and the pommel, cleaving torsos with the keen edge, smashing ribcages with the spiked guard about his fingers. If these imbeciles wanted to die in the name of their false messiah, then Rafen would be more than willing to accommodate them.

The fight ebbed and flowed, moving like an ocean swell. Figures were caught up in the morass, the press of flesh and steel sending Rafen staggering. Somewhere along the line he had lost his helmet. Several times he was forced to halt and seek his direction, and more than once he barely pulled a killing blow before a Marine from Mephiston's contingent. Rafen had already ensured that he would not suffer a similar error by burning off the spear and halo design on his shoulder pad with a discarded hand flamer. The dirty black scar on the side of his wargear paradoxically made him feel cleaner, as if the kiss of the burning promethium had purged the taint of Stele and his corruption.

Rafen's boot rang against a hollow shape and it caught his attention. There at his feet, where the spilled blood and grey rain had turned drifts of dry brick dust into tar-like slurry, a body in white and red ceramite had been abandoned. The corpse was pressed into the mud, twisted and broken by a stampede of helots, but Rafen knew it instantly.

'Sachiel…' While the fight had drifted back and forth, the dead priest had remained where he fell, the spotless and immaculate armour he once wore now ruined with bloody footprints and smeared with gore. The Apothecary's eyes were open, blankly staring up into the hissing torrents of rain. Rafen had never had anything other than antipathy for his arrogant rival, but now as he looked upon the expression of horror and despondency frozen on the dead man's face, he felt only pity for the priest. However unwittingly, Sachiel had placed his own quest for glory beyond his loyalty to the Chapter, and here in the dark mire he lay fully paid for that mendacity.

Rafen smacked away another attacker with the butt of his bolter and took a moment to reload. He glanced around as he did, finding his bearings by the actinic glow of blue mind-fire that blazed about the Lord of Death. Steam wreathed the Librarian in white streams where the rainwater flashed to vapour around him. As Rafen watched, the ethereal lightning that haloed Mephiston congealed around the upright spars of his psychic hood, coiling into rods of energy that seared his eyes to look at. Twin horned skulls at the tips of the ghost-metal psy-wave conductors flashed with barely controlled power, and the Librarian swelled beneath his blood red armour, drawing the lethal potential into himself.

Colours and shades that had no place on the plane of the living came into being, the air itself shimmering and bending like a phantom lens. Rafen saw Mephiston's target – a squad of Word Bearers Havoc Marines, bristling with heavy weapons. The Lord of Death turned his face to them and his eyes flashed. On the battlefield, Rafen had seen other Blood Angels psykers use the skill they called the Quickening, a blanket of power that could turn the user into a tornado of destruction, but Mephiston was the master of another psionic force, one that dwarfed the talents of the Librarians and codicers who served beneath him. The power of the Smite was unleashed, a blaze of insane geometry cut from liquid light fanning out into a teardrop of pure and undiluted annihilation. The witch-fire engulfed the Havocs and set them alight; ammunition packs detonated and armour split. Rafen instinctively joined in on the great cheer of approval that came from Mephiston's Blood Angels.

He waded forward to meet the psyker commander, saluting with the power sword as the Chief Librarian caught sight of him. 'My lord!'

'Rafen,' Mephiston growled, 'You live still, yet so does your errant sibling.'

'The zealots cut me off from him before I could–' Rafen began, but the rest of his words were drowned out by a roar from Arkio's ragged warriors. The slave army, driven on by some shouted command from the back of their lines, rushed forward. Rafen thought he heard Stele's voice on the wind, but then his attention was on the men tearing at him. At point-blank range he unleashed the bolt pistol, popping heads like overripe fruits, punching holes as big as his mailed fist in cloaked bodies. 'They fight like they are possessed!' he grated, the press of the charge forcing him to Mephiston's flank.

'Indeed,' replied the Librarian, his force weapon slashing a wide arc of blood and entrails. 'They rally to their "Blessed One".'

Rafen ran through a Word Bearer as it emerged from the pack, taking him from jowl to bowel, emptying a nest of blackened, stinking organs on the dirt. 'Lord, my task lies undone. Give me permission to disengage and seek out my brother.'

Mephiston eyed him. 'You wounded him and he fled. What kind of messiah is that?'

'He will return, my lord. I know the conflict inside him, but if I do not strike now, Arkio will return and lay waste to this place. I must find him, while his guard is down!'

'You understand what will occur if you fail, Rafen?' The Librarian's voice was low and hard. 'Even as we speak, my battle barge is engaged in a fight for its survival in orbit. I have left orders with the brother-captain commanding her that if Arkio's loyalists tip the balance, then Sabien is to be targeted with cyclonic torpedoes. Better this shrine world become ashes then this schism be allowed to spread further.'

'I can stop him,' Rafen insisted. 'It is what I came here to do.'

Mephiston gave him a nod. 'So be it, then.' He turned aside and called out. 'Techmarine. Bring Brother Rafen a jump pack, quickly.'

'A jump pack, lord?'

'Arkio has wings. We must give you wings of your own, lad.'

'STELE! WHAT ABORTION have you created now?'

The inquisitor whirled, Ulan clinging to his arm, as a knot of Word Bearers punched their way through the helot lines, with Garand at their head. A loyalist Marine foolishly turned his gun on the Warmaster, stepping forward to protect Stele and his retinue from the threat. Garand angrily spat acidic venom and decapitated the Blood Angel with a single sweep of his bane-axe.

'Lord Garand,' Stele said, deciding not to bow. 'Welcome.'

'My patience with this ridiculous scheme of yours is at an end, human.' Garand menaced him with the humming axe. 'You know the bargain! Bring these mewling Blood Whelps to the Banner of Change or forfeit your life.'

'Don't push me, Word Bearer,' Stele shouted, emboldened by the heat of the battle raging around them. 'My orders come from Malfallax, not you! It will be done, but by my design, not yours.'

'Your design!' Garand spat again. 'Pathetic weakling, with your schemes and your little performances, none of that matters now. In Lorgar's name, the battle is joined. These men-prey will stand with the eight or they will perish.'

'No!' Stele roared, and Garand blinked in surprise at the vehemence of the human's denial. 'I have come too far, paid too much for this moment. It is mine, and you will not usurp it, creature.'

'You dare.' Garand's eyes narrowed and he marshalled his psyker potency to chastise the ranting inquisitor – but there was a null void surrounding him, a thick weave of poisonous non-space issuing from the mind of the female trailing at the inquisitor's heels. 'Bah,' snorted the Warmaster, recoiling. 'Have your petty game, then.' The Word Bearers lord brandished his axe and called to his men. 'Pick your targets and cull the Blood Angels. Collateral kills...' and he smiled, '...at your discretion.'

Out of Stele's earshot, a tech-priest slunk forward from Garand's unit to bow at the Warmaster's feet. 'Great Witch Prince, a vox from the *Misericorde*. They have engaged Mephiston's warship, but the presence of the *Bellus* vexes the ship's machine-spirit. The crew is discontent to let a second Astartes craft go unpunished. What should I tell them?'

'Tell them...' A slow and hateful smile crossed Garand's pallid lips and he glanced at Stele. He would castigate the conceited braggart for daring to raise his voice to him. 'Tell them the *Bellus* is to be considered expendable.'

THE BATTLE IN the skies of Sabien changed from a delicate joust to a brutal, punishing fight as the three ships closed the distance between one another. In terms of tonnage the combatants were evenly matched: the *Bellus* and the *Europae* were sister ships, their keels laid down in the midst of the Heresy era, both of them cut from steel forged in the furnaces of Enigma VI, both created according to the sacred tenets of a standard template construct programme from the Mechanicus librariums on Mars. *Misericorde* was longer in the beam but slender where the battle barges were blunt axe-heads in form. Once, the battleship had been a human vessel, but that identity had long been subsumed beneath centuries of creeping mutation, the old self lost and forgotten in the warp. Garand's vessel bristled with hateful power. It was predator-fast compared with the slow, heavy hunters of the barges, but speed and firepower cancelled each other out. Had any two of the ships faced off, the battle's end would not have been easy to predict – but in a three-way engagement, all bets were off.

Misericorde powered forward, the screaming mouths of its drive bells vomiting flame. Lance fire connected the ship with *Europae*, green and red threads of coherent particles stringing between them, then gone. Spherical explosions opened like puffballs into the vacuum, spilling iced gases and spent men into the dark. As the Chaos and Blood Angels ships crossed the distance toward one another,

Ideon brought Arkio's flagship up in *Misericorde*'s shadow, allowing the powerful bow guns to rip past the ruby-coloured cruiser and strike *Europae*'s glittering void shields. The barge's ephemeral energy screens flickered and deformed under the onslaught, shedding the might of her attackers like rain, but already the enigmatic field genera-tors in the barge's heart were reacting to the pressure, sending waves of sympathetic panic into the tech-priests that ministered to them. *Europae* was strong, to be sure, but she would not resist so barbaric an assault for long.

In the depths of space, such fights took place at ranges that would swallow a star system, ships hitting ships beyond each other's visual ranges. The close-in fighting of near-orbit engagements was an entirely different game. If one was a fencing match, full of elegant moves and pin-point strikes, then the other was a dirty street brawl, punches being traded with ferocity and killer intent. *Europae* leapt forward without warning, a plume of fusion fire nova-bright and blinding erupting from her stern. She veered to port in a savage turn that stressed the hull beyond its tolerances, popping out thousands of ancient, giant riv-ets. The brutal manoeuvre bled speed and gravity away, pushing *Europae* on to a different tack and ending the lives of dozens of luckless crew caught in the wrong sections of the hull spaces.

The turn came out of nowhere and it was near suicidal. Ideon's surprise was enough that he hesitated a second too long as Mephiston's ship presented itself in passing. By the time the command to fire the bow guns had been relayed, *Bellus* was carving at empty air like an addled punch-drunk. *Europae*'s crew was prepared, however.

Secondary batteries, laser cannons with great quartz lenses broad as the eye of a kraken, spat a killing glare over *Bellus*'s starboard flank. The battle barge moaned under the impact, and Ideon felt the screech as the machine-spirit's pain analogue ripped into him. The simple, animal mind of *Bellus* hissed and spat; it lacked the intellect to under-stand why another Blood Angels ship would attack it.

Europae extended her turn, coming about on a course that would allow the ship to enter *Bellus*'s rearward arc. Even with the acres of armour and double-projected void shielding that protected it, a captain would be courting suicide to allow an attacking vessel the freedom to throw shells and las-fire into his drive nozzles. Ideon spat curses and bellowed out orders, his hands twitching into angry claws in a rare moment of physical reaction. The two barges turned into one another, matching speed for speed as they became caught in a deadly waltz. They continued to trade fire as *Misericorde* came about, sighting the bores of her lethal hellguns over *Bellus*. A human captain might have waited; a human captain might have evaluated the consequences and held his fire until *Europae* became the clearer target. But, like his ship, *Misericorde*'s captain had long forgotten his human origins and any form of fealty to weak abstracts like fidelity or compassion.

The red dagger freed its weapons to do their worst, and *Misericorde*'s starboard armaments blazed in one cascade of hot murder. Many of the shots found their true target, striking vitals all across *Europae*'s hull, but just as many punctured *Bellus*, firing through the loyalist ship as if it were some cursory piece of cover to be disintegrated.

Ideon's primary heart stammered with shock as laser fire tore turrets and minarets from the deck of *Bellus*. His head jerked on old, unused muscles in his neck, the tiny motion the first he had made with it in decades. The captain made eye-contact with Solus and saw the mute accusation in his second's gaze, then a plasma conduit burst behind him and Ideon watched Solus become a shrieking human torch.

'Return fire,' he roared above the din, the shout running into distorted crackle through his implanted voxcoder.

'Which target?' asked the gun-servitor, the dull voice at odds with the violent emotions of the battle.

'All of them,' Ideon demanded, and *Bellus* fired every gun at once, growing spines of laser light and missile fire.

* * *

RAFEN'S SKILL WITH the jump pack was hardly a match for the trained battle-brothers of the assault squads, but it was enough to guide him over the dense heart of the fighting, skipping him off the ground in steep, loping arcs of orange flame. He twisted nimbly in mid-air, avoiding the bright streaks of missiles and red bolts of laser fire. At the zenith of a leap from a broken battlement, his sight captured a glint of shining gold and brilliant white.

He skipped off the ground, sparing a moment to shoot dead a helot soldier, then powered back into the air. He spun and turned, became a guided missile himself. Rafen let the thruster pack spew flame and aim him at the cored remains of a cathedral. Only the stone walls remained, the places where great arcs of stained glass once stood now open, wailing mouths. The roof was gone, swept away by some long-faded detonation shock wave, and the endless rush of the rain cascaded over broken teeth of stone. Statues headless, bisected and shattered lined the aisles and transepts. In places, the mosaic floor had collapsed into the crypts below.

Rafen landed in a hiss of sparks from his boots and there, half-cloaked in the shadows of a huge granite altar, he saw a white spread of wings.

'Arkio.' His voice carried the length of the ruined hall. 'This must end now.'

With deliberation, his brother turned to face him, the golden armour emerging from the darkness. Where he had been wounded, a creeping purple-black bloodstain flowed like living oil across his torso. There were tiny pearls of dark matter disfiguring Arkio's face and neck. 'Yes,' he intoned. 'It must.'

And suddenly the dark was banished by a violent surge of yellow lightning as the Spear of Telesto shook into life.

CHAPTER TWELVE

BILE ROSE IN Rafen's throat as he laid eyes on his brother. The alabaster skin of his face, the noble patrician lines were distorted in subtle and cruel ways. 'What have you become?' he asked his sibling.

Arkio eyed him coldly. 'Your better, Rafen. The superior to all living things.' The rain spattered around him as he walked out of the shadows and across the church's ruined nave. 'I have banished all doubts.' He threw a cursory gesture at the altar behind him.

Sheet lightning flashed and illuminated the transept. Rafen gasped as he saw the remains of a statue of the Emperor, beheaded by a single stroke of the Holy Lance. 'Does your blasphemy know no bounds?' he said, shaking with anger, 'It is not enough that you go against your kin and your Chapter, but now you turn your back on the God-Emperor himself?'

Arkio made a lazy gesture with the humming spear. 'What need have I for gods when I am one myself?'

'You are deluded.' Rafen stabbed a finger at Arkio's side,

where the sword cut he had inflicted still festered. 'If you are a god, then why do you bleed like a man? Or perhaps, not a man... Perhaps a warp-touched thing, a pawn of Chaos.'

Arkio threw back his head and laughed. The bitter humour echoed off the broken walls. 'Chaos?' He threw the word aside. 'A childish label for something you could never understand.'

'I understand enough,' Rafen shouted back at him. 'My brother, my blood kinsman has been poisoned by the warp. Stele led you to this.' He brandished his sword. 'Recant, Arkio. While there is still time.'

The golden figure spread his arms wide and the wings on his back flowed open in a rush of wind. 'This is not heresy, and I will not recant,' he snarled. 'My eyes are open, brother. I know it all now... Men and monsters, order and Chaos...' He pointed the spear at the sky. 'Just words. There is no right and wrong, no black and white. Only the strong... and the weak.'

'And what am I?'

Arkio ignored him. 'I will not bend my knee to the Golden Throne or the Dark Gods. I pay fealty to no one!' He cocked his head, the metallic sun-shaped halo behind his head glittering in the spear's glow. 'This galaxy will fall to me... I will be the master.'

'It will not,' Rafen grated. His fingers tightened around the hilt of his sword.

Arkio's eyes flashed. 'Then I will burn it to ashes, blind every star, cull every life that defies me.'

There was no hesitation in his brother's face, not an iota of doubt within him. The ironclad certainty of Arkio's words took Rafen's breath away. 'You are mad.'

'Am I?' He drew the words out into a sigh. 'We'll see.'

Red flame exploded from Rafen's jump pack, blasting him forward, fire licking at the walls of the shattered chancel. Arkio moved so fast he faded into a yellow-white blur, both of them closing the distance down the aisle in heartbeats.

They collided with such force that the impact blew down an ornate colonnade, both of them spinning away from the point of impact on headlong trajectories. Arkio's wings unfurled and he skipped off a broken column, thundering back at Rafen. His brother clipped a wall, and used a hissing jet of thrust to mimic his opponent's manoeuvre. They met again in mid-air over the nave and flashed past each other, blades glittering.

Rafen let out a roar of pain as the hot apex of the lance ran a slice through his thigh, drawing a fan of blood. Arkio wobbled and broke through an obelisk as Rafen's power sword severed the linkage cables on his right shoulder pad, but missed his flesh. The gold hemisphere of metal and ceramite armour spun away and clattered into the shadows. Thin processor fluids leaked down his arm and the cut plastiform musculature twitched.

Rafen landed hard and opened fire with his bolt pistol, thumbing the selector to full automatic fire. Shells crashed from the muzzle of the gun, shedding spent casings in a fountain of gleaming brass. The hot casings clattered to the stone floor, buzzing as they struck the gathering puddles of rainwater. Arkio swooped and looped between the remnants of columns and arcing roof supports, Rafen's shots chewing chunks of ancient masonry from the frame of the church. He bracketed his brother with a hail of bullets, a few lucky rounds kissing his armour and keening away in orange gouts of sparks.

Arkio closed the distance, swinging the spear in a figure of eight that left bright after-images on Rafen's retina. The Blood Angel deftly changed tack, dropping back the pistol to present the power sword. He stood his ground as Arkio dove down at him, waiting for the moment of change when the winged figure would telegraph his attack.

Arkio's face opened in a snarl and he rode the lance like a jousting knight, aiming it directly at the centre of his brother's torso. Rafen bit back a grim sneer and faded into the move, turning, spinning, clashing the sword's bright blade against the adamantium tip of the spear. The blow pushed him back, striking grit and sparks from the stones under his feet, darts of bright light blazing where blade kissed blade. Arkio followed through on the strike with a reversal, sweeping the blunt end of the spear around to catch his legs and trip him. Rafen squeezed the thruster pack control in the palm of his glove for a fraction of a second and let a spurt of flame throw him clear. He flipped in a somersault and landed on a ledge, presenting the bolt pistol again. Rafen emptied the rest of the ammunition clip toward his brother, and Arkio skipped to the side, dodging between the low bulks of burial crypts and monuments.

The golden figure let out braying, harsh laughter as the rounds harmlessly spent themselves on stonework and pavement. Arkio turned on his heel and thrust the Holy Lance at Rafen, willing the weapon to release the powerful energies humming inside it. For the briefest second, the spear seemed to obey him, glowing brightly as a ball of honeyed lightning gathered at the end of the teardrop blade. Rafen sprang from his ledge, skipping off a fallen granite eagle to another naked support beam. Arkio followed him and goaded his weapon to unleash its killing force, but once more the Spear of Telesto shifted in his grip, rolling about its length. It jerked through his fingers as if it were trying to escape him.

'No!' Arkio spat, and in his anger he swung the errant weapon around him in an arc of light, slashing through two support columns and a broken statue. The spear moaned and shuddered. 'You cannot deny me,' Arkio thundered. 'I am your master!' Thick, poisoned spittle flew from his lips in his fury, and his regal face contorted. Scars emerged from his cheeks and forehead, weeping thick oil, bringing with them the hard pearls of black mutation. Arkio seemed unaware of them as they wriggled and moved beneath the surface of his skin, shifting like burrowing beetles.

His instant of rage brought distraction with it, and Rafen exploited the error to the fullest. Slamming home a fresh sickle magazine of bolt-rounds, Arkio's brother threw himself off the stone stanchion and dropped, unloading the gun in a roaring blaze of gunfire. The reports of the bolt-shells came so close together they merged into a ripping snarl of noise. Arkio brought up the spear to deflect them a heartbeat too late, and the discharge struck him in the chest. The white-hot impacts staggered him backward in jerks of motion, the thick bolts ripping long shreds of golden armour from him. Ceramite fragmented and plasteel broke away, crazing the coating of precious yellow metal.

Arkio reacted with a growling shout of annoyance and shook himself, discarding bits of spent armour clinging to his arms and his chest. Through holes cored in the plates, dusky liquids bubbled and flowed. The mark of Stele's taint was no longer concealed within the prison of his flesh. Released by the wanton hate that churned in Arkio's mind, the changed aspect of the Space Marine was revealed.

Rafen felt physically sick at the sight of his brother. The foetor of him strangled the Blood Angel's senses, and the revelation of a body irredeemably tainted by Chaos was an affront to everything he stood for. Rafen willed himself to forget that some last piece of his blood brother's soul might still survive behind that warped face, and attacked again.

Arkio was ready for him. The winged figure spun the lance and met Rafen's sword with a thunderous strike, shattering the blade of the power weapon. Rafen snarled as he felt his wrist dislocate in the impact. The shock threw him back against a fragmented piece of stained glass as Arkio reared up before him.

The flash of lightning reflected Arkio's twisted face in the age-worn glass. 'Look at yourself!' Rafen shouted. 'Look at what you have become!'

Arkio swung the spear and shattered the glass forever. 'Fool.' he bellowed. 'I know what I am! *I AM SANGUINIUS!*'

Rafen tried to dodge the blow he knew was coming, but it hit him like a falling meteor. One cut slashed across his chest, striking his armour; the second came from the blunt

pommel and it sent him crashing to the ground. The Blood
Angel struck the mosaic floor with a crash of sound and the
stonework gave way beneath him.

He tumbled into a black void and landed hard, the
breath singing out of his lungs. Air wheezed through his
chest accompanied by rips of pain and his vision fogged. Is
this death, he wondered, at last? His fingers traced the
shapes of something familiar, and in the dimness he
glimpsed the forms of skeletons. Hundreds of them – but
not human ones. These were larger, stockier. With a start he
understood: Arkio's blow had thrown him into a crypt for
Sabien's war dead, where the Blood Angels who died
defending the planet had been interred. About the walls of
the sepulchre were stone carvings of Space Marines. In the
shadows they towered over him like a granite honour
guard, mute and strong.

Rafen scrambled to his feet, ignoring the pain. All about
him were his brethren, dead for centuries in this desolate,
lonely place. A single thought burned in his brain: I will
not join them! The fury of it raced through him, igniting
an inferno in his veins. The broken sword dropped from
his fingers and he clenched his fist, feeling hot anger pour
into him. From the edges of his vision came something
bright and powerful, a glow of infinite perfection. For one
moment, he thought Arkio had followed him into the
crypt, but the light of it outshone even his brother in his
most omnipotent moment. Rafen looked up and saw the
true face of his liege lord filling the air before him, the
gene-kindred in his blood manifesting itself to him. The
vision overwhelmed him, blocking out all pain, all hesitation. *Sanguinius!*

A rage so pure it burnt white-hot swelled in Rafen's heart,
and the red thirst overtook him.

A FRESH WAVE of hooting, horned monstrosities joined the
mad throng of the ground battle, blades and guns shouting
in the clash. The square was a seething ocean of red shades,
crimson fighting against ruby, incarnadine versus scarlet,

moving and shifting in bloody tides. Mephiston and his troops ranged in a tight crescent about the remains of their Thunderhawks, pressing forward their attacks with grim determination and cold, cold rage. They faced the wild zealots of Arkio's slave army, and although the Shenlongi helots carried weapons that were mere toys in comparison to the arms of the Adeptus Astartes, the sheer weight of their numbers and the mad passion of their fervour were staggering. The warriors would not surrender or retreat. Only attrition would thin their thousand-strong horde into defeat.

The adherents of Arkio's church stood by Space Marines loyal to the Reborn Angel, but in this small number of red-armoured men the seeds of doubt and misgiving grew large. Many of them found themselves hesitant to fire on their own kind, and they became lost in the sea of conflict. Worse still, the men who had bent their knee to take Arkio's oath were shocked by the arrival of a new force of allies upon the battlefield, ruby-coloured figures who seemed to be fighting not against them, but with them. Word Bearers.

Delos saw the dark shapes of the Chaos Space Marines and felt his gut churn with revulsion. The optics of his death's-head helmet streamed with rainwater and spatters of mud as he fought to clear them. For a moment, he thought he had seen Inquisitor Stele actually standing toe to toe with a monstrous Word Bearer, then the raging mob had obscured his view and the Chaplain found himself pressed against a fallen wall. The weight of his ceremonial crozius arcanium was dead in his hand, desultory glimmers of energy fizzing around the device's ornate skeletal carvings. The weapon mirrored his mood sullen and uncertain. The Chaplain grasped it in his mailed fist and spoke a silent prayer to his God-Emperor. If what Delos had seen was correct, then the man who had been the architect of the Reborn Angel's Ascension was consorting with humanity's vilest enemy. He had to be mistaken. He *had* to be. The alternative explanation made him feel dizzy with dread and horror.

* * *

PIECES OF GOLD and tatters of blackened purity parchments
fell away from Arkio's wargear, leaving scored metal below.
The artificer armour, once unsullied and flawless, was now
webbed with scratches and scars. Yellow flecks streamed
into the wind like a dust storm, and the crazed blemishes
seemed to shift and move in the half-light, tricks of the eye
making them into vicious maws and screaming faces. New,
inhuman muscles bulged beneath Arkio's chest, and his
wings beat hard to hold him in a hover. The inky stain of
his wound was grey and pallid, lines of toxin threading
into the pinions and feathers, mottling them.

The very smallest glimmer of regret formed in Arkio's
mind as he stared down at the yawning crater in the crypt,
and he stamped on it mercilessly. No, Rafen would not be
graced with a moment more of his attention. His trouble-
some brother was ended, and at last Arkio had the freedom
he had coveted in the dark corners of his soul since childhood.

A low moan, a raw and feral sound, issued up from the
void in the stone floor. It sent the Spear of Telesto twitching
in his hands once more, as the weapon writhed and shuddered. The sky whitened as lightning flashed daybreak-bright
around him, and the dazzle picked out a man-shape in glistening crimson below. On wings of jet fire, Rafen punched
into the air and struck Arkio with all his might.

He caught his brother by surprise, and the Blood Angel
felt his bones ring with the impact as they hit. Arkio spat
out a strangled yell of anger as they flew up into the thick
grey clouds. Rain and wind lashed at their faces from the
oily banks of vapour, buffeting them. They exchanged
blows, Arkio struggling to regain the advantage, unable to
bring out the spear to strike back at so close an aggressor.
Lightning shrieked close to them, the hot ozone of tormented air searing Rafen's lungs. In the flash of
illumination, he saw new lines of the black seed-boils
emerging along Arkio's cheekbones, arranged there like ritual scarifications. His eyes were shaded with the purest,
darkest hate.

Rafen fought to bring his bolt pistol to bear, squeezing off a salvo of shots. Shells sizzled off Arkio in mad ricochets, some cutting out divots of necrotic flesh, others deflecting from the pieces of armour that still clung to his brother's changed torso. Arkio made a wordless sound of raw rage and snatched at the handgun, his fingers forming a fist around the blocky metal shape. He grabbed the weapon and crushed it to powder in a bony grip. Rafen cried out as his fingers snapped.

Arkio batted him away with a languid backhand, sending Rafen on a wild course as the rockets in his jump pack spat and laboured to keep him aloft. The winged figure turned after his target, in the clouded shadows, his aspect like an angel of death. He tried to aim the Holy Lance after Rafen, but the weapon resisted him. It bent and bowed as he pulled on it, as if the spear was frozen in the air. 'Obey me!' he shouted, yanking ferociously at the haft. 'I am your master!'

In his rage, the darkness hidden inside Arkio came flooding to the surface, the sullen beauty of his countenance shifting into an aspect as thunderous as the clouds about him. The change raced through him, down to the molecular level, the cells of the blood hammering in his veins blackening. Cradled in his grip, the potent technologies of the Spear of Telesto tasted Arkio, sampled him through the genome sensors threaded into the weapon's ornate haft. Ancient science awoke in the lance, so far removed from the advancements of the Imperium as to border on magic. It knew Arkio then, as it had known him in the first moment he laid hands on it – and this time the spear found him wanting.

It rebelled. The scent of Chaos was black and thick in the Reborn Angel, and the Telesto weapon went white-hot in his grip, melting the mastercrafted gauntlets to muddy gold slag. The pain was instant and heartstopping, and by sheer animal reaction Arkio released the burning lance, superheated steam hissing from the burning tissues of his hands. Tumbling end over end, the Spear of Telesto fell toward the ground, lightning catching the teardrop blade, wind whipping the purity seals.

The weapon landed like a thrown javelin, the blunt pommel at the shaft's end cracking the stones of the church floor as it struck them. Whirring with power, the spear came to rest upright, a naked standard in defiance of the forces that had tried to abuse it.

Overhead, Arkio swept toward his brother with his ruined hands opening into claws, the madness of kill-lust in his gaze. His rage was titanic now, and with it he would rip his sibling to shreds, spear or no spear.

Rafen shook off the dizziness threatening to wrap him in its coils and brought up his fists in a fighting stance. He bobbed as his thruster pack choked and coughed. The Blood Angel dared not chance a look at the repeater gauge about his wrist cuff for fear it would confirm what he suspected already – the jet pack was starving of fuel and damaged, and he had only moments of flight left before he fell back into the embrace of Sabien's gravity.

He blinked rainwater from his lashes as Arkio fell upon him, and then once more the two siblings were locked in a tumbling embrace, wrestling amid the storm with nothing but footless halls of air surrounding them. Arkio viciously kicked Rafen where the spear had cut a line through the flesh of his thigh, cracking open the wound again where Rafen's Astartes blood had already begun to clot. He howled and butted his brother in the face, gaining the reward of a fan of oily vitae gushing from Arkio's flaring nostrils. A flurry of punches danced across Rafen's ribcage as impacts dented his ceramite chest guard. He tasted the hot copper of his own blood as the blows rattled his teeth in his head.

Rafen clutched at his brother, raking his fingers down the thick skin over his hairless chest. The mailed red fingers of his battle gloves drew scars across the pallid and gaunt tissue; runnels of tainted blood gathered at wounds where hard marbles the shade of space protruded. He flailed as Arkio crushed him to his breast in a crippling bear hug.

Rafen heard his bones breaking with the pressure. His Space Marine physiology made him and his kind uniquely aware of their own bodies, so it was with certainty that Rafen sensed the biscopea organ in his chest burst as his ribs pressed in on it. He was bleeding internally in a number of places.

A blink of white sheet lightning turned his world into a washed-out sketch, just lines and impressions dazzling his enhanced vision. Leering out of the blindness came Arkio's twisted face, framed by the halo about his neck and the beating tides of his mottled grey wings. The sound and the fury of the thunderstorm swept away his younger brother's words, but Rafen could still read the declaration of hate on his lips:

You will die.

There was a word that no Blood Angel would ever choose to speak. It was a cognomen that their enemies and detractors had used since the day Sanguinius took up the Emperor's cause. The name was as old as Terra herself, born from times before men strode the stars, forged in the fears of superstitious hearts. It conjured all the deepest terrors of beasts that feasted upon life and bore the fangs of a blood-letter.

Vampire.

Arkio's mouth split into a smile as wide as his face, a forest of needle-sharp canine teeth blooming from his jaws. He became the avatar of the Blood Angels darkest and most horrific aspect, a monstrous parody of the predator legend. Rafen's brother was crushing the life from him, his last breaths of air escaping in choking, wheezing gasps. As the wind and rain lashed about the tumbling pair, Rafen felt his fury rise as Arkio's hot breath tickled his skin. The winged Angel pressed into him, his red maw of a mouth hungry to tear the meat from Rafen's neck and feast on the hot gush of pulsing life within.

'No!' he roared in defiance. Vision fogging, grey tunnels coiling around his sight, Rafen once again teetered on the abyss of death; and once more, he refused to yield to it.

His hands moved though motions drilled into the marrow of his bones by countless turns of muscle-memory, fingers finding and clasping the hilt of his fractal-bladed close combat weapon. The Space Marine knife had not differed appreciably in its design since the earliest days of the Imperium, the monomolecular edges of the Sol-pattern weapon as familiar to Rafen as they would have been to the first Adeptus Astartes ten thousand years earlier. Yet for all its age, the knife was no less lethal.

Rafen struck violently, bringing the weapon about and thrusting upward into the spaces between his brother's ribs. The knife slid on slick, matted skin and fell into the mouldering wound he had given Arkio in the square. He pressed the blade into the writhing, maggot-infested cut, all the way to the steel hilt.

From Arkio's empurpled lips came a scream of inchoate pain that parted the clouds around them with its force. Suddenly, it was no longer Arkio's beating wings that kept the locked pair in the air, but the chattering, dying thrust from Rafen's assault pack. The grey-white sails fluttered and curled as Arkio's fingers dug into Rafen's wargear, slipping over rain-slick ceramite.

Lightning blazed a strobe image on to Rafen's retina, freezing the instant there in shades of white, orange and purple. He saw agony on Arkio's face the like of which he had never encountered upon any battlefield, and a word, a single word, on his sibling's lips.

Brother.

Arkio's hands skidded away from purchase and his weight detached itself from Rafen in a whirl of streaming rain and falling feathers. He snapped out his arm, fingers reaching to scrape the gold sheaths on his shoulders, missing as Arkio drew away, sinking through the low blanket of boiling grey cloud. Rafen's brother, the Blessed, the Reborn Angel, the Deus Sanguinius, tumbled away like a downed prey bird, falling to earth.

Below, amid the shining wet cobbles and glistening mosaics of the ruined church's nave, the Spear of Telesto sensed him coming. The upright weapon twitched and jerked of its own accord, shifting and turning about its axis to bring the teardrop blade to welcome him. Arkio plunged from the thunderheads and his spine found the head of the lance where his shoulder blades met, at the centre of his outstretched wings. His impact sent the fatal spear through the dense altered bones of his skeleton, bisecting his primary heart and exploding out again though his sternum. A perfectly circular hollow formed in the stonework from the force of the fall, and Arkio lay in it, his corrupted blood thinning in the deluge, casting all about him with a rich pool of purple fluids.

The tear-shaped leaf glowed with golden flickers of colour, evaporating every last drop of his vitae from its immaculate, polished surface.

THE SKY TURNED to hell.

Misericorde brought her fanged flanks to bear upon the two Blood Angels warships, unleashing salvo after salvo of heavy rockets, hull-burners and laser fire into the zone of space about them. Mephiston's flagship *Europae* had speed and motion on her side, using generous bursts of vectored thrust from her tertiary drives to turn and move beneath the sister ship *Bellus*. Spinning about its axis, *Europae* weathered the onslaught, distributing the strikes that reached the battle barge across the ship's glittering void shields.

Bellus, damaged and wounded, reacted more slowly. To the untrained eye, the two Blood Angels barges seemed identical, but at close hand the injuries and scars *Bellus* carried were raw and obvious. *Europae* was fresh from Baal's orbital docks, fully crewed, perfectly maintained and at the peak of her performance; by contrast *Bellus* was tired and worn. The engagement over Sabien was just one more battle in a string of conflicts that the old warship had weathered – the wounds from the fight against the cruiser *Dirge Eterna* at Shenlong, the battleship *Ogre Lord* at Cybele and even the lasting lacerations from the mission into ork space, all of them took their toll on the *Bellus*. She was strung out and hobbled in comparison to her adversaries.

From his command throne, Captain Ideon opened up his ship like a shattered hive of hornets, releasing every weapon and warshot at once. About the barge, space became a clogged web of fire and destruction, heat haze and spheres of detonation falling off *Bellus* in radiant waves. 'Report,' he demanded, automatically turning his attention to Brother Solus's station, but Solus was dead, heaped there in a mess of plasma-seared meat and ceramite. The stink of human flesh came to the captain in a dozen different ways through the senses of the ship's machine-spirit.

Over the crashing din of secondary explosions, a sense-servitor babbled out a reply. 'Multiple critical hits along starboard hull. Breaches on fifty-two per cent of decks. Engineers report imminent collapse of the fusion core's spirit-monitor.'

'Bow guns,' he roared, thrusting his consciousness through the cybernetic links in his skull to touch the powerful ship-killer cannons in *Bellus*'s prow.

The servitor answered even as the question formed in Ideon's thoughts. 'Inoperative. Crew loss due to atmospheric venting.' The mind-wiped slave chattered in a flat monotone, as if it were discussing something no more vexing than a change in weather.

Ideon glimpsed the ragged metal where the bow of *Bellus* used to be, the tide of fragments and vacuum-bloated corpses streaming out into the black. Hate building inside him, the captain drew every last piece of the ship's offensive capability together and held it in his mind. His normally immobile form on the control throne was rocking back and forth, twitching like a palsy victim from the force of his anger. A strange, inhuman noise threaded out of his vox-coder, the peculiar ululation crossing the din of the bridge. Ideon willingly let himself fall into the screaming embrace of the black rage, his mind disintegrating into the madness of race memories from thousands of years past.

'Kill them all!' crackled the metallic voice.

Europae's patience was at an end, and with unrestrained force she opened fire with every weapon at her disposal, crossing the orbital range to punish *Bellus* for the perfidy of its crew and *Misericorde* for the crime of daring to sully the Emperor's space. In turn, the Chaos warship spat hate back at the Blood Angels, pouring it into the darkness until the emptiness was thick with radiation.

Bellus lay between them, striking out at everything and nothing around it, a mad wounded beast alive with pain and the smell of death. Arkio's flagship was caught in the crossfire of the battle and fell into the hellstorm. In the absolute silence of the void, *Bellus* detonated, breaking into huge splinters of steel, her fusion reactor giving birth to an instant new sun.

On the planet below, the light of her death was lost in the thick clouds.

RAFEN'S THRUSTER PACK ran dry when he was still a thirty metres from the ground, and he tumbled and dropped as if he were made of lead. Slamming his balled fist into the release switch on his belt, he felt the dead weight of the pack detach, and freed of the burden he turned into a spin, crashing through age-rotted beams to land with a bone-jarring crack of sound. A ring of water scattered away from him in a ripple. From his kneeling stance, Rafen rose, his eyes narrowed against the biting winds. He scanned the interior of the church, afraid of what he would see.

And there he saw it.

Pinned to the stone as a gigantic collector might exhibit some rare moth or butterfly, Arkio lay with the Spear of Telesto run through him. All about his sibling was a spreading aurora the colour of autumn, a most unearthly golden light. Favouring his injured leg, Rafen jogged across the transept and came to Arkio's side.

'Brother…'

Rafen gasped in amazement; despite so brutal an injury, Arkio still clung to life with fierce tenacity. His sibling's hands were clasped the haft of the spear, the burning glow crisping away the flesh. Arkio seemed not to notice the pain.

'Brother,' Rafen repeated, searching his sibling's face for the shroud of contamination. Arkio seemed as ruined as the shattered landscape of the city-shrine about them, hollow inside. The black trains of poison boils still seethed beneath his marbled skin, but his eyes... his eyes belonged to the Arkio that Rafen remembered from their youth, the naïve and bold soul that had given him strength and loyalty.

There was pain there, of a kind Rafen had only ever seen in the eyes of sinners and turncoats fallen to the law of the Inquisition. Before, he had never questioned it, but now he saw it for what it was. Regret, so powerful and so heartbreaking that the emotion could barely be contained by a human will.

'*What have I done?*' Arkio rasped, holding his brother's gaze. 'I have broken every compact and promise... I have turned my back on what I am and embraced the void...' He shuddered and wailed. 'Oh, Lord Emperor, I have betrayed all I hold dear.'

His hate-rage ebbing, Rafen found only one answer in the echoing chasms of his heart. 'Yes.'

The humming of the spear gently rose and fell in the fading rhythm of Arkio's secondary heart. Each peak and trough grew longer as life ebbed from him into the stones and the rain. 'I was weak...' he managed. 'I thought I could protect myself from this–' he gestured feebly and his wings jerked in response, '–from falling from the path. My arrogance... I... I believed I was... believed it...'

'I am sorry, Arkio,' Rafen said, silent tears falling from his eyes, drawing lines in dark smears of blood and soot on his cheeks. 'I am sorry I was not there to stand with you, turn you from this corruption.'

'No,' Arkio whispered. 'You share no burden with me, kinsman. I will bear this stigma...' He shivered, a drool of blood escaping from his lips. 'My error. I was weak...'

'Arkio, no… You were… human.'

He forced a wan smile. 'Fear not, Rafen. This is our fate. Both of us saw it.'

Rafen gasped. 'You knew this would be by my hand?'

'Yes. And so it was.' His ruined fingers crossed Rafen's chest plate and touched his brother's cheek. 'You weep for me? That is all I ask, kinsman. The Emperor will damn me for my folly, and I accept that without question… But you… I ask *you* to forgive me. I recant, Rafen. Please forgive me, my brother.'

'I forgive you, Arkio. On our father's grave, I swear it.'

Arkio gave a shallow, final nod of thanks. 'That is mercy enough.' His eyes fluttered closed, and the spear fell silent.

Rafen knelt there for an age, no sound in his ears but the rush and thunder of the rainstorm, no feeling inside him except the raw despair of loss. Finally, his heart brimming with its grievous remorse, Rafen came to his feet with his brother's body in his arms, the Holy Lance excised from the dead man and there at Rafen's shoulder. The warm, mellifluent light of the spear illuminated the ruins about him, and he held Arkio high. He seemed to weigh so little now, as if the burden of his tainted change had run away with his shed blood.

In the near distance, Rafen saw the firefly sparkles of bolter discharges, and on the wind came gunshots, screams and the chants of the Word Bearers. The Blood Angel's face set in grim determination and he advanced toward the fighting. He left nothing behind him but his doubts.

CHAPTER THIRTEEN

CURIOUS, THOUGHT MEPHISTON, how the passage of time became elastic in the throes of conflict. He skewered a Word Bearer and the helot soldier behind him with one swift thrust of the mindblade Vitarus, the force sword immolating them both in gusts of blue flame. Flicking the remains away, he frowned. How long had he been fighting? Crashing thunder bellowed overhead, announcing the flashes of sheet lighting that illuminated the writhing fighters in the square. Rain pelted everything, sluicing off the blood of enemy and ally alike, churning the brick dust and dirt on the ground into a muddy brown quagmire. It was difficult for the Librarian to know exactly how long the battle had been raging; every sword blow and bolt shell seemed to pass in its own small bubble of time, one single instant in the huge cacophony of wanton slaughter. Minutes, hours… it could have been days for all the Lord of Death cared. He was in his element here, an engine of destruction fuelled by the holiest of causes.

He caught the sound of a man's scream, suddenly truncated by the ripping of flesh and sinew. Mephiston whirled to see the golden helmet of a Blood Angels honour guard – one of Arkio's loyalists – sent flying by the blow of the veteran sergeant who had accompanied the pskyer from *Europae*. The Marine staggered back, shaking gore from the clogged blades of his chainsword. He caught Mephiston's eye and spared him a grim nod.

The Librarian did not need to employ his psychic skills to read the Blood Angel's mind. This was a sorry, dismal business, being forced to take up arms against men who were battle-brothers. The Lord of Death was sickened by what he and the others had been forced into, and he cursed Arkio and Stele for bringing it to pass. It was enough to purge the galaxy of turncoats and traitors, but to face men who had willingly forsaken their oath to Dante and Baal in favour of some pretender child made Mephiston weary and hateful. For each errant Blood Angel he slew, the psyker spoke a short prayer to the Golden Throne. He did not forgive these men their misjudgements, instead he tallied them as crimes to lay at the feet of Ramius Stele, the architect of this madness. However fate unfolded on this day, Mephiston vowed that the accursed Hereticus fool would not leave Sabien alive.

The sergeant fell back a dozen steps as he reloaded his bolter, before firing again into the mass of raging zealots. 'Bah!' he spat, taking three men with pinpoint head shots. 'These fools don't know the meaning of the word "retreat". We cut them down like wheat and still they come.'

Mephiston strode forward, Vitarus ending lives in sweeps of bright power. 'The wheat dares not oppose the scythe.' For every one of the Warriors of the Reborn trampled into the mud and earth, there were two more behind him, desperate for the glory of death in their messiah's name – or just loathsome enough not to care. Here and there he saw Word Bearers in tightly drilled units, and those he could not see he heard, their foul demagogues spouting dirges and songs of unhallowed praise to the Maelstrom. The

Chaos Marines took their fury to the Blood Angels, attacking Mephiston's men and Arkio's loyalists alike, ignoring the helots unless the humans were foolish enough to block their lines of fire.

'Red foes, red friends,' snapped the veteran. 'Who is the enemy here, lord?'

'Everyone,' the psyker replied, burning down a dozen more wayward souls with his screeching plasma pistol. 'This is not battle, this is chaos.'

Mephiston's Techmarine thrust his way through the morass of dead and dying, stumbling into ankle-deep pools of fluid. He killed a helot armed only with a sharpened spanner, punching through his ribcage, and threw the dead body aside. 'Lord!' he called as he approached. 'Lord Mephiston.'

Bolter fire in careful, targeted ranks ranged down on them from the middle of the enemy throng, where Word Bearers were marshalling a concerted effort. The Librarian threw back the power of the Smite, a psychic tornado ripping across the square to dismember them.

The Techmarine blinked away the after-glare of the blast and gave a jerky bow. 'My lord, we have but two Thunderhawks remaining and neither can make lift-off. The Word Bearers have six squads pinning them down. I spotted Havoc troopers in their number, although they have not attempted to destroy the transports yet.'

'They want the ships for themselves. What news from orbit?'

Gunfire drew their attention and all three of them fired back at a group of helots armed with civilian hunting lasers. 'Communication is intermittent at best,' continued the Blood Angel. 'High levels of radiation in the ionosphere prevent clear vox transmissions.'

'Radiation?' growled the sergeant. 'From what?'

'*Bellus* has been destroyed, lord,' the Techmarine said dispassionately. 'A fragmentary vox from *Europae* appears to confirm that the loyalist's ship was obliterated in the crossfire between our barge and the *Misericorde*.'

Mephiston shook his head angrily. 'Such waste. Such foolish, pointless waste.'

The Space Marine gestured with a signum, complex lines of data glyphs and warning runes marching across the device's rain-slick screen. 'We are outnumbered on the ground. Force disposition of the loyalists is weak but they overmatch us with the reinforcements of the Word Bearers.' To his surprise, the Lord of Death accepted this dire information with a clinical smile; he was unfazed by the sensor's divination. On the contrary, he seemed to expect it.

'With *Bellus* out of the picture, we can forget calling reserves from *Europae*,' grated the sergeant, shaking rain off his visor. 'They'll have their hands full with the Chaos ship, won't even be able to risk 'porting us more men. We're on our own down here.'

'As it ever was,' Mephiston added. 'So be it.' The psyker toggled a control in the collar of his arching hood and spoke into one of the bone-white skulls that decorated the throat of his armour, where a vox-unit was concealed. 'Blood Angels, rally!' he snapped, the command filtering out to the ear-beads of every man from the *Europae*. 'Your previous orders to contain this rabble no longer apply. Join the fray and leave no foe standing.'

'Aye. *Aye*!' came the replies over the channel.

Mephiston threw himself into the throng, leaving behind the hillock of rubble and stone he had defended to wade deep in the gore of his adversaries. He showed sharp fangs and eyes of fire as death rained down around him, red floods of it flashing in the air.

'Terra and God-Emperor,' breathed the veteran, as he watched the Librarian shred the unwary foes. 'He's not a man, he's a storm with a sword.'

ELSEWHERE IN THE morass, the pell-mell melee moved and shifted like a viral organism, swallowing up those that did not go with the army's flow, killing those that defied it. Delos waded through a sea of angry faces and weeping wounded, all of them merging into one pale orchestra of ghosts, eyes upturned to the grey raging sky, crying to their Blessed. The Chaplain moved among them, a black shining shadow with a grinning skull head. They flinched and recoiled from his crozius as he waved it before him, some of them automatically genuflecting toward an icon of Sanguinius, others hissing in pain as if the sight of it hurt their eyes.

A tinny rattle about his head announced the passage of a metallic servo-skull and Delos knew he was close. There, just a few lengths away, Inquisitor Stele stood in on the crest of a subsided stone dais. At his feet, shivering under a wet, matted cloak, his lexmechanic rocked back and forth, constantly babbling a endless string of words in thousands of Imperial dialects. Delos caught something of his speech when the wind changed for a moment, bringing it to his ears.

'–demnos, dannavik, dorius, delenz, dorcon, daemon, dethenex, dynikas–'

The inquisitor's servo-skulls continually described a lazy orbit around him, occasionally pausing to lance a laser bolt into a target they deemed a threat to Stele. The woman was there as well, never more than a hand's length from him, the lines of her face hiding beneath a voluminous hood. The habit she wore was cut like an astropath's, but she was anything but one of those. Delos was not cursed with the warp eye of psykers but he didn't need to be to smell the stink of the empyrean on the girl. He shook the nauseating perfume of it from his head. Odd how he had never noticed that about her before.

Gripping his crozius arcanum firmly, Delos forced himself up to the dais, his skull-helmet's sneer matching Stele's. 'Inquisitor,' he demanded. 'By the Blessed, I demand you account for yourself.'

Stele arched an eyebrow. 'Chaplain… Delos, isn't it?' He wiped a patina of rain from his bald skull. 'Leave me. I must prepare–'

'For what?' Delos shouted, startling himself with his own forcefulness. 'Tell me my eyes deceived me, Stele! Tell me it was but a mind-trick of Mephiston's!'

'What trivia are you chattering about?' Stele retorted, his attention elsewhere. He glanced at Ulan. 'The boy, the boy! Where is he?'

The psy-witch shook her head, her mind full of razors. 'Difficult….'

'I saw you and the Word Bearer.' In a blink of lightning, Delos saw something shadowing Stele's face; not a wraith or a spirit, but a haze of lines crossing and re-crossing. Eight arrows arranged in a ring. 'It is true,' Delos said, 'you consort with the corrupted!'

Stele grimaced and fixed him with a glare. 'First Sachiel and now you? This conflict is taxing me too much. Things are slipping through the gaps–'

'*Traitor!*' Delos roared, bringing up the crozius to strike the inquisitor.

'Better that than a fool.' Stele raised a hand and a column of pressure shoved Delos in the chest, pushing him back, knocking the power weapon from his grip. The air around him became dry and greasy, the rain fizzing away. Invisible tendrils of psychic force coiled about the Chaplain and slipped through molecule-thin gaps in his armour to touch his bare skin.

'The twisting path,' Stele said, leering at the kneeling Blood Angel. 'Take the path, Delos. *Take it.*'

His mind flayed open and Delos screamed, clawing at his helmet, tearing it from his head. The Chaplain saw his world fall apart around him; he watched a mirror of his life to come as he tore off his allegiance to the Emperor (*I would never do such a thing!*) as he slaughtered Dante and burned Baal's cities (*No! No! This is not true!*) as he fell, laughing with cruel abandon, into the embrace of Chaos (*No!*).

Stele broke off the mental assault and spat on his twitching victim. 'Never question me,' he growled. The inquisitor grabbed at Ulan's arm, pulling her to him. 'I won't ask again! Where is Arkio?'

'Dead.' She drew the word out into a howl.

The inquisitor's face went purple with rage. His jaw worked but no words came to him. Anger robbed him of a voice, and instead he struck out with a balled fist, back-handing the psyker-slave. Ulan stumbled and dropped to her knees, the hood about her head falling to her shoulders. Her pale and hairless pate with its tarnished brass sockets glittered dully. Overhead, the silver skull drones popped in tiny explosions.

Stele gave an incoherent roar of annoyance, the muscles in his neck bunching in tense ropes. 'That worthless, stupid fool. It wasn't enough that he could accept the gifts I gave him, he had to bury himself in the part.' He pulled at the skin of his face, barely able to contain the quaking rage inside him. 'All of it ruined by that pathetic whelp. My plans are ashes now, my greatest performance destroyed by his arrogance!'

'But... but that was why you chose him...' Ulan spat out blood and a broken piece of tooth. 'You wanted a man who could *be* Sanguinius–'

'I wanted a figurehead,' snarled Stele, 'A gaudy token messiah, not a corpse.'

Ulan shakily got to her feet. 'Perhaps he gave you a martyr instead...'

'Martyr...' The word whispered through the inquisitor's lips, a benediction, cooling his burning ire. 'I will not fail now, understand me?' he growled. 'Not now, not in the moment of my greatest triumph. I have made it my design to turn these Astartes freaks to the Banner of Change and *I will not be denied!*' Stele stripped the grox-hide battle coat from his shoulders and dashed the garment on the ground, dragging his ornate laspistol from its concealed holster. 'Plans must be accelerated,' he said. 'The turning cannot wait! It must be here and now!'

'But we are not ready...'

He ignored Ulan's warning and pressed the muzzle of his gun to the palm of his other hand. 'Open your mind to the Spite Lord, witch. Bring him. Bring him now!'

Stele jerked the trigger and the pistol blew a burning hole through his flesh, vaporising three of his fingers and setting his cuff aflame. The inquisitor screamed and clutched at his ruined hand, forcing the jetting blood from his severed veins to spatter about him in the sacred pattern he knew by heart. The geometry of the unhallowed circle came together even as he drew it.

Ulan hesitated. Stele had instructed her on the rituals that would open the conduit to the Malfallax's realm, but now the moment came to do it she found herself afraid. The psy-witch had been a slave since birth, a laboratory experiment before that, and disobedience was not part of her makeup, yet still she balked at this most dangerous command. Stele turned on her and saw the indecision in her eyes. The inquisitor snarled and grabbed her robes, dragging her close to him. The bloody meat of his hand clutched at her neck. She felt warm fluids pulsing over her skin.

'Lord, no…' She managed a weak denial.

'Open the way,' Stele shouted, and with a thrust of his arm, the lacerated fingers sank into the flesh at Ulan's collar. The pallid skin rippled like water and Stele merged his barbed digits into her bone and cartilage. The woman resisted, for what would be the first and last time in her life. It made little difference, as the inquisitor brought his undamaged fingers to her cheeks, the tips scraping away the false scars that hid the blemishes of psy-tuned metal contacts. Ulan could not scream; she could not breathe; she could only hold on and try not to die as Stele used her as a lens for his own psyker talent, magnifying his black will to cut a way into the writhing core of the Eye of Terror.

INSIDE THE NO-SPACE of the immaterium, the creature Malfallax had been waiting, floating and circling the man-filth Stele in the manner of a sea predator scenting prey in distress. Unseen by the denizens of the material world, the realm of the warp was constantly surrounding them, a layer of unreality laid across the sordid, crude matter of their wastrel worlds. The forms the live-things called Chaos, in their limited little ways of perceiving the omniverse, swarmed and thrived in this infinite ocean of mind and emotion. The daemon moved with Stele. Waiting, waiting and watching for the moment when the thrashing and chattering of the quarry was at its peak. Only then would it strike, lapping up the absolute perfection of its fear, sinking in rending teeth, tearing it to soul-shreds.

Now the prey called to him, through the conduit of the mutant abortion created by the corpse-god's science. His instrument Stele cried out for the poisoned hand of Malfallax. The warp daemon teased itself with the anticipation of the shift; it was so infrequent that the beast could find itself a vessel strong enough to contain its essence for more than a few hours. Most flesh-things in the other reality were gossamer constructs of wet, weak meats. They would burn or inflate or explode if the Malfallax issued even an iota of itself into them – but it had worked hard to prepare for this day. Malfallax, Monarch of Spite, Heirophant of Vicissitude, was weary of partial manifestations, of animating the inert or the mindless to hold a ghost of his full and awful potential. It wanted to step freely into the plane of men and run it red with their bloody terror. Malfallax missed the feel of it over there beyond the veil; it was time to return.

THE SCREAM THAT Ulan released was a sound that no human throat had ever made before. It rang from side to side of the city square, souring the deadened sky of Sabien as it passed, hammering a chill spike of terror into every life that caught the echo of it. Stele withdrew from the shaking body of the psy-witch, the oozing blood from his shattered hand wrapped about his forearm like a red glove. Mad laughter bubbled up from inside him. 'He comes!' shouted the inquisitor, the insane mix of elation and utter dread merging in his chest. Stele spread his arms in welcome as the spilt blood and mud inside the ceremonial circle bubbled and churned. 'Come to me, Void-born! Take form and heed me.'

The black-brown sludge at his feet rippled and built up upon itself, assembling the shape of a hulking figure. It grew something resembling a face and pointed it a Stele, hot coppery breath issuing from the steaming orifices. '*Sssssssssservant.*'

Ulan could not see for the blood streaming from the brass plugs in her skull or weeping in tears from ears, nose and eyes, but she knew where the creature was. The blazing power of its nova heart burned into her mind-senses. Ulan struggled to stumble away, what rationality she still had lost in a primitive desire to flee.

'Come, daemon,' Stele cried out to the mud-form. 'Bear witness with me to this victory. Take shape and release the Way of Change. The Blood Angels will turn to the glory of Tzeentch, they will know and revere him as I have always done.' He stabbed his ruined hand at the shaking woman. 'Fill this vessel and come forth!'

Ulan tripped and fell, the mud sucking at her, holding her down. She shook her head in some feeble gesture of refusal.

'*No.*' The voice was slime on cold rock. The slurry of living mire flashed forward in a wet surge, but not toward Ulan. It rose up around Stele's legs and rooted him to the spot, coiling about him like liquid snakes, filling his clothing.

The inquisitor tried to scream, but as he opened his mouth the blood-mass poured in over his lips and drowned him in thick ooze. *Your reward comes now,* said the Malfallax, each word a psionic hammer blow, *not lordship of these men-prey, not riches and powers as you were promised. You will know the glory of me. You shall carry my essence, become my mount and flesh-proxy...*

Ulan felt Stele's terrible, silent screams as the daemon forced itself into the inquisitor, turning the man into the unwilling vessel for its bloated psychic substance. As much as she hated the malignant blackguard, she found a spark of pity for the man as he was subsumed inside his daemon lord's self. Betrayal and anger, fear and terror so sweet that they clogged her throat with the backwash of their taste; the emotions flooded out of the twisting bag of skin. The creature denied his puppet the chance to frame his feelings as he died, tearing understanding from Stele's mind. He was nothing but carrion for it now: his plans were Malfallax's plans, his grand schemes tiny puzzles in the SpiteLord's rounds of parlour amusement.

And so only Ulan truly witnessed the death of Inquisitor Ramius Stele, of his flesh and his sinew, of his mind and his soul. She heard it rip through the ether and catch her in its razored wake. The psy-witch gibbered and wept, ruined by her proximity to it.

The daemon stretched at the meat surrounding it, and with slow and purposeful motion it unleashed the way of mutation upon its new organic shell. Spewing out the dead mud that had briefly contained it, Malfallax adopted the unhallowed aspect that all his kindred wore as the mark of their fealty to the eightfold way. Stele's bones shifted like putty, hollowing and distending. The pallid human flesh glittered and took on a multihued riot of colours, flashing rainbows as sunlight caught through a prism. The face pressed forward against itself, becoming a hooked beak with deep-sunk eye pits burning with ruin. Gossamer feathers burst from the remnants of the Hereticus uniform, and great scarred wings shook loose from the prison of the skin. Hooks and talons dressed the creature and it gave a long, languid yawn.

Staring out at the human world from inside its new sheath of matter, the Lord of Change glanced at the cowering Ulan and decided it was hungry. Black-barbed claws caught the psyker woman in a pincer grip and brought her to the wicked beak, as a warped voice bayed for fresh, new blood.

Malfallax ate this meal and studied the mad war ranged about it, considering where it would begin.

DELOS LOOKED ON, appalled. At first, the cleric had thought it was more of the mind-trick that Stele had turned upon him, but the stink of the shifting, sinuous beast told his senses that this monstrosity was as real as the hammering rain and the cold mud. His crozius was gone, lost and broken, but he still had his bolter and his blade. Delos drew both, running his fingers over the litany inscribed on the frame of his weapon. He came to the last etching where he had transcribed his oath to Arkio. 'All lies now?' he asked the rushing skies above. 'Have I damned myself?'

There would be no more for Delos to inscribe after today. The Chaplain blinked rainwater from his eyes and leapt at the daemon, calling out the name of his primarch.

Malfallax cocked its head in a quizzical gesture and turned to present itself to the figure in black. It stood on something wet and breakable, hot liquid spurting about its clawed feet. The daemon glanced down, shaking off the blood and organ-matter. Stele's lexmechanic had been too slow to get out of the way, and now the speaker-slave was a paste of bones and metals in the mud.

Delos's shots found purchase in the beast's hide and Malfallax swallowed the pain of them like rare sweetmeats. The daemon curled a taloned finger at the Chaplain and spoke a word of blasphemous power. A rift opened like a bloody wound before his hand and a streak of rose-coloured fire jetted forth, engulfing Delos.

The cleric wailed as the pink flames surrounded and clung to him, burning through his sable power armour. The Lord of Change left him screaming and dying there in the mud and strode away, looking for more prey. Malfallax reached into a sucking void in its chest, its hand disappearing to the wrist. It returned with a hilt in its grasp, and with slow and careful motions the daemon withdrew an edged weapon made from dead men's bones and solid delusion.

The humans had a name for such a sword – they called them warp blades, semi-real constructs existing half-in and half-out of the empyrean, raw funnels of mindform woven into killing blades. Malfallax tested the Chaos weapon in its grip, feeling the weight of it, judging the reach. Satisfied, it drew up the sword and plunged it into a mass of fleeing slave troopers, liquefying their bodies with the speed of its passage. The blade rippled and gasped in pleasure.

'EMPEROR PRESERVE US,' hissed the sergeant. 'It makes me retch just to lay eyes upon it…'

'What manner of thing is it?' added the Techmarine.

'Tzeentch-spawn,' Mephiston replied. The psyker felt the edges of the agony-sphere cast by the warp blade, and his eyes could not focus on the blurring shape of the sword, his vision slipping off the unholy geometry of it. 'A Lord of Change.' He tapped the skull medallion at his throat and spat out an order. 'Regroup. Concentrate fire on the crea-ture–'

The Blood Angels commands were silenced by a scream-ing crash of sound from the mass of the enemy force. The daemon lord drew arcane runes in the air and unleashed a flood of cold fire across the square. Men caught in the white core of the flames were instantly turned to vapour, disappearing into ash. Those on the edges of the blast caught fire and stumbled about, blind and mad with pain; the ones on the periphery became cursed with the fallout of mutation, spontaneously growing new limbs, bursting out of their wargear or imploding. Mephiston saw several men turn their own weapons on themselves rather than accede to the revision of their throbbing flesh.

Space Marines died on the tip of the monster's ten-metre sword, adding their crimson to the ankle-deep blood swamp. The warp blade left brief tears in the fabric of space where it passed, and things emerged from the hole, chat-tering with hunger. Saucer-shaped and dripping with toxic cilia, the disc-like warp freaks fell on the injured and the dying like vultures.

Emboldened by their new ally, the Word Bearers flooded forward, shoving aside or killing the hesitant loyalist Marines. Mephiston met them with Vitarus singing death, beheading and bifurcating, his plasma pistol hissing hot with discharge. The traitors met steel and died, but for the first time since he had arrived on Sabien, the Lord of Death took a step back as the press of the enemy turned tight like a ruby vice.

'THE EYE OF a hurricane,' murmured Turcio, 'we are caught in a storm.' He fired again at the gaggle of Word Bearers that sniped at them from the remains of a smouldering Thunderhawk, firing past helot soldiers who seemed oblivious to the crossfire passing through their numbers. He ducked to reload and Brother Corvus took his place, pacing his shots. 'By my life... The confusion... What are we doing here?'

'Surviving,' Corvus retorted, killing a Word Bearer with a headshot. 'We are worth nothing if we die.'

'But the Blessed... where is he? Has Arkio deserted us?'

'No!' Corvus snapped back at his battle-brother, but in truth the same fear filled his mind as well. 'He... he must be fighting elsewhere...'

'Where?' Turcio demanded, coming up to join the conflict once more. 'This day had turned to madness. Our hated enemies arise from nowhere, daemons take shape from nothing... Arkio is gone and we are fighting everything that moves.' He grabbed Corvus's arm and looked him the face. 'I don't know what I am any more! Blood Angel? Warrior of the Blessed? Traitor or loyalist? There's nothing but death here, no answers–'

Bolt-fire from the Chaos lines chewed off a chunk of their cover and both Marines threw themselves aside as lascannon shots followed through. Turcio rolled over in the mud and found himself staring up at the sky, the endless curtain of grey rain pelting them. Misgivings clouded his mind. Suddenly it seemed like everything that had happened since Cybele was being called in question. 'Sanguinius preserve me, what is our fate to be?'

'Look.' Corvus pointed toward the gutted tower of a long-fallen cathedral, one of only a few structures that still stood above ground level. There was a human figure up there on the stone canopy, atop a broken gargoyle. Lighting gave him form and colour – a Blood Angel, and in his arms a mess of golden shapes, pale flesh and white feathers.

RAFEN LOOKED DOWN on the battlefield and filled his lungs with breaths of wet, metallic air. When he spoke, his voice carried on the wind, echoing through the vox channels of every Astartes on the ground.

'Blood Angels!' he cried. 'Sons of Baal, hear me. The lie has been dispelled, our twisted fate undone. Know this, brothers. We have been betrayed!'

The conflict raged on, but Rafen's voice still reached every corner of the fight, even the helots and the enemy turning to cast an ear toward him. 'All of us hold the blood of Sanguinius inside our hearts,' Rafen called. 'Every man of us is the Pure One in some small corner of his soul... But our primogenitor, our lord and founder... He lies *dead.*' The word thundered across the sky. 'Sanguinius is ashes, millennia gone, no bones, no heart, only blood! Sanguinius died at the hands of hated Horus, he perished at the blade of *Chaos.*'

Angry howls bubbled up from the throats of all the Blood Angels, to a man all of them stirred to violence by the stark truth of Rafen's statement.

'And now the archfoe seeks to turn us all, to drag us to their blasphemy by a false idol...' He held up Arkio's body, high above the throng. 'See. Look at what has been done! My blood kinsman, mutated and warped by the hand of a traitor...' Rafen's voice was choked with emotion. 'They made him think he was the Pure One Reborn... They made us believe. But he was corrupted, poisoned by the pawn Stele! The daemon that walks among you did this, so we would follow blindly, blindly into the abyss.'

A chorus of denials came up to Rafen on the wind, anguished refusals from men who now saw the lie they had granted their fealty to.

'See the truth!' Rafen screamed. 'See my brother fall.' He tipped Arkio's corpse over the edge and let gravity take the winged body from him. In a moment of terrible silence, only the rain spoke as the dead man tumbled end over end, ruined wings flapping, to land in a broken heap on the cathedral steps.

TURCIO SCRAMBLED TO the body and turned Arkio's face to his. He recoiled with horror and stumbled away.

'What do you see?' Corvus asked, his hearts tight in his chest.

'Ruin,' Turcio said in a dead voice. 'Ruin and damnation. Our messiah is black with untruth, brother… Rafen does not lie.'

'ARKIO IS DEAD!' came the cry from the tower. '*My brother perished for this mendacity and it dies with him!*' Rafen drew up the Spear of Telesto and let the weapon's golden light haze the sky around him. 'By the Holy Lance, reject your flawed allegiance to Arkio and remember the true lord, Sanguinius.' He pointed the weapon into the melee and felt it turn hot with willing power. 'See the foe among you and destroy them.'

ON THE STEPS, Turcio stood back and called to the sky. 'Aye. *Aye.* I renounce the Reborn. I am a Blood Angel!' The battle-brother leapt off the cracked stones and threw himself into the helots and traitors. 'For the Emperor and Sanguinius!'

Corvus yelled the same oath and followed him and across the square, Arkio's loyalists threw off their misguided devotion, the burning power of the spear tearing the shroud of Chaos's confusion from their minds.

MALFALLAX'S ANGER PIERCED the Warmaster's mind like a white-hot arrow, the thread of psychic communion between them so strong it killed two lesser Word Bearers beside the Witch Prince.

'Garand! The man-filth's ridiculous catspaw is cold meat! You promised me this elaborate charade would be a success!'

The Word Bearers commander glanced in the direction of the shambling Lord of Change, far across the battle, and bowed. 'The fool Stele, great heirophant. I tried to control his scheming, but his vanity was his undoing.'

'I have consumed his flesh,' said Malfallax. 'I know his goals. This day may still be won by us, and we may still turn the Blood Angels for our master's pleasure.'

'Forgive me, excellence, but how? With the boy dead, these Blood Whelps will not follow us into darkness.'

Psychic laughter battered at his senses. 'You see only the battle to hand, Garand. There is another way.'

Realisation flooded into the Warmaster. 'The Flaw. The gene-curse of the Baalites.'

'Yessss,' murmured the daemon. 'I tasted it on Cybele through my bound psy-slaves. We will conjure it from these fools and let it consume them – and when they are deep within the black rage, I will lead them to a well of blood the likes of which they will never escape, to the very heart of the Maelstrom itself.'

Garand nodded, awed by the daring of it. 'Your glory, Lord Malfallax.'

THEY MADE WAY as Rafen walked from the cathedral's interior to the place where Arkio's body lay. In his mailed fist, the spear glowed as it had that day on the *Bellus*, when the light of the primogenitor had touched every soul aboard. Gently, he curled the broken wings around his sibling's corpse in a death shroud, while Mephiston's men looked on in silence.

Rafen rose to find the Chief Librarian at his side. The Lord of Death proffered a thick glass injector in his hand. 'Your wounds are severe, brother,' said Mephiston. 'Take this. Corbulo himself gave it to me. It will lend you the strength of the lords.'

He gathered up the exsanguinator and turned it in his fingers. Thick, heavy blood glistened inside it, drawn from the highest Sanguinary Priest of the Blood Angels Chapter. Once this blood mixed with Rafen's own, the essence of Sanguinius would flow even stronger in his veins.

Mephiston nodded at the dead man. 'The time has come to avenge him.'

'It has,' agreed Rafen, and with one single sweeping motion, he plunged the needle into his chest and emptied its contents into his heart.

CHAPTER FOURTEEN

For hundreds of years the landscape of the shrine world Sabien had been silent of human voices, the desolate ruins speaking only with the mournful winds that chased dust and rain through the streets and open spaces. In its own way, Sabien was a mournful twin to the planet Cybele, a sister sphere light years distant toward the coreward marches of the galaxy. Both worlds were markers for the dead, and both had run crimson with the life of both Astartes and traitors. Fate, if such a thing existed, had cast a circular path for Rafen and his brethren to follow. Their journey into darkness had begun among tombstones and memorials, and here and now it would end among the same.

Sabien had known the unbridled passion and fury of the Sons of Sanguinius all those centuries ago, when the long-since dead had fought and perished in order to hold this planet against the legion enemies of the God-Emperor. That power had come again to the silent world, raising up against the thunder of the storm clouds in a brilliant tide of virtuous malevolence.

The Blood Angels did not simply attack, they *detonated* across the war zone in a wave of unfettered rage, a red tide of men plunging into the lines of the Word Bearers and the maddened helot soldiers. They rushed to the fight, rejecting the relative safety of a stand-off battle, throwing caution to the wind in shattering chants and war cries. The unholy hymns of the Chaos Marines were drowned out by the lusty roars of their opponents, and then by the massive crash of the two forces meeting like a hammer on an anvil. Metal on metal, chainsword against ceramite, bolter striking flesh, the hissing snap of laser fire – and the screaming. The horrible, heart-chilling screaming. All of it came together in an orchestra of unchained war. The earth quaked beneath the awesome release of mayhem and destruction.

The Blood Angels had returned to Sabien, and a crimson hell came striding with them.

ONLY IN THE crucible of close combat could a man truly understand the measure of himself. It was nothing to stand aside, in the cockpit of a fighter or behind the barrel of a ranged cannon, to press a button and watch a distant foe vanish in a puff of smoke. How could a Space Marine ever know the colour of his heart unless he stood toe to toe with his most hated enemy and took their life as they looked him in the eyes? What truth was stronger than the final moment of reckoning, when weapon matched weapon and the pulse of shed blood sang its symphony?

Mephiston knew this; it was the greatest glory of the Lord of Death's existence to cast the aberrant and the reviled into shreds. He was at the very tip of the arrow of red ceramite that marked the Blood Angels advance, slashing through the lines of Word Bearers and the helots who dared to assault the Marines that towered over them. The psyker killed a man, a commoner whose mind had been addled by the Chaos demagogues, killed him with a look from his flinty, iron-hard eyes. The over-spill of Mephiston's Quickening brushed the errant fool and stopped his heart, bursting blood vessels all over the slave trooper's rough-hewn robes. The hot fluid spattered the psyker's muscular body armour and droplets found their way to his cheeks. Mephiston wiped them from his pale, sallow face and licked the blood from his fingers. It was the most perfect wine, a lustrous red vintage filled with heady adrenaline. The Blood Angel's fangs drew out over his thin lips. He was suddenly filled with the anticipation of more, more, *more*!

He threw aside the dead man and cut wet streaks through a Word Bearers Havoc trooper, bisecting the barrel of the lascannon he held and cutting into the pallid white meat of the enemy Marine's neck. The force sword's downward fall did not end there, blue lightning clashing and spitting into the body, severing it into unequal chunks. Black liquids issued up from the gaping voids he cut in thick, oily fountains. This was an altogether different draught, raw with the pollution of a thousand years, stinking and putrid. To let such a libation touch his lips… The very idea made Mephiston ill.

Across the falling corpse of the ruby-armoured traitor came more of the Warriors of the Reborn. All of them were throwing off their loyalty to Arkio now that the winged golden figure had been shown dead, their weak little minds turning to the eightfold way as their new saviour. So pathetic and desperate, they were.

Mephiston shouted a hate cry at them and struck out with Vitarus. He held a special place in the rage he carried for the feeble of devotion and the cowardly; these wretched mundanes were thrice damned in the eyes of the Lord of Death. They had allowed their world to be soured by a Word Bearers invasion, they had lacked even the strength of character to stay true to the Emperor's light when Stele had brought Arkio forth as an erstwhile messiah, and now they ran gladly into the embrace of Chaos when that lie was shown to them. These Shenlongi rabble were like broken children, beaten so often by vicious parents that they had come to believe that it was a sign of love. Another man

might have found pity for them in his heart, but both of
Mephiston's were filled to the brim with only vehemence.
He killed them all, cutting and slashing with the sword,
taking up those that did not run from him with his free
hand to rip their throats from their necks. He drank from
their veins to feed the predator-self inside him.

In his frenzy, the psyker glimpsed his brother Space
Marines doing the same, rending and tearing, burning down
the soldiers of Chaos where they stood and taking the hot,
frothing blood from their screaming lackeys. A dark and
potent miasma enveloped Mephiston, clouding his reason
even as it thickened his wrath. He felt the red thirst beckon-
ing him, opening up to flood the battle with its crimson
mist. The black rage was welling up within him, boiling and
furious, and the Blood Angels warlord tipped back his head
and roared with laughter. Mephiston embraced it.

THE REMAINS OF the half-eaten corpse twisted through the
air and landed in a heavy heap near the base of the bomb
crater where Turcio and Corvus were bogged down. Corvus
shrank back, pacing shots from his bolter, barely glancing
at the body. Turcio's gut knotted as he examined the dead
man. Like the carapace of some exotic shellfish, the Blood
Angel's armour had been cracked open and peeled back to
reveal the meaty innards it protected. A slurry of molten
bone and liquefied organ meat oozed from the holes
where arms and a head would have been. There were licks
of glutinous spittle and teeth marks from where the body
had been turned into a food morsel.

A wet belch of blood turned Turcio's attention up to the
lip of the crater and there he saw the bloated shape of the
Malfallax. It eyed him, spitting out an intact human femur
from the side of its wide mouth with callous disdain. The
newly assimilated flesh of the dead Marine bubbled to the
surface of the creature's body, merging into the panoply of
glittering skins. The Lord of Change moved like oil over
water, stagnant rainbow hues shimmering hypnotically.
Turcio blinked furiously to shake off the mesmeric allure.

Malfallax picked at the grove of sickle teeth in its mutant mouth. 'Stringy,' it said, sniffing at the discarded corpse. 'Old and tasteless.' The beast winked at Turcio. 'You'll be a better catch.'

The Blood Angel refused to grace the hellspawn with even the most insulting of ripostes and shot at it instead, his bolter hammering in his hands. Malfallax growled and spat as a couple of lucky shots hit home. It moved with unnatural grace, flowing through the air rather than simply stepping through it, glittering through the constant rods of rain in a weaving dance.

'Stele!' spat Corvus, suddenly recognising some vague aspect of the inquisitor still apparent in the corpse-skin worn by the daemon. 'You took him.'

'He wanted it,' retorted the creature, slapping aside a fallen metal stanchion. 'The imbecile desired to know the warp... and my kin are the warp made flesh.' It plucked at the stretched skin about its face, flapping like grotesque wattles.

Turcio and Corvus reacted without thinking, laying down corridors of concentrated fire to pin the monstrous beast between them, but the daemon whooped with wry amusement and let the bat wings at its back lift it clear. They bracketed it with shots, but again Malfallax shifted and merged into the rain, always appearing at exactly the point where the bolt-rounds were not. There in its breast glowed a green oval with a yellow disc in its centre; a boon from its god, the Eye of Tzeentch grew like a living electro-tattoo, and through it the creature glimpsed a measure of the skein of time. Malfallax saw enough of fate's complex weave to know where the Space Marines would shoot, veering here and there to avoid the burning bullets. It was like firing at smoke.

Turcio's gun ran dry and he twisted towards cover, but the beast was already there with unfolding talons as big as the claws of a fire scorpion. It batted him with the blunt of the nails, knocking Turcio into his battle-brother and throwing them both down into ankle-deep mire. Malfallax hooted with delight and clapped its hands together, a disturbingly human gesture for something so alien. The daemon could have easily struck with a killing blow, tearing Turcio open and eating him, but that would have been too quick, it would have lacked finesse. Malfallax loved the sensuous feeling of its new flesh husk and it wanted to revel in its play as long as it could. It opened a number of mouths across the scarred face and torso, and all of them spoke with the same arrogant and chilling voice. 'Where is your angel now, man-prey?' it mocked.

'*Here!*' shouted Rafen, lightning framing him in a flood of blue-white at the crater's edge. The Marine pointed the Holy Lance with one outstretched hand. From the tip ran thick streams of Word Bearers blood, and the haft was steaming as it burnt out the taint of the dozens of Chaos dead it had already claimed. Malfallax spied the Spear of Telesto and let free an atonal shriek. Even the proximity of the hallowed archeotech device was enough to enrage the daemon.

'You denied me the chance to bring my revenge to your lackey, warp scum,' he hissed, 'so I will grant it to you in kind.' Rafen twirled the spear above his head and leapt into the air, turning himself into an arrow aimed at the archfiend's beating black heart.

Malfallax's clawed talon came up to protect itself with the speed of a striking shellsnake, catching the haft of the lance as it fell toward his chest. The carvings of Sanguinius cut into its fingers, but Rafen's headlong flight ended with an abrupt jerk, shaking his bones. The spear pressed forward against the daemon's grip, ready to penetrate the mutant skin; the creature held on. Rafen twisted the weapon and the tip of the teardrop blade scarred the sacred eye branded on Malfallax's chest.

The Eye of Tzeentch wept pink liquid and popped like a burst blister, drawing a murderous howl from the daemon. Ignoring the burning agony from its own flesh, Malfallax gripped the lance hard and shook the golden rod. Before Rafen could even let go of his grip, the Lord of Change had used it to slam him into the mud. The Spear of Telesto stung him with gold fire for his viciousness and the daemon screeched again, tossing the holy weapon away into the quagmire. Rafen scrambled after it as the beast mewed, licking pitifully at the crisped ruin where its hand had been.

Turcio fumbled his last clip of ammunition into his bolter's gaping slot and turned the muzzle on the monster. Its attention distracted by Rafen, it presented an unprotected flank to the Space Marine, and the blinded brand robbed the creature of its second sight. Hot bolts stitched blossoms of brackish blood where the hits found their marks. Necrotic skin peeled from yellowed bones, embrittled by the rapid mutation forced on them, and loops of grey intestine emerged from what had once been Ramius Stele's abdomen.

Malfallax twitched and flashed forward, instinctively homing in on the source of the new pain. Pink fire looped about its scarred claw, and the other limb brought up the shrieking bone sword, the warp blade falling in an iridescent arc. The prismatic shimmer was a thing of beauty in its own ever-changing way, and it rooted Turcio to the spot with its majesty until the keening weapon slashed through the breech of his gun and his right forearm.

The Blood Angel was thrown back by the shock of the pain, the consecrated and hallowed icon of his bolter instantly destroyed and his severed limb spewing jets of incarnadine fluids. The reflex reaction saved him from being shredded as Malfallax followed the strike with a downward sweep of his claw. The talons tore through the pauldrons of Turcio's armour and opened his wargear to the navel. A strong grip yanked him back. Corvus dragged Turcio by the neck ring of his torso plate, firing over his battle-brother's stumbling form into the advancing daemon. Malfallax chewed on the bolt shells that struck it, picking the flattened humps of tungsten rounds from the holes in its chest.

There was a flurry of wet motion behind it and the beast craned its elongated neck over a crooked shoulder. Rafen rose from the mud with the spear in a two-handed grip and stabbed forward into the meat of the daemon's exposed thigh. The sparking blade buried itself in the flesh and opened it to the air. Maggots and writhing alien parasites spilled from the cut.

Malfallax spat and turned its attention to Rafen once again. 'Still alive?'

'Still,' Rafen grinned and slashed again, cutting at the creature's hide. The daemon parried the lunges with a swipe of its freakish sword and came forward, heavy hooves punching into the churning puddles gathering in the crater. Rafen saw Corvus dragging the injured Turcio from the pit and threw them a nod.

The beast saw him do it and cackled. 'You are persistent, human, I will grant you that, but then dogged obstinacy is a trait of the corpse-god's kind.' Hot breath coiled in clouds from its mouths. 'You resist the changing way and that is why you perish.'

Rafen replied with a swooping attack, dancing the tip of the spear about the questing warp blade, slamming it in savage stabs at the daemon's legs. It blocked every strike, trying each time to trap the Telesto weapon in the barbs that lined the edges of the sword. The Marine channelled his effort into the spear, letting the lance become an extension of his arms, looking beyond the apex of the glittering teardrop blade, seeing only the points where the daemon bled and wept ichor; but still it fanned the warp blade, the mesmerising arc of colour becoming a dome of mad light. He worked the spear just as he had been taught on the courtyards of the fortress-monastery, blocking, parrying, advancing, thrusting, sweeping, but never gaining more than a cursory bite from the monster's flesh. In his mailed grip, the raw energy of the spear hummed and pulsed inside the ornate shaft and golden crossguard, throbbing with power every time it cut into Malfallax – but still it would not respond to him as it had to his brother Arkio.

There had been a moment there on the rooftop of the ruined cathedral, after he threw Arkio's body to the throng

below, when Rafen had thought the Holy Lance was about
to open its secrets to him. It glowed in his hands, lighting
the world around him. For a fleeting instant, Rafen had
known the thrill of connection with the Spear of Telesto,
just as Arkio must have, just as the lord Sanguinius himself
did in the ancient conflict with Morroga. But it fled as
quickly as the flashes of lightning in the steel-grey sky overhead. The lance was a superlative weapon, perfectly
balanced and keen enough to slice a hair down its centre;
but unless he could unlock its inner power, it was only a
relic.

How? he demanded of himself. *How can I open the spear
to my will?* Arkio had been changed beyond all normality
and the Pure One himself… There was no way that Rafen
could compare himself to the Angelic Sovereign. He parried another flurry of violent strikes by the daemon, and
one too quick to dodge severed a nest of power conduits
on his trunk. He felt the icy cold as super-cooled liquid
spurted from his damaged backpack. Patches of frost
formed on Rafen's backside and thigh, turning the ceramite
and plasteel brittle. The daemon slashed through a toppled
stone column to snap at the Blood Angel and he avoided
the blow with only a hand's span to spare.

Rafen swore angrily, half in frustration at himself, half in
adrenaline-fuelled hate for the Malfallax, and took off a
strip of skin from the beast's shoulder, forcing it to stagger
backward. It released a gush of cerise flame from its hand,
the roseate fire turning broken stone to slag, crawling over
the tilled earth like a live thing. A spark of hard rage stiff-
ened Rafen's heart as he attacked again – and the spear
responded with him, suddenly melting into his assault,
flowing with the press of his muscles. Brief, tiny flares of
gold sparks chased each other down the length of the haft.
Sudden realisation shook him: *the rage! The gene-curse was
the key!*

Malfallax's eyes for the future were blinded but the beast
still knew how to play the harp of the fates. All things were
under the motion of invisible strings that ranged from birth

to death, past to present; they pulled all life and matter like wayward marionettes. This man-thing, this Blood Angel, was as much at the mercy of clockwork destiny as were the stars in the sky, the falling rains, the rising and setting of Sabien's sun. With the paingift of its master denied, the Malfallax's sight of the human whelp's fate was cloudy, but it knew there were many outcomes where Rafen lay dead and ruined, far more of those than the ones where he stood in victory or where he turned to worship of Chaos Undivided. The daemon knew how the Marine fought, it had toyed with him and watched his motions. It saw the hesitation telegraphed in his moves, the resistance of the lance in his hands. Rafen was ill at ease with the deadly, pestilent, hateful spear – so Malfallax would use that against him.

In Rafen's split-second instant of indecision, the creature caught the weapon in a toothed niche in the warp blade and twisted. The alien sword sang and left nicks in space-time as it drew back and up, dragging the Spear of Telesto from Rafen's shocked grip before he could react to halt it. Malfallax thrust him back with a pulse of pink fire and tossed the Holy Lance away. It spun into the wet ooze and started to sink.

The Blood Angel beat at the writhing hellfire and stumbled, aware of the chorus of noises around him. Sounds coiled over the arena of the bomb crater in waves, the shrieking of dying men mingled with shot and shell, harsh thunder and sacrilegious war prayers.

'A poor adversary,' rumbled the daemon. 'Such limited sport. Perhaps the mind-witch Mephiston will provide a better challenge, or even your wastrel Lord Dante...'

Rafen's anger flooded out of him like a torrent from a broken dam. 'Chaos bastard! I'll choke you on those words.'

'With what?' it demanded. 'Come, little man-prey, attack me with tooth and claw, if you believe that will make your death have more meaning.'

With a rush of speed, the Malfallax shimmered toward him, fast as mercury. The warp blade spun about in its grip and the calcite stone of the heavy pommel whacked him in the face, splitting his skin and lighting fireworks of pain inside his skull. Rafen staggered backwards and fell. The beast-thing advanced. It towered over him, blocking out the light from the myriad battle fires and the sheets of white in the tortured sky. The burnt, meat-stinking claw pressed Rafen into the cold mud, holding him there so the daemon could finish him with one last slash of the bony sword.

'The spear rejects you,' it chuckled, jerking its head at the bubbling mud pool. 'You are a failure to your Chapter, Blood Angel, just like your craven brother.'

The pressure pulled all the air from Rafen's chest and with it a final, heartfelt denial. 'No,' he hissed, pulling together the burning embers of his blood-tinged fury. 'No! *No!*' Throughout his service to the Adeptus Astartes, Rafen had restrained the black rage within him, holding the reins of the red thirst, never once allowing it to overwhelm his rigid, unbending self-control; now he gave it the freedom it wanted so badly, unleashing the bestial frenzy that was the darkest secret of the Blood Angels.

The red thirst unfurled about him in a storm of seething crimson, a fog of bloodlust madness descending on the Marine. The raw energy of his primarch set a flash-fire in his veins, the traces of Sanguinius's genetic code engorged with preternatural power. The heady cocktail of Astartes blood and the potent flood of vigour from the Lord of Death's blood-gift merged into Rafen, filling him with a fury that blazed with unbound, inchoate hate.

The ropes of fate unwound before Malfallax, spinning and snapping in his blinded mind's eye. *Impossible!*

Rafen roared and broke free of the beast's grip, shattering claws as big as scimitars and ripping scabbed skin into rags. He moved at the speed of wrath, an unstoppable bullet of red. The Marine's spirit plunged into the rage-sea about him, and there he found the glittering beacon of the Holy Lance. From the slime of the mud swamp, the weapon flew to him, crossing the distance to his waiting

grip in an eye-blink. Golden fire, shards of lightning dazzling like fragments of suns, ripped from the air and
collected at the hollow heart of the teardrop blade. The
weapon was awake, the beating pulse of the sacred spear
tasting Rafen's holy anger and knowing it as true.

Malfallax launched itself at him, leading with warp
blade, opening rents in reality with cerise darts of fire; it
threw the veil of the Twisting Path at the Blood Angel, but
every attack fluttered and died against the glory of the
Telesto lance. The daemon saw its fate-path curl into black
formlessness and cried out in despair.

A wash of mellifluent light flared, and for a brief
moment Rafen's battle-ravaged crimson wargear was
replaced with golden armour, crested with wings made of
white steel. The righteous vengeance of his primogenitor
stared out from Rafen's ice-blue eyes and carried retribution into the Chaos spawn's heart.

The Spear of Telesto entered the Malfallax's chest and
sank into the writhing morass of corruption inside. Rafen
pressed forward, forcing the blade through the beast's gut,
up through the decayed lungs and organ matter, piercing
the withered black meat of its heart. The creature screamed
to the clouds, and still the Blood Angel advanced, pressing
the haft of the weapon into the dying enemy until the
teardrop burst from Malfallax's back, between his drooping, bloodless wings.

'I… am… undeath!' it sputtered. 'You cannot kill a child
of the warp.'

'*Begone!*' Rafen bellowed, his fangs flashing. 'Your cursed
realm awaits!'

'Aaaaaaaaa–' Malfallax's death rattle was deafening from
its dozen mouths. 'You have not won,' spat some of them.
'Your rage will be your ending–'

'*Die!*' Rafen shouted, one final shove of the spear cutting
the daemon's link to its fleshy vessel. Streaks of sizzling
ectoplasm burst out of Stele's carcass, ripping away
through the blood-misted air and flashing into nothing;
glistening jags of ethereal warp matter, unable to sustain

permanence for even a second on the human plane of reality, banged and vanished, taking the weave of the creature's wrecked self screaming back into the madness of the immaterium.

The mutant body turned to powdery black stone, trapping the lance inside a deformed statue. Rafen tore at the spear and it went hot in his grip, giving out a shock wave of heat that obliterated the ashen form.

'Wait,' he cried, a sudden shadow of fear passing through him; but his call came too late. Like a tornado made of nails, the black ash exploded outward in a perfect concentric ring, each tiny particle of the contaminated matter impregnated with the void-born antipathy of the Ruinous Powers. A surge of mad hate passed through Rafen and threw him into the air. The tide of rancour moved over the square, touching every single Blood Angel on the surface of Sabien, tearing the veneer of humanity from each of them, debasing the Space Marines. The noble character and high honour of the Sons of Sanguinius fled before a madness that made them all animals. Malfallax's laughter echoed as his death curse exposed the insanity of the Flaw in his enemies, and to a man they fell into the horrific grip of the red thirst.

IT WAS NOT battle; it was butchery.

Among the gales of driving rain and cracks of thunder, men fell in their dozens under the frenzy of the Blood Angels. Still-beating hearts were torn from the chests of helot troopers and crushed like ripe fruits, the nectar of heavy arterial blood drained into gaping, hungry mouths. Blood Angels nuzzled at the throats of corpses, fans of crimson covering their chins and necks, barking and growling at one another like jackals fighting over fresh carrion. Lakes of vitae poured into the square, turning the damp air sharp with the rusty, metallic tang of its scent. Blood, blood and blood; there was no end to it, torrents of the rich red fluid slicking the mud around the feet of the combatants.

The errant slave warriors were not the only ones to come to murder by the rage of the maddened Astartes; Word Bearers found themselves shocked silent from their impious revels as the Sons of Sanguinius threw all caution to the wind and fell on them in waves. The Blessed of Lorgar faced foes that were little more than a force of nature now, a living, breathing, killing storm of men without fear or compunction. The Blood Angels were berserkers, spirits of scarlet destruction that gave no quarter and asked none in return.

Warmaster Garand shot hellbolts into the bodies of the red-armoured Astartes that came in range, but the death's head shells did little to stop the crazed tide. Blood Angels with limbs missing and great fists of meat torn from them still roared on in battle frenzy, the light of humanity inside them extinguished by the Malfallax's parting gift, its ruinous hate wave. The Witch Prince of Helica had seen this sort of behaviour on the battlefield before, but never from a human opponent. In his forays into the Eye of Terror and sorties where the Word Bearers found themselves matched with other followers of the eightfold way, Garand had been cursed with the misfortune to fight alongside the World Eaters. Madmen among a culture of psychotics, the berzerker bands killed ally and foe alike in their unending lust to claim skulls for the Skull Throne of the Blood God. The Warmaster saw the same stripe of insanity here and now among the Astartes legion, a revelry in the slaughter for slaughter's sake.

'They fight like Khorne himself,' grated one of Garand's lieutenants. 'I have never seen the like…'

'I have,' spat Garand, and he snarled with anger. 'The warp take this blighted scheme. That daemon wretch has fled the field.'

Hymnals from the Unhallowed Books were turned into gurgling screams as the wild Blood Angels assault touched the Word Bearers line and necks were torn open. Garand watched in fury as a squad of his handpicked aspirants vanished under a surge of red armour, falling like cut timbers.

'Lord. Lord!' cried a voice, and he glanced down from his vantage point as a war-priest crashed toward him through the melee. 'Lord, the veil has closed to us!'

In his anger, Garand grabbed the Word Bearer and dragged him to his eye level. 'Speak plainly, fool.'

The Marine writhed in his grip. 'Our summonings have been ended, Lord. Every daemonform we called to be for the battle has fallen dead and inert!'

'Malfallax.' Garand released the war-priest, cursing the Lord of Change's name over and over. 'That pestilent wraith. This is his doing!'

'But how?' demanded the lieutenant.

Garand swept his hand about. 'It drew back its essence when the host-body perished, and with it all the warp-matter from the field of battle. Nothing remains. We are becalmed, lost to the empyrean here.' He shoved the war-priest aside and snatched at his lieutenant. 'Our battle here is ended. Rally. Rally!'

'Lord, you cannot mean to–'

'Retreat?' The word thundered from his lips. 'The mad ones cannot be stopped by our numbers, fool.' He tore a rod-shaped teleport beacon from the Marine's belt. 'We go.'

'No,' sputtered the war-priest, his ardour overwhelming his better reason. 'Ever forward, never back! That is the Word Bearers code. We do not retreat.'

Garand struck him with a brutal punch and threw him aside. 'Imbecile! Leave these freaks to themselves and what will they kill? Each other.'

'No…'

The Warmaster pressed the activation glyph and felt the warm tingle of the *Misericorde*'s teleporters reaching for him. His last action on Sabien was to shoot the war-priest in the leg and leave him there for the madmen; punishment enough for daring to speak against the Witch Prince.

MEPHISTON DID NOT notice the departure of the Word Bearers. Some, those who were injured or none too quick to run for the glowing bubbles of the teleport fields, died the moment they turned their backs on the Blood Angels, their meat and their armour joining the endless slurry of corpses littering the ruined landscape. Perhaps, in some far distant corner of his night-black soul, the part of Mephiston that was still the man who had been Brother Calistarius existed. That tiny fragment of lucidity cried and screamed for the red thirst to abate, desperately trying and failing to halt Mephiston's headlong rush into the bosom of the black rage.

On Armageddon, the Lord of Death had been transformed after seven days and seven nights of wrestling the gene-curse, but now even his iron will had snapped, caught in the maelstrom of bloodlust that filled his soul. He was not conscious of the hot weapons in his hands, only that he could kill and kill and kill with them, unstoppable and furious in the glory of it.

'Mephiston!'

The name meant nothing to him; he had no identity now, only an all-consuming hate.

'Mephiston, heed me. Reject the darkness.' A red shape moved into his blurred vision. '*Reject it!*'

With an incoherent howl, Mephiston dropped his force sword on the man-form, seeing only the pulsing flesh and hearing the beat of a warm heart inside. The mindblade Vitarus met a rod of golden light and stopped dead, the power of the impact rocking the Lord of Death back on his heels. Fangs flared, Mephiston pressed against the glittering haft and for the first time, he saw who dared to defy him.

Rafen crossed the Holy Lance, blinking away the sparks that emerged where Mephiston's sword scraped back and forth. The barbed tip of the blade was at Rafen's neck and he felt the icy cold of the crystalline blade touch his skin and open it. The Marine's blood pooled in the lee of his clavicle and glistened on the sword tip.

'Raaaaaaa!' There was no humanity in the Lord of Death's gaze.

'*Mephiston!*' It was the Spear of Telesto that had protected him, Rafen was sure of it. When Malfallax's hate had consumed all his battle-brothers, he alone kept his mind intact, the warm touch of the lance clearing his vision of the suffocating rage. It was he alone who could stem the tide of the madness, before his comrades tore each other apart. 'Step back from the abyss. In the name of Sanguinius, *release your rage!*'

Golden light gushed from the spear and struck Mephiston like a physical blow. He staggered backward, his sword falling away, the dull glitter of insanity cast from his sight. All around them, the roars of frenzy and murder subsided into the rushing murmur of the rains. The water sluiced spilt blood from the Librarian's face and chest as he looked up from his hands and into Rafen's eyes.

'You…' It was difficult for Mephiston to speak at first, the words hard and heavy in his fogged mind. 'You reclaimed me from the brink… How?'

The spear's bright colours began to fade, growing quiescent. 'I do not know,' Rafen admitted. 'I was only the instrument. My hand was guided…'

The warrior-psyker shook off the lingering taint of the thirst and shuttered it away deep within. He watched Rafen examine the silent lance, his mailed fingers tracing the shape of the carving of their primarch. The lad had, for one moment, touched the soul of the most holy weapon, and with it he had drawn his kinsmen back from the edge of a soul-killing void. Although his expression betrayed nothing, inwardly Mephiston marvelled at the potential of one who was so blessed with the touch of the Pure One.

EPILOGUE

THE SKY HAD begun to rain ruby tears when the rescue ships blasted down through the cloud cover. The grim faces of the Space Marines from the *Europae* told the tale of their inner thoughts. They saw the carnage that lay about in the city streets and did not speak of it. None of them would shame their brothers by asking after what had taken place there beneath the curtain of grey clouds, while the battle barge and the Chaos warship went back and forth with salvos of laser fire and missiles.

Rafen watched as Mephiston accepted the report of a veteran sergeant with a solemn, serious mien. A lucky hit from the *Europae*'s main guns had torn open a wound in the *Misericorde* that vented directly into her weapon store, and the red-hued battleship had been hobbled. There had come a moment, the sergeant said, when something peculiar happened to the Word Bearers ship; the codicers and Librarians aboard *Europae* had cried out as one when the shock of something horrible resonated out from the shrine world below, a spillage of a black and potent evil. *Misericorde* had felt the undertow from the warp schism as well and things had died aboard the enemy ship from the pain of the passing. It was all the barge's captain had needed to press the advantage, and soon after the Word Bearers, the proud and arrogant demagogues who swore they would never fall back, disengaged from the fight and made best speed to the outer face of the debris ring. Her engines damaged, *Europae* was unfit to catch the Chaos craft and so the crew watched *Misericorde* reach free space and fall into the phantasm of a skull-formed warpgate. The snarling face hung in the dark for long seconds and then faded.

Rafen glanced at the dull sky and then to the Librarian. 'Is this victory, Lord Mephiston?'

The Lord of Death walked away toward the waiting Thunderhawks. 'For now,' he said quietly.

THEY STAYED IN orbit for another solar week while the Chapter serfs and indentured crew expedited *Europae*'s repairs. Task forces of Space Marines expert in vacuum environments were sent out into the disc of fragments that marked the site of *Bellus*'s infernal death, charged with searching the wreckage for any survivors or materials of interest to the Chapter. Those few sealed escape pods that were found contained panicked groups of Shenlongi citizens, members of Arkio's thousand who had broken when the fighting had started.

The Blood Angels treated them in the manner of all enemies of the Imperium, offering them the choice of bolter or airlock. Most chose the former, weeping on their knees in the name of Rafen's brother as they died from point-blank headshots. One of the teams located the hardened steel module from the interior of *Bellus* that housed the ship's progenoid capsules. Many of the clerics aboard *Europae* were of the opinion that the gene-seeds were tainted and fit only for the fires of the fusion furnace, but Mephiston spoke otherwise. The vital organs were placed in secure holding for the journey back to Baal; it would be Lord Commander Dante alone who would decide the fate of the pods of genetic matter.

Rafen thought on this and wondered. Did his old mentor Koris's soul still hide somewhere in his progenoid gland? And what of Bennek, Simeon and the others? Would they live again one day, or be cursed by proximity to Arkio's insurrection?

The Blood Angel knelt in a small sub-chancel off the central transept of the *Europae*'s main chapel. The vast chamber mirrored the one aboard the *Bellus* in line and form, although the decoration, the stained glass and the scripture across the walls and mosaic floor were different. Being there made Rafen feel strangely displaced: it was almost as if he were in some parallel world, an alternate version of the now where paths had been different and outcomes altered. He heard footsteps approaching behind him and raised his head, for one giddy moment expecting to see Arkio coming toward him – not the golden, winged avatar, but the strong, proud Marine he had met on Cybele.

Mephiston slowed to a halt and nodded to Rafen. The psyker's battle armour was absent now, and instead he wore the sacred robes of his high order. 'Brother,' he said, by way of greeting.

Rafen returned a slow nod. 'My lord.' He went to stand, but Mephiston shook his head, and bade him remain where he was. 'What do you wish of me?'

For a moment, the psyker was silent. 'We lick our wounds, Rafen, in our own ways we heal and move on. The Chaplains tell me you have not left the chapel in days.'

'No,' Rafen admitted. 'I felt it… necessary.'

'Many would agree. After the ceremonies for the fallen and the rituals of purgation, your battle-brothers have spoken to me of the need to expunge this sorry incident from our chronicles.'

'That would be a mistake,' Rafen said quietly. 'To do that would mean we have learned nothing.'

Mephiston continued. 'The ship is ready to depart, and I have ordered the astropaths to make space for Shenlong. It will be… necessary to expunge any lasting traces of the heretic Stele's plans.'

'You will destroy the forge-world.' It was not a question.

'*Exterminatus*,' breathed the Librarian. 'A sad but inevitable conclusion.' He glanced up at the altar in the main section of the chapel. Held in a magnetic field bottle was the Spear of Telesto, quiet now but still dazzling as it slowly turned about its own axis.

'Am I to share that fate as well?' Rafen asked in a level voice. 'I am no more or less tainted than the people of that wretched sphere.'

'Some would argue thus,' Mephiston admitted. 'There are voices from Baal that counsel your execution along with the loyalist survivors gathered from Sabien. They are afraid that you may take the same path as Arkio. The knowledge that you were able to wield the Holy Lance…'

'Briefly, lord. Only briefly.'

The psyker eyed him. 'Indeed. But cooler heads have prevailed. Your dedication and honour to our Chapter, however unorthodox, was unparalleled. Commander Dante will give you an audience when we make home port, but rather than hold until that day, he has given me leave to grant you a field promotion in respect of your selflessness. The leadership of a full company of men is yours. The late Captain Simeon's command, the Sixth.'

Rafen let out a breath. 'With your permission, lord, I must respectfully decline Commander Dante's great accolade.'

'You *refuse*?'

He nodded. 'If I am to earn captaincy, it will be on my terms. I do not feel I deserve such rank… not yet.'

'Then what am I to do with you, lad? This will not sit well.'

The Marine looked up at the Librarian. 'May I ask a favour instead, then?'

'Name it.'

'I ask for mercy, lord. Grant clemency and compassion to my battle-brothers who strayed, those who followed my sibling unwittingly.' He thought of Turcio and Corvus as they had been brought aboard *Europae* stripped of their wargear and in manacles. 'Their only error was to be blinded by their belief in Sanguinius. Their faith was turned against them and misused. They are not to blame.'

Mephiston considered his request. 'There are rites of cleansing and purification that might be employed... They are quite arduous. Many would not survive.'

'They will,' said Rafen, 'and their faith will be twice as strong for it.' He got to his feet and approached the altar. As Mephiston watched, the Marine reached into the mag-field and ran his bare hand over the haft of the spear. He gripped the lance and for a moment, Rafen felt the weight of it in his hands once again. He peered at the teardrop blade – the metal seemed to run and shift in the light, glistening with the blood of the dead upon it.

'What do you see?' asked the Lord of Death.

Rafen saw dark red there, and he knew that it was his brother's blood upon the blade, glittering and then gone. 'Great Angel, hear me,' he whispered. 'Take my brother Arkio to your side, bring him to the Emperor's right hand. Forgive his folly and forgive mine. This I beseech you.' He bowed his head. 'My life and my soul for the God-Emperor, for Sanguinius... For the Blood Angels.'

He closed his eyes, and there in the depths of his soul, he felt the mark of his liege lord, indelible and bright as a golden sun.

In the blackness, *Misericorde* limped onward, gushing gas and vital fluids into the vacuum of space, slowly bleeding to death as it crawled ever closer to the Maelstrom and the lair of the Word Bearers. Garand smacked at the chirurgeon-servitor attending to the damage on his arm and stood up. The writhing energies of the ship's teleporter had turned the Warmaster's limb into a distorted mess of bone and muscle. He had already killed the serf responsible for the error by feeding it to the two-headed monstrosity that had been three of his best Marines... At least, before the botched beam-out from Sabien.

At his feet, Garand's personal vox-servitor cowered. He had allowed the slave to keep some measure of its personality when he had taken it for his retinue. It made little sense to the Warmaster to have servants that could not be afraid of him. 'What?' he demanded of it.

'A signal from the Eye, your darkness,' it chattered. 'The burning psy-mark upon the message bears the loathsome sigil of his most foul and hateful self, the Despoiler of Worlds.'

'Abaddon,' Garand said, suddenly weary. He ignored the squealing of the servitor as he openly uttered the High Warmaster's name. 'Of course.' The Word Bearer laughed with harsh, brittle humour. 'And what am I to say to him? Tell me, little man-slave, how I shall phrase my words to inform the Despoiler that the allies promised him for the Thirteenth Black Crusade have been denied? With what sweet lies do I conceal the failure of the Malfallax and Stele... and myself?'

'I... I do not–'

'*Silence!*' roared Garand. 'I alone survive. I alone must take the blame!' As quickly as it had arisen, the Warmaster's anger subsided. 'Bring my death-shroud. I will have need of it.'

THE FORMLESS REALM of warp space could turn a man insane at the sight of it. The frothing mass of alien energies defied the minds of organic lifeforms. It was a raw landscape of twisted emotion, peaks and troughs cut from the stuff of nightmares. In this small pocket of the immaterium, in the churning and unknowable hell that was the nest of the dread Malfallax, screams and shrieks of anger built cages of hate from the psychoactive matter. The disembodied consciousness of the daemon, wounded by the brutal severing of its link to Stele's host-corpse, hooted and howled its pain to the endless mad vista. Its towering fury would last for uncountable ages – but then in the warp, time had no meaning and correlation to other realities.

There would come a moment when the Malfallax would calm enough to begin conceiving of revenges both subtle and gross, nursing an anger that only the most inhuman could contain. An anger directed at one man, at the single being who brought its complex schemes to ruin.

One day, there would be a reckoning for the costs of the Malfallax, and every Blood Angel would pay a thousand times over for the daemon's defeat at Rafen's hand.

About the Author

James Swallow's fiction in the dark future of *Warhammer 40,000* includes *Deus Encarmine*, several short stories for *Inferno!* magazine and *What Price Victory*. His novels include the *Sundowners* series of 'steampunk' Westerns, *Judge Dredd: Eclipse*, *Rogue Trooper: Blood Relative*, *The Butterfly Effect* and the horror anthology *Silent Night*. His many other writing credits include guides to genre television and animation, scripts for videogames and audio dramas, and *Star Trek: Voyager*.

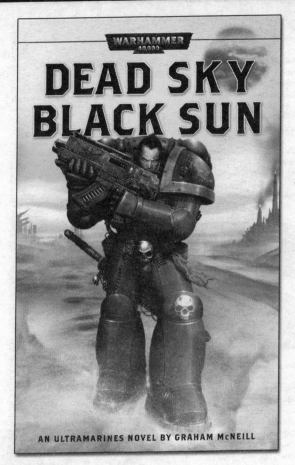

WARHAMMER 40,000

DEAD SKY BLACK SUN

AN ULTRAMARINES NOVEL BY GRAHAM McNEILL

DEAD SKY
BLACK SUN

ISBN: 1 84416 148 X

www.blacklibrary.com

Read till you Bleed
Do you have them all?

More Warhammer from the Black Library

EISENHORN

by Dan Abnett

In the 41st millennium, the Inquisition hunts the shadows for humanity's most terrible foes – rogue psykers, xenos and daemons. Few Inquisitors can match the notoriety of Gregor Eisenhorn, whose struggle against the forces of evil stretches across the centuries.

XENOS

THE ELIMINATION OF the dangerous recidivist Murdon Eyclone is just the beginning of a new case for Gregor Eisenhorn. A trail of clues leads the Inquisitor and his retinue to the edge of human-controlled space in the hunt for a lethal alien artefact – the dread Necroteuch.

MALLEUS

A GREAT IMPERIAL triumph to celebrate the success of the Ophidian Campaign ends in disaster when thirty-three rogue psykers escape and wreak havoc. Eisenhorn's hunt for the sinister power behind this atrocity becomes a desperate race against time as he himself is declared hereticus by the Ordo Malleus.

HERETICUS

WHEN A BATTLE with an ancient foe turns deadly, Inquisitor Eisenhorn is forced to take terrible measures to save the lives of himself and his companions. But how much can any man deal with Chaos before turning into the very thing he is sworn to destroy?

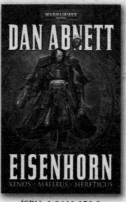

ISBN: 1-8446-156-0